PROLOGUE

No one chooses to live on the streets. No one willingly gives up the roof over their head. No one enjoys spending nights in search of shelter and no one should have to beg, steal and borrow just to feed themselves. Each day without a home is spent in the uncertainty of what dangers might be faced, in the certainty that nothing good lies ahead and that there is nothing in life to look forward to. In Ireland, there have always been people without a home, since the times of the potato famine, but today's number is the highest it has ever been. One of those statistics was Joanna Quinn. She had hoped her darkest days were behind her, until she reached rock bottom. She had never felt so hopeless. So useless. So worthless. She spent every day in a constant state of despair but even so, she had always considered herself a fighter. She had suffered post-natal depression with both her children. One day her partner walked out without warning and was never seen again. When she was a child, Joanna lost her father to a heart attack. She had never come to terms with why the world took him so young. She believed that what didn't kill her made her stronger. Ending her own life was not an option that had ever entered her mind. But today death seemed like the only outcome.

She had dreamt of freedom, of putting this living hell behind her. Times were not always so bad for Joanna. A few years ago, she was happy at home. She lived with her mother and her two daughters, who worshipped her. Sure, her job was stressful, but at least she was doing what she loved. She had started her own company, she imported wine from small boutique vineyards in France and sold them to shops and off licences. Wine was her biggest passion in life. The work was gratifying and when it was going well, she was able to provide for her family. She realised that perhaps the main reason her daughters forgave her for her minimal hours spent at home was that they wanted for nothing and knew her long hours were all for them, or at least somewhat for them.

But things had been going badly. Joanna had been spending long hours travelling to keep selling her products. In the few months before it all went so horribly wrong, she spent hours in vain trying to save her company from going under. Then, one day she left her rented office for the last time with her work laptop under her arm, knowing she would never return. She went home and disguised her heartache as good news that she had finished early and was ready for family time. She had no idea how she could tell her family, or anyone. It would break their hearts. Joanna didn't want to be a disappointment to her family or a failure in the eyes of her friends. She put off telling them until they were asleep. She whispered the truth to her eldest daughter as she breathed deeply and when morning came she put on her suit jacket, had breakfast, got in her car and drove to nowhere in particular. She hadn't a single case of wine to sell and couldn't afford to import any more. She had run up a massive debt she'd never be able to repay and was essentially bankrupt. She would have to hand the house over to the bank. She parked the car she'd also have to give up and thought about her ordeal. She decided the only way to save face was to get a job with a competitor, any job, and pretend it was a better job than it was and tell everyone they made her an offer she couldn't refuse. Using her car as an office she operated from a different car parks each day, sending her CV to whoever was hiring. However, it went nowhere as that month was not good for jobs in her industry. Neither was the next month, nor the month after that. When she returned home one day to be confronted by her mother, who had learned the truth about her failed business from a local off-licence, she realised that she

could no longer hide the truth from her distraught family.

Overcome by embarrassment, feeling she had let everybody she loved down, Joanna got in her car and fled, believing they would be better off without her. She brought shame on her family. With her gone they would have a better chance if they were rehomed with someone that could take better care of them. She headed to Dublin city centre and with one case in her hand, checked into a decent hotel with a beautiful view of the Liffey. A few days later she changed to a more affordable hotel with an interesting view on the adjacent apartment block and the following week to the cheapest accommodation in the city with a view of the building's moss infested galvanised roof. Two weeks had now passed and for the fifth dawn in a row Joanna had awoken on the streets. She knew that above anything else it was her pride that got her to this point, but she believed two things to be true. That her children missed her more than she deserved and that today would be the last day that she would wake up on the streets. She was determined that today would be the day she would take action. Their smiling faces were the last things she thought of as she descended from the wall and the cold water of the Liffey punched her like a powerful breath-seizing blow to the chest. Then everything went black.

CHAPTER ONE

ONE DAY EARLIER

The shrill beep of Fionn Fagan's alarm cut through the haze of his dishevelled consciousness, assaulting his senses like a distress signal from a trawler lost at sea. It had been just after 5.30am when Fionn Fagan unlocked his door and staggered into his Foley Street apartment. He had known that going for a drink after work would be a bad idea, but he had a problem. Deep down he knew this, but was yet to admit it to himself or anyone else. The one pint of Guinness that turned into six wasn't so much the problem, although he knew *that* alone was a bad idea, especially on a weeknight. It was the fact that come midnight, when everyone else was happy to call it a night, the real thirst came. The thirst for the thrill. The thrill of the chase. Outcomes that are as of yet unknown. The hunt for the adrenaline rush that comes with each new flip of the coin. The exhilarating prospect of making himself a fortune.

"2.5 hours until alarm" his phone screen had read when he set it three hours ago. He had already hit the snooze button twice and was now running late. He moaned to himself. Half in anguish, half in self-disgust. Today was going to be hard to get through. As a Detective Garda with the Gardaí Síochána his work of late was mainly driving distinguished individuals from A to B. Escorting Ambassadors, Government Ministers and Judges that needed diplomatic protection was the extent of his work. Usually it bored him to death but today he was going to welcome the opportunity as his low functioning brain was going to be able to handle little else.

The first person Fionn spoke to upon arriving at work, or rather, the first person who spoke to him was his friend and colleague Detective Neeve Bello.

'You're in water hotter than that coffee you got there buddy.' Neeve said half flippantly in a way Fionn knew was to make light of a fairly heavy situation. Neeve had been Fionn's friend for years. He regarded her as one of his few true friends and had a huge amount of admiration and respect for her. Her Nigerian immigrant parents wanted to give their daughter an Irish name to help her fit in, they loved the name Niamh but not the spelling. Neeve always described herself as a proud Irish woman and claimed to love her country and its people, however Fionn witnessed her face adversary from all directions on her journey through the ranks of the Gardaí. Both her gender and the colour of her skin meant that she was met with patronisation at best and verbal abuse at worst from colleagues, superiors and members of the public. However, it didn't stop her keeping on Fionn's heel all the way through Garda College. They were a huge support to each other throughout and they would regularly end up consoled in each other's arms. There was a magnetic attraction between them from the moment they met and it didn't take long until that attraction was acted on. As the physical desire faded between them a romantic void began to appear which was replaced with a close platonic friendship like neither had ever experienced before. Neeve had seen a side to him no one else had and that made them even closer. He always judged his closeness to a friend on the awkwardness complete silence would bring. With Neeve, silence was a blissful break from reality. Like all friendships they had their ups and downs through the years. Ups such as when they both finished their training top of their class. Downs such as the distance put between them by her ex-boyfriend who disapproved of their friendship. Downs such as having to go head to head for the same promotion even though both knew the other deserved it as much as they did. Ups such as another position becoming available and them both being offered the job after all. After years of love, hate, lust, resentment, adventure and boredom they now felt like an old married couple, except they weren't married and they weren't old. They were in fact both thirty three, Fionn being nine months Neeve's senior although it often seemed the other way around.

'Ah, what now?' He said with defeat already in his voice.

'Bagman is out for blood, your blood. He's after getting it in the neck from upstairs because of your report on the Milligan case.'

'What? I never mentioned him by name, what's his problem now?'

'Well...' The volume of Neeve's voice went down a notch. 'I'm not supposed to know, obviously, but apparently you noted that there was a discrepancy in the itinerary between the house being searched and what we declared in contraband. That came back on him. The team that looked into it found out that the search happened on his watch.'

'For God's sake, what, he thinks I was trying to get him in trouble? Or insinuate that he was up to something? What did he expect me to do? I was just giving objective facts' Fionn said as his voice quivered from equal parts tiredness and frustration.

'I suppose he thinks you shouldn't have put those details in your report.'

'I can't lie in an official report, come on.'

'I don't know Fionn, maybe you should have given him a heads up?'

Fionn waved his hand in front of his face to swat away an invisible fly. 'I didn't even think about who submitted the count, I didn't care, if I left that out it would be me getting it in the neck, this is so stupid, Bagman's a prick.'

Because Det. David Lyons started off his career stationed in the money laundering section of the financial crimes unit, "Bagman" was a perfect nickname. Had it been the reason for his nickname he may have liked it but he hated his nickname and people rarely called it to his face. His nickname preceded his beginning at financial crimes by several years and happened to alter organically over time from when someone called him "Tea Bag" after noticing he shared his name with a

8

popular brand of tea. At some point "Man" was added and "Tea" was dropped but David Lyons' loathing of the name never altered. He was without doubt a good detective and his hard work and results were well respected throughout the force. At the same time however he wasn't well liked. He had a dog eat dog attitude, acted only with his own interests in mind, his colleagues threaded on eggshells in order to not piss him off and his superiors went out of their way to avoid grief from him.

Fionn silently considered the implications of Neeve's information. 'I guess I better lie low. Where am I being sent today, do you know? The boss told me yesterday at 7pm he wouldn't know what the story was with the car until this morning.' 'I don't know.' Neeve responded. 'I got to get moving, go see the boss yourself, I'm not your PA.'

Neeve scurried down the hall and Fionn stood staring at his coffee which he had felt zero effect from so far.

Fionn gave two quick raps on the door and waited until he heard a loud 'Yep' from the other side before entering. Nobody ever looked forward to the walk upstairs when summoned by Superintendent Tom Corcoran. Although Fionn quite liked his facetious and impatient tone it was never enjoyable to be on the receiving end of it. Tom Corcoran was one of the youngest Superintendents the country had ever had and he was promoted quickly through the ranks based on merit. He was efficient and good at his job, however, in order to use these traits to the best of his ability he had to be ruthless and made no friends along the way. This also helped him to be objective and he would never make a decision in order to do someone a favour.

'Sit down Fagan,' Corcoran commanded with his thick bushy grey eyebrows forming a V shape, the base of which was disappearing underneath his thick framed glasses. 'Look, this is a pain in the ass for me as it's pointless work, but I have to deal with it now. I'm going to have to have you investigated.'

Fionn's eyes widened and his bottom lip fell from his top lip leaving a gaping mouth like a fish forcing oxygen into its gills. 'I assume this is about the section in the report?' Fionn asked with confidence. 'I'm sorry if it's causing extra work for you boss but I'm not sure what else I could have done?'

'How about doing your job properly?' Corcoran suggested rhetorically.

'Pardon me boss, I don't understand. I did do it properly, I noted the discrepancy in the count which has regretfully left Det. Lyons with the responsibility of explaining. Can you please clarify what it is I have not done properly?'

Tom Corcoran stared blankly at Fionn for several seconds before shuffling in his chair to adjust himself to a higher view point. His forehead was simultaneously changed into a redder colour than usual. 'What - In the name of God - is happening inside that soft skull of yours to think that I - for one second - would discuss that with you right now?'

Every new darker shade of red washing over Corcoran's face could have been stolen from Fionn's as his own face started to lose colour fast. 'I'm sorry Sir, I don't follow.' He was addressing him as Sir now, he noted to himself.

'Evidently you do not, Fagan. I called you here to talk about a very serious accusation regarding the Malloy murder case last year.'

The whites of Fionn's eyes widened like a sheet of snow engulfing the ground and a tight knot started to form in the pit of his stomach.

'It has been alleged that you did not follow procedure when Det. Lyons was conducting his final interview with the prime suspect. He claims you abandoned your post leaving Lyons alone and in a compromising position.'

Fionn sat silently in confusion. He started to scan the metre radius directly in front of him as if searching for something important, as he tried to make sense of what the Superintendent was talking about. Just over ten months ago a seven year old girl had been kidnapped from Jervis shopping centre. She had wandered off as her mother played with cosmetic samples at a stall. Four days later her body was found in an abandoned skip down by the docklands. The investigation did not take long to find a suspect as CCTV footage captured Barry Malloy leaving the shopping centre with the child. Tests found traces of her DNA in his Mayor Street apartment. Together with several witness statements the case was pretty open/shut and Fionn had been tasked with compiling the report for submission to the Director of Public Prosecutions in the presence of Lyons who was the arresting officer, and the suspect. Lyons then requested to take a coffee break and leave the room; Fionn knew exactly why and it was not out of consideration for his desire for a coffee. Lyons wanted to rough up the suspect while alone in the room with no one to witness it. Fionn decided that Malloy deserved a lot more than being knocked around a little and left the room so if Malloy lodged a complaint at a later date there would be his word against Lyons'.

'What exactly am I supposed to have done?' He said with a crackle of despair in his voice. It suddenly dawned on him that Lyons was now manipulating the situation. He knew he shouldn't have left the room, there should have been two Guards there at all time, and now Lyons was reporting this, intending to deny that it was his idea.

'Either you don't know because you haven't done anything wrong, in which case you have nothing to worry about, or you know exactly what you did wrong, in which case you're asking questions you already know the answer to.' Corcoran leaned back in his chair and pressed the palm of his hands together under his chin like he was about to pray.

'This is Lyons doing this isn't it? He's already under investigation so he's deflecting the attention onto me,' the anger was starting to show in Fionn's voice. 'It's bullshit. Will you speak to Malloy to get his memory of it, and ask what happened when he was left alone with Lyons?'

'Why are you asking a question you know I won't answer?'

'I was doing the bastard a favour.'

'In what context is that supposed to matter to me?' Corcoran slid a white envelope across his table to Fionn.

'Your meeting is next Tuesday, you know you'll get a slap on the wrist for being an idiot. Just take it like a man. I see no need to suspend you but for the next week. I think it's best if I get you out of here, to give you some breathing space as it were. I'm putting you on a case. It's a no brainer but the media are all over it, so we need to be seen to be doing something about it.'

'What about Lyons I suppose he...'

'Will you shut up and listen to me?' Corcoran interrupted. 'This is happening. Stop whining like a baby and get on with it. Here's what we have gathered so far.' He flung a file across his desk for Fionn to pick up. 'What we have are three men, all believed to be homeless, who don't seem to have any prior connections. Within an 8 day period they all throw themselves into the Liffey from the boardwalk and drown. First assumption is that the suicide rate among the homeless increases dramatically as the evenings get colder, big deal. But the papers are hassling me for a comment on what we're doing about it, you know how much they love a human interest story on a marginalised community. So you will be what we are doing about it. Got it?'

Fionn conceded with his body language and his tone of voice. 'Yes boss, I'll look into it'.

CHAPTER TWO

Fionn stood on the boardwalk and leaned on the railings with his back to The Italian Quarter and the Millennium Bridge to his right. All there was to hear was the low hum of slow moving traffic and the squawk of seagulls circling overhead. The crime scene tape had been removed and tourists were strolling along unaware it had ever been there. A forensics examination revealed nothing substantial and Fionn had no further info than the fact all three of the deceased were of no fixed abode at the time of their death. Fionn decided to call his partner, Billy McGinty, so he could hear something other than his own thoughts, which were starting to annoy him.

'Hello to you,' said Billy in a jovial voice.

'Hi Billy, how's things?'

'Good man chief, fine thanks and yourself?' Fionn was not his chief, or anyone's chief for that matter. Billy called everyone chief. He had been Fionn's partner for two years now and Fionn quite enjoyed his company. He often tested his nerves but so did most people, and unlike most people Fionn knew Billy never really meant it and so usually let it slide. Billy was a good detective but was always too soft as a Guard. He was a pacifist at heart so although he was great at catching lawbreakers he would avoid getting hands on when things came to a head. Billy was one of those people that had an unforgettable face simply because it was so unique. It was noticeably asymmetrical and weathered looking but yet there was a friendliness in it. He had pale skin, fair hair which was balding and cropped tight, he was always clean shaven, slightly overweight, owned a mouthful of crooked pearly white teeth, a slanted smile and a pair of intense blue eyes. Physically, Billy had very little in common with Fionn.

'Where did they send you in the end?' asked Fionn.

'Croatian embassy, Peter Street, one man job, no worries, I don't miss you too much yet. How are you getting on with your thing? Have you calmed down yet about the Bagman situation?'

'No, never, and not going very well down here either. I don't really know what I'm looking for, if anything. Let me just bounce some info off you. Within eight days three homeless people jumped in the Liffey. No suggestion of foul play and I went back over all the witness statements from those that heard the splash and saw the body in the water and none of them remember seeing anyone on the boardwalk so they were alone when they jumped in. It's not the first and not the last time that someone will jump in, but three? And so close together? It looks like a coincidence but we're trained not to believe in those, so where do I start?'

'Wait for the toxicology report', suggested Billy. 'Considering the way we've noticed that illegally obtained prescription medicine is being dealt more than hard drugs these days, it could be that there is a sudden supply of some new opioid stuff knocking around and well, maybe it's helping them sleep? Why it's causing them to end up with lungs full of water I don't know. Maybe the first one did it and the second thought it was a good idea and so on.'

Yeah that's exactly the same logic I came to,' said Fionn. 'But they all jumped in at some point along the boardwalk.'

'Where else would they be? After 10pm the general public stop using the boardwalk and it becomes a sanctuary for the addicts of the city.'

Fionn was always an appreciator of Billy's logic. 'I suppose, but our crowd usually comes and moves them along don't they?'

'They hadn't moved these ones along it seems,' replied Billy.

'OK, fair enough, I guess my next step is to try and understand why they jumped, I will have a chat with some of the people on the street,' proposed Fionn with a tone that revealed he was fully aware of his purposely bad pun. 'I'll catch up with you later,' he said and hung up.

Fionn took the boardwalk back towards O'Connell Street and up ahead noticed a middle aged man slouched on the benches looking worse for wear and half asleep. He was wearing a black beanie hat, a black hoodie, blue and white tracksuit bottoms and what were once white runners. None of his clothes, nor his face and hands, looked like they had been washed in the recent past and he was clutching a can of cheap cider.

'Hello there,' Fionn said with vigour in order to establish what level of response he was going to get from the drunk man.

'Howaya' the man responded cautiously. 'Spare some change for a hostel?'

Fionn flashed his badge. 'Can you tell me where you live please, Pal?'

'Ah here, I haven't done anything wrong, Guard,' responded the man slowly with an emphasis on each individual word.

'No, not yet anyway. Answer my questions and keep this trend going though, yeah?'

'What do you want?' the man asked.

'Where did you come from today?'

'I bleedin' come from right here, don't I? Can you not see me sleeping blanket? What do you think I'm doing here, on me holidays?'

'Are you telling me you sleep here every night? What's your name?'

'Me name's Buzzer, and yeah most nights, I have nowhere else to go, I'm homeless aren't I?' Buzzer was looking through Fionn as if he wasn't there, or at least as if he was wishing he wasn't.

'Most nights? What about the other nights?'

'Well, when I get enough money together I spend the night in the hostel.'

'Which hostel?'

'Lowes, down there on Gardiner Street,' answered Buzzer reluctantly.

'Always that one?' Fionn's questions were coming at a rapid pace.

'Yeah.'

'Why only that one?'

'It's safe,' replied Buzzer bluntly. 'It costs a bit more than the others but even the streets are safer than those places.'

'How often do you stay there?'

'Once a week maybe, when I can, don't always have any money on me you know.'

'No, I suppose you spend it all on drink?' Fionn asked, nodding towards the can in Buzzer's hand.

Buzzer's tone got defensive. 'A few cans are all I have to keep me warm, Guard. Most of the other homeless people around here are all on heroin or meth or snow or all three but I've never touched drugs. I have me few cans and me spot here and I don't touch anyone unless they touch me, so piss off and leave me alone.'

Fionn smirked at Buzzer's vague threat. 'Calm down now or I will touch you. I'm not finished talking. Why do you always sleep here?'

'Because I get left alone. At night time people don't walk down this way because they think it's full of junkies and junkies don't walk down this way because they think it's too open plan and the Guards can watch them so that leaves me here in peace. I've been homeless over ten years, I'm good at this game. Good at surviving. I'll do what it takes.'

'Were you here on the 11th, 15th and 19th of this month?'

'What? I don't know,' replied Buzzer, holding his hands out like Jesus in Da Vinci's Last Supper. 'What days were they? I'm not very good with numbers.'

'Saturday week, last Wednesday and Sunday,' stated Fionn from memory.

Buzzer squinted and sat pensively for almost a minute as Fionn stood over him studying his train

19

of thought. 'And what day is today?' Buzzer finally asked.

'Jesus Christ, it's Tuesday. On those nights someone jumped in here,' Fionn said as he motioned to the river behind him. 'Did you witness any of that?'

'Some guy keeps jumping in there? The mad yoke, what, does he love swimming?'

'No, three different people,' replied Fionn, not entertaining the flippancy. 'And they won't swim again, I'm afraid they all drown. Wouldn't you have noticed something if you were sitting here?'

'Jesus, I would have.' Buzzer's eyes were widening in genuine surprise, or, what Fionn considered to be just as likely, the act of seeming genuinely surprised. 'I must have been in the hostel those nights, I have been there a few times recently, alright.'

Fionn raised an eyebrow to show he wasn't going to be convinced that easily. 'And if I pay Lowes a visit they will confirm you stayed on these nights?' Buzzer nodded sheepishly. 'What's your real name by the way?'

'Buzzer is me real name, I haven't had any other name in years!'

'Fine,' Fionn said as he took his mobile out of his pocket and proceeded to take a photo of Buzzer's puzzled and cantankerous face. 'I'm sure they will remember that unique mug.'

'Ah here guard, you better not be selling that to a modelling agency now or anything'.

'No fear of that,' responded Fionn. 'A fetish website, maybe? But listen, don't think about

20

uprooting your home any time soon, I need to check if you're a filthy lying bastard or just a filthy bastard.'

Fionn turned and walked away from Buzzer with an arrogant swagger, not noticing the middle finger Buzzer was holding up in his direction. But he presumed there was a gesture of some sort being made behind him.

Fionn had walked the short journey from O'Connell Bridge to Lowes Hostel on Gardiner Street. He wanted to clear his head of the resentment and anger he was feeling towards Bagman and that whole situation. He also figured that by the time he walked back to his car and found parking up here it would have taken longer. Lowes was a narrow Georgian building with a small reception just inside the front door. It was a hostel but pitched on travel websites as an inexpensive and centrally located hotel. Fionn was familiar with the various accommodations that were regularly frequented by homeless people and had never known here to be a place someone would usually spend their hard begged for money. If Buzzer had been staying here, like he had claimed he had, then he had a unique taste. Just inside the door he noticed a Trip Advisor certificate boasting four stars proudly displayed in a gold frame. He approached the man behind the desk holding his badge in his right hand and his mobile, displaying the photo he had just taken of Buzzer, in his left. He could tell the middle aged man had already guessed what he was going to be asked as he glanced quickly at the badge, looked straight at the photo and then began to consume his grey moustache with his lower lip, formulating an answer to the unasked question.

'Hi there, Sir. Fionn Fagan is my name and I'm currently conducting an investigation. Can you please tell me if you recognise this man?'

'Yes of course, that's Buzzer,' replied the man politely. 'What has he done, is he OK?'

'Yes, he seems to go by Buzzer alright and yes, he's OK,' replied Fionn. 'He claims he has stayed here a number of times over the last week or so, is this correct?'

'Yes indeed, our Buzzer is a long-time guest. He's been coming here once a week or so for years. We don't usually let undesirables stay here, if you know what I mean. We run a reputable hotel here, but we can trust Buzzer.'

'Hotel eh?' Fionn said in a flippant tone the middle aged man seemed instantly insulted by. 'What's your name please Sir? And please tell me what you know about Buzzer.' He took out a pen and pad and stared down at it as the man spoke.

'Brendan Kelly is my name, I'm the owner and you'll find me sitting here seven days a week, usually. We renovated this *hotel* about six years ago.' He put an emphasis on "hotel" in retaliation to Fionn's remark, then paused and stared. Fionn continued to look down at his pad and scribble, so Brendan continued. 'It was falling apart. There were fights every night, drugs were everywhere, we couldn't keep staff for more than a month and it was costing more to maintain the place than what we were making. We closed down, refurbished and then raised the prices so as to attract the right clientele. We had gotten to know Buzzer and he was never any trouble so when we reopened we continued to allow him to stay. We didn't have the heart to tell him we had doubled the rates so we continued to charge him the same price as before, €35 a night. We tried to get him help, a permanent roof over his head and such like but to be honest I think he prefers the streets. It's his home. He says he feels claustrophobic sleeping in a bedroom but he needs a shower once in a while so I think that's why we see him.'

'Who do you mean by "we"?' Fionn asked without lifting his head.

'Maureen, my wife, she makes the beds and cleans the place,' replied Brendan.

After a few seconds of silence Fionn looked up for the first time since he started writing. 'Have you got a record of the last, say, three times he has stayed with you?'

'Sure thing, Guard. Give me a minute. Let's see, where did I put it?' Brendan rummaged around for the information. 'Here we go, we've seen him more than usual recently, actually. He was here Sunday gone, the Wednesday before that, and, two seconds, the Friday, no, the Saturday before that.'

'So the 11th, the 15th and the 19th of this month?' Fionn asked. 'Can I have copies of your records?'

'Sure, no problem, just let me print.' A concerned expression suddenly appeared on

Brendan's face. 'Can I ask if this has something to do with the drownings last week?'

'You can ask but I can't answer that directly,' replied Fionn as he flipped to a page in his notepad and handed it to Brendan. 'But what I will ask you if any of these names seem familiar to you? Perhaps they are regular guests too?'

Brendan looked at the names of the three homeless men that had recently drowned and typed them into the computer as he waited for the records to print. 'No, I'm afraid not, these names mean nothing to me. Also, I can tell you Buzzer didn't need to be here for me to know he had nothing to do with any of it. He wouldn't harm a fly. He likes a few cans and will never hassle anyone. Sure the homeless seem to fight among themselves but Buzzer is a very smart guy and always seems, I don't know, one up on all the others we get around here.'

'Thank you for your time, I'll keep that in mind,' said Fionn, putting his pen and pad away.

'He has a friend. Works for one of the charities, Shelter Ireland I think. Jim is his name, Buzzer always tells us Jim gives him new clothes and blankets and I believe he works with the homeless in the area so he might be able to help.'

'Yes, perhaps,' Fionn replied, removing the pad once again. 'Do you know Jim's surname?'

'I'm afraid not, I've never actually met him, just heard about him. Is there anything else?' Brendan asked, but Fionn was already halfway out the door.

Fionn was walking back in the direction of his car and took his mobile out to give Neeve back at the station a call.

'Hi Neeve,' said Fionn jovially.
'Hi. Fionn? Where are you?' Neeve sounded surprised.

'I'm in town, Corcoran has me looking into something pointless. That's why I'm ringing actually, I need your help. Can you get in touch with Shelter Ireland and ask them for details on one of their staff, a Jim something, who works with homeless people on the boardwalk? I need his help with a couple of enquiries'.

'OK,' Neeve replied. 'Have you got any more info than a first name?'

'No sorry, can't imagine how many Jim's they have working the boardwalk though'.

'No worries, leave it with me, I'll call you with what I get,' Neeve chirped.

'That's it?' Fionn asked, sceptically.

'What do you mean?'

'I expected "piss off, I'm busy, get back here and do it yourself". What happened to "I'm not your PA" from earlier?'

'I assume you need my help because, you know, you don't dare come back here today'.

'What?' Fionn asked with loud surprise. 'What have you heard? Corcoran told me he was sending me out on a job for some air, he never gave me the impression I need to stay away indefinitely.'

There was a couple of seconds of silence as Neeve considered how much she should tell Fionn. 'Bagman is going around saying you are staying away from the office because you are scared of him and guilty for getting him in trouble. He's just messing with your head, don't worry, no one is listening to him. But when you rang and I heard you were outside, I assumed you were avoiding him'.

'I was just being lazy.' Fionn heard his own voice and realised he didn't sound convincing. He had that halfhearted conviction people took when they were lying. 'But now I'm definitely coming in after lunch, I'm not giving him the satisfaction.'

'I wouldn't if I were you, you know?' The tone of Neeve's voice got high pitched towards the end of her sentence and her native Cork accent that she tended to repress came through loud and clear. This was unusual considering she usually toned it down and pronounced each word individually rather than roll her sentences together, so that people could better understand her.

'Yanooooo,' Fionn mocked and then chuckled even though he himself had been accused of having an unusual country accent in the past. 'Oh I'll be in, I'll see you real soon,' he said with conviction, 'let me know if you get anything on this Jim guy, and, thanks'.

Fionn hung up and in the interim of his walk back toward his car he realised he had veered off course and was heading over O'Connell Bridge away from the correct direction. He had made a subconscious decision, or a conscious decision he chose not to analyse, to walk in the direction of Amusement City on Westmoreland Street. Just a quick stop, he told himself. He was a frequent customer of the Casino. He had spent thousands of Euros through the years. He had won big several times, but didn't like to think about how many hundreds of Euros he spent for every hundred he won. He walked in, nodded to Li, the friendly fat faced Chinese girl that greeted him almost every time. He swiped his card and walked on through. He did a lap of the slot machines, deciding whether or not he was feeling a connection with any one in particular. Fionn had learned to always trust his gut. It was a skill he mastered through many years of gambling, although a skill may not be the right word as he was often wrong. Nonetheless, he had a tendency to obsess. Obsess over his work and obsess over his pleasures. Corcoran compared him to a dog with a bone. Once something grabbed his attention he would not relent until he wore out every aspect of what made it interesting to him and it became redundant. His colleagues often mistook this for perfectionism. He walked through into the back room, and then decided to loop back towards the roulette machines. He resented the automatic spinning wheels. There was something so mechanical and impersonal about them. He only had the miserable faces of the other players to keep him company. He much preferred the human aspect of being served by a live person but there was not a single croupier in Amusement City day or night. Unfortunately, because of the less than liberal gambling laws in Ireland, there were no better casinos in Dublin. Nothing like he had experienced in Vegas anyway.

Oh, Vegas. The greatest city in the world. Fionn had been only once and had wanted to go back ever since. It wasn't even his idea to go. He had been gunning for New York but Ian, his friend from school, insisted. He had argued to the others that seven nights in Vegas was too long, but by the end of the week he didn't want to leave. That was where the monster was born. They stayed in Caesars Palace as they had seen it in one of their favourite films, "The Hangover". In the first few days they had played a few slots, picked up how to play roulette, drank a lot and only saw the inside of one nightclub, deciding not to go to another after paying $100 each into a mediocre venue on the first night. As the week went on they spent more and more time in the casino. They had tried Blackjack and were impressed with the croupier, patiently talking four drunken Irish guys through each hand. Then Craps came along. On the fifth night Fionn wandered off from his friends and watched a game, trying to understand the rules. He had no idea what the crowd around the table were cheering at. A pair of dice were being propelled to the other end of the table like they were hot stones being released from an agonising grip. Sometimes the way the dice fell caused an eruption of applause, sometimes hollers of disgust. The unknown cause of the extreme fluctuation in emotion was the most fascinating enigma he had ever witnessed. He stood transfixed on the spectacle before him like it was witnessing a miracle of biblical proportions. Eventually one of the croupier manning the table invited him to join so he just went with the flow. His chips started to accumulate far quicker than his understanding of the game but several hours later he was up several grand and had realised he had found the best game in the world in the greatest city in the world. He had never experienced such a thrill and he was instantly addicted to it. He soon figured out that Craps is a game where everyone was playing together. Even the croupiers were cheering when a point number was rolled. He had been by far the luckiest roller of the night and had made a lot of money for other players, including a stunning blonde from one of the Scandinavian countries that ended up back in his hotel room at 4am after the group decided to call it a night. By then their thousands of winnings had diminished by a few hundred and they decided their lucky streak was over. Or it merely moved from a table to a bed. He had only ever been with Irish girls, apart from an English musician he met in a club one night. He didn't know what it was, but there was something different about Scandinavian women, or certainly this one anyway. She seemed more open. More spiritual. More electric. She had gotten up early the next morning and informed him she had to go back to her room and freshen up before her boyfriend arrived. He was flying from Canada and was due to arrive 15 hours later than her. She thanked him for a lovely first night in Vegas and wished him as much luck with whoever would be his good luck charm that night. Sin city eh? He hadn't even thought to ask her if she had a boyfriend. He wondered in hindsight would it have made a difference and decided it probably wouldn't have. It was quite frustrating that none of the others witnessed any of the previous night's events. He had nothing to show for it except a wallet full of cash. He could tell they didn't believe him. He could have got that from an ATM or spent double that to get it back. There were no photos of his Norwegian, or was it Danish lady friend and his friends implied she could have been a hooker. Since his trip to Vegas he had lost touch with his schoolmates, but he still had an eye for tall blond girls and was forever chasing a rush to beat that night in Vegas.

But they didn't even have a single Craps table in the whole of Ireland. Certainly none of the casinos he had been in. They barely had Blackjack so he had to take what he could get and what he had right now was a Roulette machine. He was distracted by his fury over Bagman's comments around the office so he wanted to get back and confront him as soon as possible. He usually had a long game for roulette but decided he didn't have time right now. Go big or go home. He took €50 out of his wallet, fed it into the machine and observed. He needed to study the form before his gut started talking to him. A maths teacher friend of his had said each spin had its own odds. Each time there's a 50/50 chance of either red or black he had said. Nonsense. First of all there is a green 0 and a green 00 so it's a 49/49 chance of red or black. Also the odds are a lot higher that red would come in five times in a row than four times in a row. 27 red. 12 red. 32 red. 23 red. He thought about putting it all on black. It was only €50. All he stood to make was €50. Anything less wasn't worth playing for. Anything less didn't get the heart beating fast enough. Anything less didn't give him the rush. Still, his heart rate was picking up and the rush was almost here. It was just loitering outside the door to his soul, waiting patiently to be invited in with the simple press of one button. Should he do it? Was it the right time? He decided to wait it out. If it came up black he would know he missed his chance. The wheel spun like a colourful whirlpool vigorously pulling caution into the abyss. 3 red. He had made the right decision. The train he was riding would have got off one stop too early and he would have to make the long miserable walk home. Now was the right time. He could feel it. He believed it. It was as if he was communicating with the wheel in his mind and it was telling him what it was going to do next. All on black. Always bet on black. Especially when the last five numbers were red. Red? Black? Green. 0 Green. Bringing him down to zero. In that moment of deflation, all seemed lost.

CHAPTER THREE

David Lyons 'mind was racing and his thoughts were fast, frequent and in vast quantities. He had so many problems and worries and the line of cocaine he had for lunch didn't even seem to have helped his energy levels. His usual self-prescribed dosage of the beautiful white powder was starting to have less impact of late so he decided he would have to start upping his intake. He probably would have done so long ago, but he had been freaked out since that nose bleed a few months back and worried snorting even a little extra up there might be more than his thin nostrils were able to stand. He quite liked his nose because girls seemed to like it. He had been compared to a young Kevin Bacon but assumed it was mainly because both of them had similar thin pointy noses. Regardless, he still took it as a compliment and had come to associate a woman's observation on his striking resemblance to the Hollywood actor to the inevitability of them ending up back at his place. It had happened on a number of occasions. Once at a bar. Once in a nightclub. Once at a wedding, and once from a girl in this very office who's desk he was about to pass. He had four simultaneous thoughts going through his mind as he headed past the desk of the detective he once slept with but no longer talks to. He needed more cocaine. He had gotten away with a wicked thing. He would call an escort later. And he had sufficiently bad mouthed Fagan enough to get their colleagues on his side and quite rightly as it was as much his fault for being a rat. As he approached his desk he noticed someone was sitting in his chair.

'Fagan, what are you doing in my chair, you rat?' he said angrily as if the action violated him to the highest degree.

'Ah Bagman, I'm just sitting here doing nothing, isn't that what this chair is usually used for?' Fionn replied calmly. David Lyons spoke through gritted teeth. 'Ok. Here's what's going to happen. You're going to get out of my chair and then get out of my face'.

'Why's that?' Fionn responded, glad that several colleagues had stopped what they were doing and were giving this discussion their full attention. 'Because I'm so scared of you that I dare not come in here today and face you? Or because I should cower with shame because I outed you as being a stupid prick? You're pathetic.'

'You're pathetic. You have your head up your arse. You should know better than to mess with me. If I'm going down you're going down with me, dickhead.'

The two men stood a foot apart. As they were both the same height neither had the advantage of looking down at the other. The first physical contact made was initiated by Fionn as he placed a hand patronisingly on Lyons' shoulder.

'Listen Pal,' Fionn said, putting a sarcastic emphasis on "pal" to show his resentment of Lyons' passive aggressive use of the word. 'You need to get over yourself. Do you think I gave a shit who did what when I filed that report? You're a paranoid bastard and you need to lay off the coke,' he said with a half grin on his face.

Lyons swung his right arm with one firm and swift chop, digging into Fionn's forearm with a blunt thud, forcing Fionn's hand off his shoulder. 'Don't touch me,' he exclaimed with anger in his voice.

Fionn recoiled his arm into his chest and rubbed it vigorously to take the sting out of it. 'You don't touch me,' he replied as he gave him a firm but controlled shove in the chest with both hands, forcing Lyons to take a step back.

'I can sue you for harassment, you idiot.' Lyons said as he stepped forward and brought his face to within an inch of Fionn's.

Fionn took a step back. 'Sue me for this you little bitch'.

As if in slow motion, Lyons saw Fionn's right palm come up towards him, turning like a corkscrew. He then felt Fionn's wrist dig into his left cheek, following through and forcing him to whip his head to his right in order to take the sting out of it. He slowly rotated his head back to face Fionn. He stood silently and stared at Fionn as the nostrils on his small nose flared up and the white of his eyes became enlarged. Fionn could see a demonic glint come into Lyons' dilated pupils as if a raging fire had just been ignited behind his eyes. He pulled back his hand and jabbed Fionn square in the mouth with a clenched fist. Fionn hadn't noticed yet but the inside of his bottom lip had burst open and he had blood filling his mouth and running down his chin. He didn't have time to feel pain as in the meantime the back of his head had hit the desk on his fall backwards and the sudden dull pain far outweighed any feeling coming from his lip. He shuffled around on the floor uncomfortably trying to find some sort of balance. Neeve had been walking over from the other side of the room to defuse the situation as soon as the first piece of physical contact was made. By now she had reached them and was standing adjacent to both of them. Assuming the argument had concluded Neeve was about to tell both men what she thought of the little pageant when Fionn pulled his knee towards his busted mouth and kicked out heel first at Lyons' shin which brought him to the ground with a thud and a yelp. Both men were on their knees and lunged at each other with their arms flailing as each attempted to get the other in a headlock. The altercation soon ended when Neeve grabbed a chunk of lock hair from the front of each man's ear just like her granddad had told her his teachers would do to punish him in school. She pulled both men apart and shouted at them. 'Cop the hell on you saps. The problem with measuring who's got the bigger dick is you might find out neither of you actually have one.'

'You're a dead man, Fagan,' Lyons said venomously.

'Piss off,' Fionn replied with a lisp, as he dabbed his bloody lip with the palm of his hand.

'What the hell do you absolute children think you're doing?' Corcoran sounded strangely calm as he spoke from behind the small group that had gathered around the altercation. No one had noticed him approaching. 'How did this happen?'

'Fagan hit me first and I demand his suspension,' replied Lyons immediately.

Fionn stared at Lyons in shock, the white of his eyes forming a saucer shape. 'I absolutely did not, does anything else come out of your mouth apart from bullshit?'

Lyons was quick with a reply once again. 'You injured my shoulder, I think you may have broken something, it was self-defence boss.'

'Are you actually for real? I'm so sick of you, you little weasel shit, you think you're fighting fire with fire, but I've got so much dirt on you I'm going to bury you with it.' Fionn said, immediately wishing he had at least rephrased in his head before blurting it out.

'Fagan,' Corcoran exclaimed. 'I will not tolerate blackmail among my staff. This behaviour is unacceptable.'

'But boss,' protested Fionn. 'Lyons is unnecessarily aggravating me, I should not have to put up with this corrupt asshole.'

'Fair enough, you poor little petal' replied Corcoran sarcastically, 'I know exactly how to solve this problem.' Corcoran arched his eyebrows and gave Fionn a judgmental grimace.

'Ah, you can't suspend me, I swear, he hit me first and he's been talking shit about me all day.' Fionn pleaded.

'That's not the way it looks to me, Fagan. I come over and see you kick Detective Lyons to the ground and then threaten him with blackmail. You have some serious behavioural issues. It's not the first time you have been in trouble with me and it remains to be seen if it is the last. I'd like you to leave immediately, you're suspended until your investigation meeting which I will inform you about in due course. Get the hell out of my face and thank your guardian angel I already had my third coffee or this may have gone a lot worse.'

Fionn faced Corcoran with a look of plea in his eyes and then glanced over at Lyons who was smiling patronisingly. He glanced over at Neeve who was staring at him with a look of concern but also what seemed to him to be disappointment. He then looked back at Corcoran.

'So, go.' Corcoran commanded.

Neeve was walking Fionn out to his car. 'You're an idiot,' she proclaimed as if it were a revelation. 'You let him wind you up and he came out on top. He played you like a fiddle.'

'What does that even mean?' Fionn replied with a glum tone of self-pity in his voice.

'What's really up?' Neeve asked.

'What do you mean?' Fionn replied in genuine confusion.

'There's obviously something more to this. You're usually cool and calculating, and I mean that in a good way,' Neeve said, immediately regretting her choice of words.

'Of course,' Fionn said, as he dismissed the comment as causing no offence.

'You absolutely flew off the handle today. Bagman really screwed you over, but the Fionn I know would have sat back and thought about the best way to handle this, you came straight in here looking for blood like you had just lost the plot. I mean, how did you think this was going to go?'

'I don't know,' Fionn admitted. 'I just wanted to come in and face the lying asshole. I'm so sick of him and his bullshit. He should be in prison for some of the shit he's done over the years, everyone knows it. I just had enough.'

'Yeah but something is different, come on Fionn I know you. Is everything OK with your parents? You were down visiting them at the weekend right?'

Fionn shook his head almost shamefully. 'I didn't go in the end.'

'Oh, right. Well, look on the bright side now you have plenty of time to go visit.' Neeve smiled as she tried to put a positive spin on Fionn's suspension.

'Nah, that won't happen, I was informed not to visit home until…'

'Until what?' Neeve coaxed.

Fionn looked at Neeve blankly until she came to the likely reason.

'Ah Fionn, how much do you owe them?'

'Not that much,' Fionn lied. 'I'm just in the bad books at the moment, no big deal, it'll blow over.'

'I know you have a gambling problem, Fionn, I know you spend every spare Euro you have on it but I didn't realise you're working yourself into debt?'

'I'm not, I swear, I'm just a bit slow paying the folks back and they've taken the huff with me, honestly, no biggy,' he lied again.

'Look, if you're having money trouble I can help you out a little bit if you really need it, for a short while, I suppose?' Neeve said unconvincingly.

'No not at all.' Fionn replied just as unconvincingly. 'It's honestly no big deal. Please, stop thinking it is, I'm not in debt, Jesus, if anything I have more money than I should, no, no, stop talking about it now you're making me out to be a charity case.'

Fionn had promised himself a long time ago that he would never ask Neeve for a loan after previously losing two close friends and now being on the verge of losing his whole family through unpaid debt, he did not want to lose her too.

'Ok, well look, here's that info you wanted earlier. I found a Jim Rogers who volunteers for Shelter Ireland. They told me they only have one 'Jim' and he works mainly in the city centre, here's his details,' said Neeve as she handed a folded A4 page to him.

Fionn held up his hands defensively as if touching the page would hurt him. 'That's no good to me now, I'm suspended, besides it's a bullshit investigation to get me out of the office.'

Neeve stamped her foot and took a chastising tone with Fionn. 'Hey. Take the bloody information. I went to the trouble of getting it for you, not that I had to, you have a partner to treat as your lap dog, at least humour my effort.'

39

Fionn reached out and took the page with a sheepish grin. 'Love you,' he said jokingly.

'Asshole,' replied Neeve as she made an exaggerated turn on her heel to start marching away from Fionn. 'You'll be OK, this too shall pass, I'll call you later,' she said loudly to him as she walked away without looking back.

Fionn opened the page and briefly scanned the information. Name, Address, DOB, etc. One piece of information jumped out at him above all others. His full time job. He owned a bookmaker on Dame Street.

That is why Fionn decided the best way to take his mind off his suspension was to immerse himself in his current case. In an unofficial capacity.

CHAPTER FOUR

Fionn walked it in the direction of Dame's Dime Bookmaker on Dame Street. He had a rigid, upright and confident posture as he walked with his head held high and his phone to his ear.

'Rohypnol?' he exclaimed into his receiver. 'Very interesting.'

'Each one of them had high traces in their system,' explained Neeve. 'You'll need to find out if this is normal among the homeless community. Sounds suspect.'

'Yeah, obviously,' retorted Fionn.

'Not today, I mean tomorrow or whenever,' continued Neeve ignoring his remark.

'Yeah sure, tomorrow or whenever,' he said glibly. 'I'll keep you posted, thanks for letting me know and call me later.'

As he pulled the phone away from his ear he heard her say 'I will' before he hung up and continued walking down Grafton Street. He noted that it seemed busier than it usually would at this time. He was always observing the people and places around him. It came with the training but he believed he had always been like that. When he was a child, his father used to tell him that he had eyes like a hawk. As he got to the end of the street it occurred to him that he had not noticed a single person he knew during his brisk strut. People always scoffed at him when he brought up his theory but he believed Dublin was so small that if you stood in one spot on Grafton Street you would see someone you know, or at least recognise, within ten minutes. He felt his theory was compounded by the fact that most of the time when he walked the street he would notice someone he recognised without even having to stop and wait.

As he entered Dame's Dime his first impression of the interior was that it wasn't as dreary as he was expecting based on its appearance from the outside. He had almost missed it, as compared to the big bold doors of The Mercantile Bar which he passed first, its old dark unassuming entrance almost disappeared into an alcove. He looked around the seemingly well-kept Bookmaker and noted that although it was quiet and empty there was a musky smell of sweat and money in the air that suggested the space had been recently packed with an active crowd. The member of staff attending behind the window and an old man with thick glasses and a farmer's cap reading a paper were the only other people present. He scanned the TV screens. There were approximately twenty different TVs covering three of the four walls and almost all of them were showing horse racing. Horses were not Fionn's favourite sport but he was still partial to the odd bet when he would get a good tip. He stopped in front of a screen and read the paper that had been placed in front of it detailing all the horse races as well as all the sport fixtures that were happening later that day. He scanned the horses looking for a name that jumped out at him like a moment of inspiration, but none

42

did so he started picking out some 10/1's to study the form of and see if any were worth the bet. He always preferred 10/1 odds on horses as if those odds were his lucky numbers in themselves. He had found horses with better odds of winning weren't worth the bet for the amount he stood to win, whereas horses with higher odds almost never won for him.

The process of studying the form and deciding on which horses to back took up a good ten minutes before Fionn finally made his decision. The irony of the horse's name may have played a part in the selection but he was completely locked into his choice as he approached the window with a handwritten slip of paper.

'€50 on number two, 'Bad Chances' in the 5.15,' said Fionn as if the information was not already on the paper he was holding.

The owner could be accused of being pessimistic for giving their horse a name that suggested it didn't have winning potential. However, Fionn thought it was brave and believed it to be a statement of having such faith in the horse that the ironic name would only serve to show that names mean nothing. If the horse wins it's the winning he'll remember, not the name.

Fionn stared at the bet slip intently for one more moment before the man behind the window reached out, placed his hand on it and pulled it towards him. With one swift movement he fed it into the machine beside him for processing, not looking at Fionn once during the entire transaction. He had short cut silver hair which Fionn thought made him look well over fifty, even though he probably wasn't quite that yet. He had smooth, sallow skin and deep dark circles under his eyes that sunk to his cheeks, like he was wearing Native American war paint.

Upon hearing the details of Fionn's bet, the old man in the farmer's cap looked up from his paper and over at Fionn with a satisfied smile. 'Good choice, young lad,' said the old man. 'A sure thing, and it's at 10/1. That was one of the first bets I placed today.' Fionn gave the old man a wry smile and turned back to the window. 'Is Jim Rogers working today by any chance?' Asked Fionn in an almost whisper.

The man looked up at Fionn for just the second time. 'And who wants to know?' He asked defensively, visibly taken aback by the request.

Fionn opened his wallet which he was already holding, having just handed in his €50. The man looked at the badge for a long moment, his eyes widening and then looked back up at Fionn.

'Don't worry, no one is in trouble,' Fionn said in an attempt to abate any distress the sight of the badge had caused. 'I just have a couple of questions I think he can help me with.'

'I'm Jim Rogers. I'm the owner,' said the man with a squeak in his voice that would better suit a teenager going through puberty. 'How can I help?'

Fionn looked back at the old man who was pretending not to listen to the conversation but had his ear cocked in their direction, so it was obvious he was paying attention to little else. He decided to

44

raise his voice so the old man could clearly hear. 'I understand you are a volunteer with Shelter Ireland Mr. Rogers? I am just gathering some information on homelessness in the city centre area and I was hoping you could help me?' Jim still seemed to be tense but that was to be expected. Many generic reactions come hand in hand with the introduction of a Garda badge, even for those with nothing to hide. Sweats, pale faces, red faces, quivering voices. Everyone assumes the worst thing they have ever done has come back to haunt them. He looked back at the old man who had become bored of the subject matter and was now devoting all his concentration to the current race he probably had thousands of Euro riding on.

After a long pause, which Fionn waited out, Jim beckoned him back behind the window so they could talk in private. He stepped in front of the closed door and noticed it was damaged. There was a mark underneath the slit of the door. It looked like someone had tried to force it open. Although still intact, the door had obvious signs of wear, tear and damage and didn't appear to be overly secure. He put his hand on it and gave a firm push but as it didn't budge he realised it was more secure than it looked. He waited for Jim to gingerly make the journey from his chair to the door to open it and let him in. A friendly smile and an offer of a hand shake awaited him as he stepped across the threshold.

'How can I help you, Garda?' Jim asked with a note of inquisitiveness, drawing out the end of his sentence by way of asking his name.

'Fionn Fagan, thank you for speaking to me.' He took out his notepad but left it on his lap, suggesting he had no intention of taking any notes. 'I won't keep you long Mr. Rogers, I just wanted to ask you a few questions regarding the homeless around the city centre area which I understand you work with quite often?'

'Yes that's correct,' replied Jim. 'Once a week I go around the area offering tea, sandwiches and blankets and just generally have a chat with them. And please, call me Jim.'

'And how long have you been doing this?' asked Fionn.

'Almost a year now, I suppose,' replied Jim. 'I just want to be able to give something back to the community,' he added in a tone as if it were a job interview.

'OK Jim,' said Fionn, flashing a smile. 'You may or may not know that over the past week or so several members of the homeless community have been tragically found drowned in the Liffey. I was wondering, as someone who works so closely with the homeless, if this seems unusual to you?'

Jim shook his head. 'No, not really, to be honest. Some of the poor unfortunate people I meet have admitted that they think about doing that every day. Jumping off a bridge. Into traffic. In front of a train. Ending it all. Have you any idea how hard life is on the streets? I'd say the first guy did it and the others just thought, "yeah, that's probably the best idea." He paused and bowed his head briefly. 'Tragic really. As much as I try to help, sometimes I feel useless.'

Fionn had only just picked up on an unusual twang to Jim's words. Like he was making a poor attempt at an English accent. 'Each of the victims had rohypnol in their blood, does that seem unusual to you?'

For a split second Jim seemed surprised but then his tone turned serious. 'Unfortunately they will get their hands on whatever they can to numb the pain. Alcohol, prescription drugs, heroin. My guess is someone got their hands on a bunch of those things and passed it around among them, or swapped for booze, or for a prime spot for begging where they can sit comfortably and watch their cup fill with change.'

'Forgive my bluntness, but why don't you bring them to a homeless shelter, instead of letting them sleep on the streets?'

'They prefer the streets,' Jim replied sharply. 'They consider the streets safer than shelters. They get robbed and beaten in shelters, of course we do encourage them to go to one but all we can do is try to make them as comfortable as possible.'

'OK, I see,' Fionn said with an empathetic frown. 'All the same, it's very admirable, the work you do.'

'Thank you,' replied Jim.

'I think you're right, that's all there is to it but I still have to ask the questions, you understand?'

'Of course,' Jim answered with a wry smile. 'I'm just glad I can help. Help you and help them. It may not be much of a help but I'll do what I can.'

'No, no you've been more than a help,' Fionn said as he removed a pen from his inside pocket. 'But I want to ask you about a man that seems to go by the name Buzzer.'

'Oh,' Jim replied with a tone of worry in his voice. 'Larry? Is he OK? He's not in trouble is he?'

'Not at the moment Jim, no,' replied Fionn. 'What is Larry's surname?'

'Larry Flynn. He's an old friend.'

'Can you tell me about him? How long have you known him?'

Jim looked down for a few seconds as he thought about where to begin. 'I know him from London. I worked with him on building sites in the 80's. I was a plasterer and he was a labourer. We are and were actually quite different but in London in the 80's the Irish very much stuck together. I suppose we felt we had no choice. Back then if you met another Irish person in London you were automatically friends. I spent twenty-five years over there, until the Celtic Tiger allowed me to come home.'

Fionn had started to take some notes. 'Did you work with Mr. Flynn during your entire time in London?'

'No, I'd say eight to ten years. At some point in the early 90's he lost his job. He had turned up for work drunk one too many times. I tried to warn him it was coming but there's no reasoning with an alcoholic. I had heard he lost his apartment and was sleeping rough in London for many months, possibly a couple of years, until the British

Government finally paid for a one way ticket for him back to Ireland. I don't think he had any family to come home to. I don't remember him ever speaking about any family during our time working together and when I spotted him on the streets a couple of years ago I tried to help. I was surprised to see him, he looked like he had aged twenty-five years in the ten odd years since I had last seen him. I wanted to help. I bought him a cup of tea and a sandwich and gave him some money for a hostel. When I asked him if there was anyone I could contact for him he told me no. It's awfully sad really, the position he's in and I wish I could do more.'

'How often do you cross paths with him and how would you describe him as a person?' Fionn's meeting with Buzzer earlier had left a bad taste in his mouth, so because there was something he felt wasn't right about him he wanted to gather as much information as possible. Here he was, obsessing over something again.

'I see him almost every time I'm out working with Shelter Ireland but if I'm not here at work I'm in or around my home in Ranelagh, so I never see him other than that. And as for him as a person, he's harmless. Stubborn, but harmless. I don't think he's ever been in trouble with the police. Maybe he's had to defend himself against other homeless people or troublemakers in the past but that's it.'

Fionn gave an exaggerated hum. He still wasn't sure about Buzzer but he proceeded to put his pen and pad away. 'Thanks for your help Jim. That's all I need for now.'

'No problem,' Jim said with a smile.

'I think it's great, what you do, highly admirable.'

'Thank you,' replied Jim with a nod of his head.

'Can I ask you, what made you get involved with the homeless?'

Jim seemed to think hard about the question before he answered. 'I suppose it's because of Buzzer, er, I mean Larry, really. We were both in the same place when we worked in London together and I've been lucky with my decisions in life and he hasn't and I think the least I can do is to give something back to the part of the community that needs it most.'

Fionn leaned his head back slightly and arched an eyebrow. 'Hmmm, very noble,' he said.

'Hey, look,' Jim said with a sudden burst of excitement as he opened his till and took out a €50 voucher and handed it to Fionn. 'Members of the Gardai get a free first time bet here, that's the rule'. He then offered a friendly wink.

Fionn held up his hands in protest. 'No, absolutely not, I can't accept that, thank you but I could lose my job for taking bribes.'

Jim gave a wink. 'What bribe? Your business is finished with me right? You're not asking me questions about this place so this is merely a voucher you are being given. Call it a prize?'

'Thank you but I'm not comfortable being handed €50.'

A grin like a Cheshire cat came over Jim's face. 'I absolutely understand. Best of luck with your bet.' He stood up to open the door and let Fionn out.

Fionn was halfway out the office when stopped dead in his tracks and turned, as if a magnet was pulling him back in. 'If there's anything else I need, can I call back in to you Mr. Rogers?'

'Oh anytime,' Jim replied. 'I'm here almost every day.'

Fionn waited for the 5.15pm race and spent the time between studying who was due to be playing in each of the football matches that were among the night's fixtures. He knew a decent amount about Premiere and Scottish League, a little about the European leagues and had a minimal knowledge on much else, including his home country's football league. He also called up his partner Billy to inform him on the day's events. Billy seemed to be already aware of everything, which didn't surprise Fionn in the slightest, as word travels fast in An Garda Síochána. He then returned a missed call from Neeve, who had kept true to her word about calling him later. He omitted the fact he was sitting in a bookies when speaking to both of them and other than him moaning about how he felt he was being screwed over, none of the three had anything else of significance to discuss. He had told both of them that he was continuing to informally look into the homeless cases just to tie up some loose ends and arranged for all three of them to meet for drinks at the weekend. 5.15pm finally came around and Bad Chances started out well. The rush kicked in strongly for Fionn over the course of the first few lengths. He could feel the joy beginning to manifest in the pit of his stomach. Each time it came it felt like a year of Christmas mornings in one moment. The thrilling feeling of a day ending on a high was on the near horizon, an easy €500 in the bag. However, the taste of victory started to rapidly deplete around half way through as his horse started to fall significantly away from the leading pack of four. Always the optimist, Fionn would never give up hope until the race was over but when it finally was and Bad Chances finished fifth, Fionn was left feeling deflated.

He looked around at the old man who gave him a commiserating smile, knowing full well the disappointment he was feeling. His eyes were then caught by Jim who was waving him over from behind the counter. He reluctantly strolled up to the window fully expecting a jeering from Jim for not taking his €50 voucher.

Jim smiled at Fionn before speaking. 'Sorry about that,' he said.

Fionn gave a weak fake smile. 'Not to worry,' he said.

'I know you don't take *bribes*, but I want to offer you something you can work with.'

Fionn said nothing but looked at Jim with confusion.

'They say 80% of first time customers will not revisit a place if their experience was bad. I like to make sure my first time customers come back.'

Fionn continued to just look at Jim. He wasn't sure if that was a legitimate statistic, and even if it was, whether it applied to Bookmakers, but he wondered what form of bribery Jim was going to attempt next. As a Guard he was used to being offered complimentary treatment. People seemed to think having a Guard in their debt would get them off anything they had done or protect them from anything they were about to do.

'Look, I'm not offering you anything for free, I just want to give you the opportunity of redemption.'

'Redemption?' Fionn asked as if he was confused as to what that meant. He realised Jim had an excellent understanding of the psychology of a gambler.

'You could call it double or nothing. We only have football for the rest of the night, but you put down a €50 bet, and I'll give you double the odds.'

Fionn made a humming sound while he thought for a moment. He found this interesting. It wouldn't be against regulations to accept this offer, it wasn't a bribe or a freebie, it was just a good deal. He cast his mind back to the fixtures he had studied earlier while trying to pass time. He knew Chelsea were playing away to Real Madrid and that pundits had all but given up on the London team. He never particularly liked Chelsea, in fact, being a Spurs fan since he was given a hand-me-down jersey as a young boy, he disliked The Blues more than any other team but he had felt that Chelsea were being written off in Europe too soon. He picked up a fixture sheet and reminded himself of the odds he had read earlier out of interest. '7/1 on Chelsea to win 0-1,' he finally said. 'That would be 14/1 for me?'

Jim said nothing, just smirked and nodded.

'I guess I'll have to take that. It would be rude not to.'

CHAPTER FIVE

It was twenty four minutes into the second half. Just over three quarters way through the match and there was still no score. Fionn's nerves were shot. If Real Madrid scored, it was all over. Chelsea needed to score or else when the match was over, so were Fionn's hopes. The match had been tense so far. Chelsea had been by far the weaker team but seemed to be holding their own and Fionn continued to believe all the way through that a one nil win was entirely possible. He looked away from the TV screens and noticed a man that had been there since the start of the match made his way out the exit, so he decided to give the room a fresh scan. Several dozen people had come and gone but besides Jim and himself, only one other person remained. The man was short and was wearing tracksuit bottoms and a cheap looking fleece. He was standing calmly with his arms folded in an upright steadfast and rigid position, whereas Fionn on the other hand was slouched on a stool with both knees twitching and the palm of his hands moving around his face like he was discovering it for the first time. He could not figure out what the fellow gambler had money riding on but was sure it couldn't have been much as he didn't seem fazed by the ball being in either team's goal area. He wouldn't have been surprised if he was just a football fan and either didn't fancy watching it in a pub or wasn't able to. Fionn hadn't observed him place a bet in the time he was there but that wasn't to say a bet wasn't placed at an earlier point. The man in the fleece took a phone out of his right trouser pocket and began slowly texting. Fionn focused his attention back to the game as Chelsea began a charge on goal. A feeble long shot resulted in a corner kick after a defender put a foot on the ball to clear what was already quite hopelessly drifting wide. It was from the corner kick that followed that a header from Chelsea was punched by the goalkeeper to his left with a long stretch but only enough to hit the inside of the left post, bounce directly down and roll across the back of the goal line. 0-1 to Chelsea. Fionn gave a brief but loud cheer that reverberated around the room. He looked over at Jim behind the glass who smiled at him but was clearly trying to hide the panic that the match would stay this way and he'd be paying out €700 to Fionn. He then caught the eye of the other man who appeared to be giving him a dirty look. He was either the type of person who resented other people's good luck, had a bet on a different outcome or he was a Real Madrid fan. With fifteen minutes left in the match it was the last piece of action Fionn would get to see as his full attention was suddenly redirected elsewhere.

It all happened incredibly quickly but Fionn observed every second as it unfolded. The first thing he noticed was the urgency with which the door to the bookmakers opened and the two men entered. It was like a gale wind blew in and filled the room with perilous tension. Both men were wearing black balaclavas, shades and army combat style clothes. Besides a slight variance in height, the only other difference between the two men was what they were holding. The taller of the two had a thick black heavy looking crowbar and the other was holding what seemed to be a fake gun, although whether or not it was fake was an assumption he was not going to make. It wasn't until they had charged into the middle of the room that one of them spoke.

'Hands up high, don't move a muscle or you'll die,' shouted the one with the gun. Fionn held his hands up and stood still. His eyes darted around the room for the location of the nearest fire extinguisher. His partner Billy once told him that using one would disarm a gunman at point blank range. He had been sceptical but he figured now was the time to find out. Billy had said that when you release the foam towards the gun it seizes the internal mechanics, causing it to misfire and rendering it useless. The size and weight of the extinguisher also made it an effective weapon to knock someone out, once they were disarmed of their gun. He finally spotted the extinguisher but it was the other side of the room. He wasn't going to get to either prove or disprove Billy's theory today. He quickly assessed the likelihood of a successful interception without the extinguisher and decided that the odds were against him. He figured the best case scenario would be a crowbar to the back of the head as he would go for the guy with the gun first, just in case it was real. The man in the fleece had ignored the request to not move and had slowly moved towards the door and then stood directly in front of it practically blocking it. The man with the crowbar stood facing Fionn, about a metre in front of him. Fionn looked straight into his eyes, which were dark brown with a deep deadness. He was holding the crowbar in his left hand and away from his body in a way that he was ready to swing it like a baseball bat and make contact with skin and bone at any second.

The man with the gun was standing on the other side of the glass and pointing it towards Jim. 'Open this door now,' he commanded and gestured his gun towards the door Fionn had entered through earlier.

'Here, take this, it's everything that's in the till,' Jim said with a quiver in his voice as he started to briskly shove several dozen notes of all denominations through the gap at the bottom of his window.

'Never mind that, I want everything in the safe,' he said as he gestured with his gun to an area down and to Jim's left. 'Open the door now or I'll blow your head off and make do with this,' he said while pointing to the small mound of cash on his side of the window.

'It's no good,' replied Jim. 'The safe is time locked and the window is bullet proof. You'll have to just take what's there and go.'

The man with the gun walked towards Fionn, pointed the gun at his head and shouted towards Jim. 'What about this lad's head? Is *it* bullet proof?'

Jim looked at Fionn for a moment as he considered what to do next. Fionn tried to communicate the thoughts in his head using just the expressions in his face. *Just give them the money, don't be a hero, you're insured. Right?*

Jim finally spoke after a few long seconds. 'I'm sorry, this is all I have access to. Just take it and leave, the police are on their way. He's one in fact,' he said pointing towards Fionn.

Both men in balaclavas immediately turned to Fionn and gave him an attentive stare while they tried to assess if this was true, and if so, did it matter? The man with the gun who Fionn noticed had the exact same lifeless brown eyes as the other seemed to be losing his patience. 'Bollix to this,' he shouted. He walked over to the window and proceeded to stuff the money into a small camouflage shoulder bag that Fionn thought might have been bought as a matching set with his outfit. He then stuck his hand along with the gun through the gap in the window. With limited room to manoeuvre, he still managed to point it in Jim's direction. 'Just open the fucking safe asshole,' he said calmly. At that moment Jim, who had been standing beside the safe, went rigid with fear and clumsily dropped to the floor. He frantically started to type in a code and when it finally unlocked the man with the gun ordered him to open the door to let him in. Jim jumped up and made a dash for the door to open it and once the man with the gun was inside Jim pressed himself up against the far wall like he was hoping if he leaned hard enough the wall would consume him into it, protecting him. The man with the gun bent down at the safe and vigorously stuffed his shoulder bag to the brim with wads of cash. In one swift movement he swung his body on his right foot like he was attempting to break-dancer and made a dart through the door and towards the entrance. The man with the fleece ducked out of the way, letting him through and stayed in an unblocking position until the man with the crowbar also made his exit. He then slowly side stepped, glanced coolly back at Jim and Fionn and reached for the entrance door.

'Wait, stay where you are,' shouted Fionn, but the man with the fleece edged out the door. Fionn ran to the door and looked out. The two men in the balaclavas had already gone out of sight. Fionn thought a getaway car in city centre traffic would be a ridiculous idea so he assumed they had already ducked down an alley towards a prearranged escape route. He saw the man in the fleece about fifty metres up Dame Street heading in the direction of Christchurch Cathedral. Fionn shouted back into Jim, 'Call the Guards,' and didn't wait for a reply as he began to give chase. Fionn caught up by the ever bustling George's Street junction as the man in the fleece pushed heavy-handedly through a dense crowd of pedestrians. Fionn was closing fast but was also decelerated by the same crowd. Once he negotiated through he was about thirty metres behind the man when suddenly at the top of Dame Street, he saw him turn left and disappear. He had gone out of sight less than ten seconds but once Fionn got to the corner and looked around, he realised that he had lost him. If the man in the fleece had kept running he could only have gone in one of two directions. He had not run ahead nor had he crossed the road because Fionn would have seen him. He could only have hung left and double backed on himself down the narrow and desolate Castle Street or else carried on up towards the red brick lined Bride Street. Fionn ran on a little further so that he could see down both streets but with the man still not visible in either direction it was as if he had vanished into thin air. He must have gone inside somewhere. Fionn scanned the vicinity and deducted he must have entered either of the two adjacent pubs he was standing directly outside. The old fashioned and regal Lord Edward was facing him and the stylish Bull and Castle was behind him. He flipped an imaginary coin in his head to decide which pub to check first. Deciding on the Lord Edward, he briskly walked up to the door as he started to feel his heart beat in his neck. He placed his hand on the door and before pushing it open he took several long deep breaths in an attempt to slow his heart rate. The door swung open with such vigour that it crashed against the inside wall with a loud thud. He carefully scanned the room but could not see the man in the fleece. He examined the faces of the patrons that were sitting quietly enjoying their drinks and then looked to the man that was serving behind the bar. He was an older man with a full head of snow white hair and a face full of wrinkles, each of which probably had its own story to tell. He looked at Fionn inquisitively. As one by one each customer looked in his direction to inspect what the sudden commotion was about, Fionn made the decision this was not the man's choice of refuge as it seemed the clientele and staff of The Lord Edward were too confused to see him. If someone else had just come running in ahead of him they wouldn't have looked so interrupted. Fionn launched himself backwards out the door as a rewind button had been pressed and he headed straight for the doors of The Bull and Castle. He repeated his pantomime entry and noticed the look on the faces of these patrons were slightly different. There was the same confusion but there was a look of surprise lacking in their facial expressions. Instead, it seemed to be replaced by an element of fear. As he tried to take in the body language of the whole lounge at once he noticed a couple of people looking from him to the stairs and back. The automatic glance towards the stairs from a couple of people told Fionn he had gone that way so he headed in the same direction. As he approached the top of the wide wooden stairs to the first level he peered over the final step and scanned the room. He saw that the room was almost empty. It took him several seconds to spot the man in the fleece who was sitting in the unlit end of the bar, almost as if he was hiding in the darkness. Fionn had hoped he would be blocking the only exit but he could see another door just behind where the man was sitting. Fionn made a bolt for the man and in just as fast a speed as he was moving the other man leaped off his stool and bolted for the door behind him, no different to any other predator and prey confrontation found across the animal kingdom. He reached out and pulled the big wooden door ajar while edging vigorously through the narrow gap in order to be able to step out. As he got most of the right side of his body out the door Fionn had caught up to him and with a ferocious blow threw all his body weight shoulder first into the door winding the man and probably badly bruising several parts of his torso. The man hit the ground like an over packed coat stand being knocked over. His body fell crumpled in a heap as he let out a sharp grunt from the impact. Fionn knew he wouldn't have to chase him any further.

Forty-five minutes had passed by the time Fionn got back to Dame's Dime. Jim was still in his little office behind the glass and as Fionn entered two uniformed policemen were on their way out.

Jim looked over at Fionn with an inquisitive look. 'That's him, that's the detective that was here,' he said as he exited the office and walked towards Fionn. 'Did you catch either of them?'

'I wasn't after them,' Fionn responded, which perplexed Jim. He then turned towards the two Guards. 'Detective Fionn Fagan,' he said, pulling out his badge.

'What do you mean you weren't after them?' asked Jim interrupting both Guards as they attempted to ask Fionn to recount the events from his point of view.

'They were long gone, believe me, they had their escape route well planned out. I became more interested in the other *witness* so I chased him.' Fionn put a sarcastic emphasis on the word witness.

'You chased *him*? What for?'

'He was in on it. Obviously. He wasn't the inside guy, that was the taller of the two but you'd know better, did you recognise any of the men?'

Jim gave Fionn a stunned and confused look and his eyes shifted from him to the two Guards and back as he tried to decide which of the questions in his head he wanted to ask next but one of the Guards beat him to it.

'Detective Fagan, can you just back up a little and start from the beginning. Mr. Rogers here has told us what happened from his point of view and I'm sure the CCTV will help but maybe you could share your observations?'

Fionn took a deep breath and exhaled slowly. 'OK, but we need to start at the beginning. Jim, can you tell me about your recent robbery? The scuff marks on your door I noticed earlier look quite new and they look like they weren't exactly your idea.'

'Yeah, I was broken into a couple of weeks ago as well,' replied Jim. Two addicts. They forced the door open with a crowbar but I managed to convince them the money in the till was the only cash I had in the building. They didn't even spot the safe. Anyway, I had a deadbolt put on the door the next day, so once it's locked it can't be open with anything less than a bomb.'

'Right, well that raises some interesting points,' said Fionn as he scratched his chin. 'First of all, the robbers knew full well they weren't getting into the back. When you refused to let them in I assumed they would go straight for the door with the crowbar. I mean, the marks from the last time are right there almost like a clear step by step instruction on how to gain access.' Fionn then motioned with an invisible crowbar. 'Place crowbar here, apply pressure here, door opens there. But they never even bothered trying. I was surprised. I would have assumed they were really stupid if it wasn't for a couple of other things. Like the fact they knew you had a safe and they knew exactly where it was.'

'They did?' Jim asked as his eyes widened. The two uniformed Guards remained silent as they scribbled intently on their notepads.

'Absolutely. I noticed that the man with the gun gestured towards it when he was demanding you let him in. He motioned towards the corner in there, it was the moment I was educated as to where the safe was or even that you had one. I was in the back myself earlier and if the guy held a gun to my head and told me he would pull the trigger unless I told him where your safe was…' Fionn paused for a beat. 'Well, I would tell him, because *I* notice it, but I have very good observation skills, so you can be sure most people would be unable to tell him. It is well hidden for sure.'

'Jesus,' exclaimed Jim as his jaw sank revealing a crooked and yellow row of bottom teeth. 'I never noticed that.'

'Nor would you, it happened so fast, your adrenaline would have had your body concentrating on other things, such as staying alive.'

One of the Guards looked up from his pad and started to speak. 'Thank you Detective, you've been extremely helpful so far, but can we get to the part...'

'I'm not finished,' Fionn interrupted. You don't have a panic button do you Jim?'

'No, actually I don't. How did you know?'

'They knew. They didn't seem worried that you might trigger something. Usually in an armed robbery situation in a place this size the robber would be particular that you would put your hands on your head and keep them there as they carefully observe your movements. They were letting you roam free in there, you could have speed dialled a direct line to Batman on speaker phone for all they seemed to care.'

'Mr. Rogers,' said one of the Guards. 'We will need details of all your employees and any contractors that would have had access to your office or knowledge of it over the last, say, three months to be on the safe side.'

'Don't bother, it was the guy that put in your new lock,'

All three looked at Fionn in unison and asked the same question at the same moment but with varying degrees of puzzlement. 'How do you know?'

'The guy who you paid to put in the deadlock was quite the opportunist it seems. I'll also bet he was in this place earlier. The one with the crowbar, he said nothing the entire time, I bet he didn't want you to recognise his voice. He was looking at this place very carefully indeed when he installed the lock. Did you get a look at him?'

'No, not really,' replied Jim. 'I only remember the guy with the gun, I don't even know if I'd know him again if I saw him.'

'Yeah fair enough, anyway give the Guards here the details of the guy you hired for the lock, they'll soon get answers for you.'

'I'm afraid we can't be sure it was definitely him,' suggested one of the Guards. 'We best take a more detailed list of names so as to cover all bases.'

'It was definitely him, I'm one hundred percent sure of it,' protested .

The other Guard folded his arms and spoke with a gentle tone. 'That's amazing if it's true Detective but...'

'Nah it's not that amazing,' interrupted Fionn. 'The third guy admitted it to me after I bent his shin half way under my foot.'

'What third guy?' asked the first Guard.

'The so called bystander I gave chase to, I'm getting to that part now. I knew there was something weird about him from well before the two men entered, but couldn't put my finger on it. When they came in I thought he was trying to make for the door to escape but he was actually there to not let anyone else in. I eventually caught up to him after I gave chase and even though he might need a new hip, the little weasel was saying nothing. I had to bluff with what I already assumed and eventually tricked him into giving me a name. "Lockie." He shut straight up after saying it. He realised he shouldn't have said the name and did not mutter another word. Which he should have done from the start really if he wasn't such a moron but I took the phone out of his pocket and went through his contacts. I found a *Lockie*, the gobshite didn't even attempt to disguise the number. I waited for a police car to arrive and on the way back did a search on my phone for his mate Lockie's number and got several hits for John McLoughlin, locksmith. I don't need to ask what the name of the guy you hired to put in the lock was, do I Jim. It will be far more impressive if I don't'

Jim gave a wry smile. 'No. No you don't, that's him.'

The second Guard unfolded his arms. 'Thank you very much Detective, it was lucky you were here to help. Is there anything else we should know?'

'Nope.'

All four men stood silently until the Guards decided to be the first to leave. After offering their farewells and reassurance, Fionn turned to Jim with a scrutinising look.

'You were putting your money over my safety back there, Jim. When you told him you couldn't open the safe and he was standing there with a gun to my head. That was a bit shitty of you.'

Jim instantly hung his head and blushed. 'Oh, God, is that what I said? I don't really remember, you know, it happened so fast, I didn't mean to. As you said, adrenaline and everything.'

'Yes, so I did.' He gave Jim a tense extended stare.

'I'm really sorry. I didn't mean to... I don't know why...'

'It's a tough situation to be in, I understand.'

'It really is. You would think after it happened before that it would be a little easier the second time around.'

'Having a gun pointed at you never gets any easier, believe me.'

Jim nodded and gazed over Fionn's shoulder at nothing in particular.

'I best be off,' declared Fionn, breaking the silence.

'Oh. Yes. Of course, thank you so much and I'm sorry, I don't know what to say I'm just...'

Fionn waited for Jim to finish but the sentence seemed to be over. 'I'll catch you soon Jim. Don't be worrying about anything, they won't be back, we'll have them arrested tomorrow.' Fionn was heading for the door but stopped and turned back towards Jim. 'Can I ask you something though? What's the real reason you work with the homeless?'

'What do you mean?'

'It wasn't just because of Buzzer. You knew him as homeless a long time before you got involved. You didn't just wake up one day and decide to do charity work, there must have been something specific that happened?'

69

Jim gave a brief forced laugh that sounded more like a cough. He then stared briefly into the middle distance for a few seconds before answering. 'You're right actually. There was one thing. Buzzer was a factor of course but there was something else. One day I was on the Quays at an ATM taking out money. It was pretty late but there were still quite a few people around. I took my money and as I turned around there were two homeless people right behind me. I had noticed someone behind me but assumed it was the next person to use the ATM. I didn't notice that one of them was holding something until he said, "give me the money or I'll give you the virus." I remember very clearly the man was so gaunt and dirty looking and had a desperate look on his face. At first I thought he had asked for help until my eyes fell to his hand and I saw him holding a dirty syringe. I realised he must have been HIV positive and was ready to jab me with his needle. I don't know if he was lying or not but I just froze. I have never felt as much fear in my life and I hope I never will again. I could feel the blood drain from my head but at the same time felt this enormous pressure build up. My legs nearly went from under me and I could barely get my wallet back out of my pocket because I was shaking so much. I handed over my wallet, I can't remember how much I had in it but I didn't care. They grabbed it and ran away to the best of their ability, which wasn't that fast at all but I ran in the opposite direction. I felt like I dodged a bullet that night. After the dust settled and things got back to normal

I thought about what sort of desperate situation they must have been in to resort to that and I realised that after the fear and anger, what I felt most was pity for the people that robbed me. I decided that the only way of stopping this kind of thing happening was to try to help them.

Fionn waited a few seconds before he responded. 'I can only imagine how tough that must have been for you. But did you not want to catch them?'

'Well yes, of course. I suppose I skipped a lot of the story there but yeah, I was angry. I went out looking for them in the streets. I went back to where it happened and around the city but never saw them again. What I did notice was a lot of people in genuine need of help. It kind of touched me I suppose. I don't believe in God but I suppose you could say I'm just trying to be a good Christian.' Jim then gave a quiet chuckle at how strange those words sounded out loud to him.

Fionn offered an understanding smile in return. 'I see. I'm sorry I asked, it's none of my business, I couldn't help it. I get an itch and I have to scratch it.'

'No, don't worry, I don't mind. You've already done so much for me today, you can ask me at what age I had my first wet dream and I'll scream it from the roof of Dublin Castle. Make sure and come back soon, you're getting plenty of free bets as long as I stay in business.'

Fionn gave a smile and rubbed his hands together. 'That's so nice of you to offer. I'm half tempted to take you up on it, actually. God damn

Chelsea went and won 2 – 0. I was so close to cashing in.'

CHAPTER SIX

The sudden pulsating shudder of metal on wood startled Fionn. His phone vibrated on his bedside locker many times but not often at 3am. He rolled to the side, nudged the phone sideways with the tip of his fingers and saw it was Neeve calling.

'Neeve? Are you OK?'

'Yeah fine, did I wake you?'

'Of course you did, it's 3am. It's been a while since I got a late night booty call off a randy cow.'

'Hah,' replied Neeve without any hint of amusement. 'You don't sound like you were asleep. Look, I've been called out to an incident in town. A woman, homeless it seems, has ended up in the river. It's happened again. I was wondering if you got anywhere at all with your investigation earlier that could help me?'

Fionn sat further up in his bed, pushed his laptop aside on which he had enough credit left for two more spins on Wolf Run, his favourite online slot machine game. Just before his phone vibrated he was already contemplating a quick try on another virtual slot machine before calling it a night. But he decided to stick with this game. He wasn't sure why he always played that particular game with hundreds to choose from but there was something about the sound of the wolves in the game howling that he felt drawn towards, as if he could understand them. It was raw and primal and he'd come to subconsciously associate the sound with the thrill of online gambling so much so that now they both came hand in hand. The sound of a computerised slot machine with the stock audio of a wolf's howl.

'No, not really,' he replied. 'I met an interesting fellow who calls himself Buzzer. I looked into him as he tends to base himself around the boardwalk but he wasn't able to tell me anything. Did this happen in the same place?'

'Yep, Aston Quay, just a few metres beyond O'Connell bridge. We are running a toxicology report now, no bet that we find the same stuff in her system.'

'The drugs can be explained by a supply being shared among the homeless community, and the suicides can be explained as a psychological domino effect from when the first guy did it. Not much to investigate from what I saw, all that can be done *is* being done by the various charities that are there to help stop people thinking it's their only option left. Like this poor girl obviously did, whoever she is.'

'Joanna Quinn, thirty-seven, originally from Wexford.'

'Wow, you got a quick ID on her, you must be on your fourth coffee already?'

'She told me,' replied Neeve matter-of-factly.

'What?'

'She's still alive, she was rescued. Four Spanish tourists here on holidays were walking along the other side, heard a splash and saw her floating. One of the men is a lifeguard and jumped in to save her. He's actually being treated for shock at the moment, I don't think he realised how much colder the Liffey is compared to the beaches along the Costa Del Sol.

Fionn started to slouch back down into the half sitting half lying position he had been in before the call. 'I see, that's quite interesting, but not interesting enough that you should call me at 3am I'm afraid, so I'm going to have to go ahead and enter your name in the bad books, in fact it'll go in under the chapter I'm calling "Neeve".'

'No that's not the interesting part at all,' Neeve said bluntly, to show no tolerance for his banter.

'Oh no?'

'No. See, she claims she had no intention of jumping in the river. She's adamant she was pushed.'

CHAPTER SEVEN

'So basically, the way Neeve explains it, she's making it sound like some sort of hypnotising was involved,' exclaimed Fionn as he twisted his coffee cup in his hand trying to collect the remains of his cappuccino into one foamy mound. 'Derren bloody Brown himself is touring at night to the homeless of Dublin, bending their heroine spoons and making them think they're swans so they'll jump into the water.'

Neeve nodded her head unfazed by Fionn's negativity. His opinion was too low on her priority list. At this particular moment her focus was on stopping herself from nodding off into a micro-nap as she rubbed the dark shadows surrounding her bloodshot eyes which were the result of not sleeping in over 24 hours.

'What do you think, Adam?' asked Fionn as he watched his criminal psychologist friend stroke his greying stubble as he let the situation that had just been described to him sink in.

Adam Kelly had been a friend of Fionn and Neeve for over ten years. They started out in Garda College in Templemore together but Adam ended up branching off into a different direction from his other two friends, being far more academic, having a higher tolerance for paperwork and being far more of a people person. He was described by his friends as posh and a little pompous, yet he was also considered charismatic and charming, which was helped by his unconventional good looks and rugged build.

'What you need to understand is,' he began in a tone like he was about to deliver a lecture, 'there are traditionally four main types of hypnotism. Classical hypnosis, Ericksonian hypnosis, new hypnosis, and humanist hypnosis. Now, classical hypnosis is the original. It's the old school "follow the pocket watch with your eyes" technique that you see in old films. You had to be bold and brash and quite authoritative to pull it off but it often doesn't actually work. Ericksonian style is what you see modern "mind control" entertainers use. The power of suggestion and that type of thing. The ideas are planted and the person thinks they have come to the conclusions themselves. New hypnosis is what is used in self-help books. It's about retraining the mind. Overcoming fears, becoming more confident, quitting smoking and so on. Humanist, well, that's basically yoga and bullshit. But the one thing none of them share is the use of drugs or sedatives. What you're describing suggests to me a different approach to mind control. Quite a dark style, obviously, considering what this guy's aim was. Tell me exactly what the woman remembers and don't leave anything out no matter how small. I haven't completely ruled out that you may be overthinking it, although I hardly share Fionn's dismissive attitude either.'

Neeve squeezed her eyes tightly together and reopened them, as if she was trying to regain focus both in her vision and in her mind. 'She wasn't at all talkative. A highly distrustful lady, especially of the police, I suppose. All I got from her was that she said she was sitting on the Ha'penny Bridge most of the night. She was getting the usual few coins in her paper cup when at one stage, she made no attempt to even guess exactly when, but we estimate about 1am, a friendly man brought her a cup of tea and offered her a pill. She said she asked him what it was, but the man just said he knew how hard nights were on the street and it was just something to help her relax. He apparently said he takes them when he can't sleep. She said she took it and a while later started to feel really sleepy. Apparently she regularly uses the bridge to ask for money and uses a sheltered doorway beside the SIPTU building to sleep and so she has no reason for walking along the south of the Quays. Despite having no idea why she decided to, she got up and walked along Aston Quay. The walls at the banks of the river are quite low along here and the next thing she remembers was what felt like someone pushing her causing her to fall in. That's everything she shared, she wasn't that good with the little details. I asked her to try to remember any distinguishing features about the man that gave her the tablet but she couldn't remember. He was Caucasian, that's as much as she was sure about.'

'Chances are that she wasn't exactly sober before she took the pill but when will we find out what it was?' asked Fionn.

'Hopefully we'll have the full toxicology report later today.' Neeve shook her head and sighed. 'Look, I believe her OK? I've met enough people on the street and seen enough despair and madness to know the crazy from the lost. I see a fight in her to survive. I know when people are talking shit and I don't believe she is. She is shook by what happened and there is just something not sitting right about it all.'

Adam perked up in his chair. 'You're right to trust the gut but how can you be sure the same person that gave her the pill tried to throw her in, and for what purpose?'

Fionn jumped in to answer. 'To be fair, the first time a homeless person with drugs in their system drowns in the river it's an accident. The second time it becomes an incident. The third time in eight days it becomes a coincidence. I'm starting to think that after a fourth time now we are dealing with a situation we need to treat as suspicious. Foul play needs to be assumed until we can prove otherwise.'

Neeve looked at Adam and nodded to portray her agreement with the sentiment.

'Just not so sure our number one suspect is Derren Brown,' Fionn continued.

Neeve just shrugged, still looking towards Adam.

Adam made a V with his thumb and forefinger and then rested his chin between the space it created. 'I do actually agree with you. I'm just playing devil's advocate. How do you know she was heading back to the SIPTU building when she was...' Adam made bunny ears in the air with fingers, '...pushed in?'

'Well she assumed she was, she didn't know where else she could be going.'

'Anywhere really, with the power of suggestion. I'm interested to know what was in her blood, but Flunitrazepam is my bet. It's simple enough to persuade someone to do something when they're under the influence of roofies, as long as your ability to convince is top notch, and can be done before they pass out. So I do think there is an amateur level of professionalism at play here, if you'll allow me to coin that phrase?'

Neeve and Fionn looked at each other and rolled their eyes.

'Your contradictory word play is mesmerising Adam,' mumbled Fionn.

'Mesmerising?'

'I was being sarcastic.'

'Obviously. It's just interesting to me as you probably didn't realise we get that word from the father of hypnotism. Franz Mesmer.'

'I did so realise,' replied Fionn, sarcastically.

'Anywhere where was I? Oh yes, usually with this practice I've read that as well as using a drug they would need an instrument, like the swinging watch. It acts as a tool to which they get your full attention and control your decisions through suggestion.'

'I just don't understand what the point is, if someone is actually doing this', declared Neeve.

'I think you should go back and talk to her one more time,' said Adam. 'I have a few more questions I think you should ask, the first one being what route would she usually take back to the place she sleeps by the doorway of the SIPTU building. If you're going to give a roofie to someone in order to drown them you'd want to be sure they are in a place they can be easily thrown in and you couldn't even throw a cat over the railings of the Ha'penny Bridge. You'd convince them to go elsewhere. You'd also convince them not to swim. Whether they could or not.'

CHAPTER EIGHT

The hospital room was bright with florescent lights yet bleak in tone and smelt excessively sterile. Fionn and Neeve sat side by side facing the physically gaunt woman that looked like she hadn't slept in weeks.

'Hi Joanna, thanks for letting us talk to you again. Just to remind you, my name is Detective Neeve Bello, and I'd like you to meet my colleague Detective Fionn Fagan.'

Fionn tried to give the best empathising smile he could muster up but feared it was coming across as more of a grimace. Joanna returned the smile with her own suspicious one. It was always his experience that when the Guards tried to help members of the homeless community, they assumed there was an ulterior motive.

'Hi Joanna,' Fionn began. 'I know you have shared as much as you remember with Neeve here already but I would just like to go over a few things again and I would like you to remember as best as you can and please don't leave out any details, no matter how small or insignificant you might think they are.

Joanna made a "tut" sound and rolled her eyes. 'I'm actually quite sick of this now, I've told her,' she said, gesturing towards Neeve. 'Don't you people talk to each other?'

Fionn was taken aback, she didn't speak like he expected her to. She spoke clearly and sounded sharper than she looked.

'Of course we do,' replied Neeve, 'but we would like to talk to the man that gave you the pill, we have some questions for him.'

'I thought the man was just trying to help me, he seemed so kind. I can't understand why he tried to push me in.'

'You could have died, Joanna,' said Neeve. 'We really need you to give us as much detail as possible because we don't want him to get away with this.'

Fionn leaned forward in his seat. 'Anyway, the pill was probably prescription and as you didn't purchase it from him, nothing illegal happened so you have nothing to worry about. Tell us about him.'

Joanna shook her head as her voice cracked. 'You're just like all the others. You think everyone that's homeless is a junky or a wino or a criminal or all of the above. I'm not a criminal but you assume I am before you know anything about me. Do you have any idea what it's like to be looked down on like you're literally an inconvenient lump of shit in someone's way? Like you're stealing their oxygen. They assume every homeless person ends up like they do because of drink and drugs. Many don't even touch the stuff, and for those that do turn to it, it's *because* they're homeless, not the other way around. I ended up on the streets to save my family, simple as that. They will have a better life without me.'

A feeling of embarrassment washed over Fionn as he looked away sheepishly. He made a mental note to pass on this information to a councillor and to involve social services as there may be a family out there trying to make contact with Joanna. He then looked back at the weak bodied but strong willed woman sitting up in her bed. 'I'm sorry Joanna, you're right,' he reluctantly conceded. 'I made an assumption and I shouldn't have. You haven't done anything wrong and your assistance is both appreciated by the Guards and vital in our investigation to ensure we stop this person. I'd really appreciate it if you could tell us as much as possible that you can remember about the person.'

'OK, fine,' replied Joanna. 'But it's hard to explain. It's like I can't describe a single thing about him right now but I know if I saw him again I'd scream.'

'So you do remember what he looks like?' asked Fionn.

'Yes. But no,' explained Joanna.

'Young or old? Skinny or fat?' Fionn asked as gently as he could.

'I don't know. Not young but not old. Middle sized weight, I'm not sure, average looking. Have you not got any CCTV footage of it?'

'Unfortunately not,' replied Neeve. 'We did look into it but the only cameras in the area belong to businesses and they have them all pointing at… their businesses.'

'Hah, well that's funny,' quipped Joanna. 'I'm always being told to move on from wherever I'm sitting because there are CCTV cameras watching me, obviously bullshit!'

Neeve turned to Fionn and smiled wryly.

84

Fionn put his palms together and raised them to his chin. 'Were there any distinguishing features about this man at all that you remember?'

'What do you mean?'

'Was there anything unusual about his voice or accent?'

'Not really. He sounded like you I suppose. A little funny.'

'So not Dublin, from down the country?' said Fionn.

'You're a culchie?' Joanna asked, sounding surprised. 'So am I.'

'Go on the culchies,' said Fionn in jest. 'OK, so he's definitely Irish?'

'I guess so,' she replied. 'He said his name and I remember it was an Irish name.'

'He did?' asked Fionn with alarm in his voice. 'That's really useful, what was his name?'

'I'm sorry, I don't remember,' she confessed. 'I just remember his voice was unusual but I thought he was Irish because he said an Irish name.'

'What kind of Irish name?' pushed Fionn. 'A long or short name?'

'All I remember is thinking that it was an Irish name.'

'What, like Liam? Oisin? Cormac? Fiachra? Fuinneoige?'

Joanna looked at Fionn blankly.

'She doesn't remember, let's move on,' said Neeve.

'OK nevermind, what about his hair?' asked Fionn. 'Colour, short, long?'

'I think he had a hat or a hood.'

85

'OK that's good, which was it?'

'I can't remember.'

'OK,' Fionn mumbled in frustration, mainly at himself for not being able to ask the right questions. He was getting nowhere. He studied the woman in front of him. Looking much older than thirty-seven he wondered if living rough had aged her faster. Her dark green eyes were quite beautiful but yet there was a certain emptiness in them. Her matted hair was fuzzy and dirty and although it was mostly an intense red, her roots revealed a prominent mousey brown, her natural colour that was growing back through. 'Did you notice a tattoo or what his watch looked like? Or any distinguishing scars?'

'No, nothing like that, I'm sorry.'

'OK, never mind, tell me what he said?'

'He was very nice, he just said he knows how hard it must be for me. He brought me a cup of tea and said he uses these tablets to help him sleep and that they will make the night go faster.'

'Did you believe him?' asked Fionn.

'Yeah, why wouldn't I?'

'What happened next?'

'That was it, the next thing I remember he's pushing me into the river.'

Fionn raised his hands. 'Hang on, go back to when he was talking to you, did he say anything else?'

'No.' she replied sharply.

'Not even goodbye?'

'Yes, he said that, or take care, or see you soon or something like that.'

'Which?'

'I don't know.'

Fionn and Neeve exchanged a look as if to acknowledge how difficult this was. Neeve decided she wanted to take over asking questions. 'Tell me everything you remember about what happened next. Please include any small detail you can think of.'

'I don't remember,' protested Joanna. 'It felt like I sort of blanked out.'

'Had you taken anything earlier that may have caused this?' Fionn asked.

'No way,' exclaimed Joanna.

Neeve shot Fionn a dirty look for asking the question so insensitively.

'OK sorry, no judgement I was just asking,' he said.

'I'm not a junkie, if that's what you think,' protested Joanna. 'I've never taken a drug in my life. I had my own business until recently, you know?'

Neeve intervened with a calm tone. 'Please continue recounting the events of last night Joanna. What happened next?'

'People passed me, some gave me some coins, then, I'm not sure how much time had passed, I felt like I had to get up and walk.'

'Why did you do that?' asked Neeve.

'I don't know,' she replied with a confused tone in her voice.

'Where were you going?' asked Fionn.

'I don't know.'

'Were you going to where your shelter was?' asked Neeve.

'Yeah, maybe.'

Fionn gave Neeve a look and she knew he was thinking that this wasn't very helpful to the investigation. She ignored him and continued. 'What route would you usually take to walk back to your shelter?

'Straight up the Quays obviously.'

'On which side?' asked Neeve.

'North side, obviously. SIPTU is on the north side isn't it?'

'Yes, but you were on the south side quays when you were pushed in,' reasoned Neeve.

'I don't know, I don't remember, I just felt like I needed to get up and walk. Like a real need to. Like the kind of need when you...never mind.'

'OK, tell me about what you remember about being pushed in?'

'I was in a daze, but the same man definitely pushed me, I didn't jump in, OK?'

'OK,' replied Neeve who was trying to keep Joanna calm.

Fionn was still of the opinion that the interview was going nowhere so he stood up. 'Thanks for your help and sorry for any offence caused, we'll let you get some rest, you look like you need a decent sleep.'

Joanna lay back on her bed. 'Yes, thanks, I haven't been able to close my eyes properly since it all happened.'

'I can only imagine how traumatic the whole ordeal must have been for you,' said Neeve. 'Such a shock to the system to almost drown. Do you have any family that you could call?'

Joanna closed her eyes and turned her head. 'I don't think they would want to see me.'

'Of course they will want to see you, you should call them,' said Neeve.

Joanna remained silent with her eyes closed. She appeared to be drifting off to sleep.

'Come on, let's go,' said Fionn.

As they turned to leave, Joanna gave out a short gasp and they immediately turned back towards her.

'Oh God, that image,' she exclaimed. 'I can still see it. Every time I close my eyes, I can't get it out of my head. It's like it's there all the time, burnt into my brain.'

The two detectives stopped in their tracks and in unison turned on their heels back towards the hospital bed.

'What do you mean, Joanna?,' asked Neeve. 'Tell me about this image. Where do you think it came from?'

'It was on his ring.'

'What?' Fionn said, so loud it startled Neeve.

'Who's ring, Joanna?' asked Neeve.

'The man that gave me the pill. There was something about his ring that haunts me.'

Fionn walked back towards the bed. 'Why didn't you mention this ring before...'

'You didn't ask,' interrupted Joanna.

'OK, fair enough? So is there anything else...'

'Fionn, shhhh,' said Neeve. 'Joanna, how did you come to notice the ring?'

89

'He showed it to me. Told me to look at it carefully, that it would guide me where I need to go, or something like that. I wasn't listening properly, I didn't really care what he was saying but afterwards the symbol just stayed in my mind afterwards, do you understand?

'What did it look like?' asked Neeve.

'Like...shapes.'

'Shapes?'

'Circles inside triangles. I can try to draw it if you want?'

'Yes, please,' answered Neeve as she removed a pen and her notepad from her pockets.

Joanna started to badly draw what looked like a game of x's and o's without the grid lines. Fionn took a long look at what she had drawn. 'Excuse me, may I try to tidy this up?' He took the page and started to re-sketch Joanna's attempt by drawing a circle inside a triangle inside another circle inside an upside down triangle. 'Was this it?'

'Yes, that's it,' confirmed Joanna. 'Oh God I hate it, it torments me, it's like an evil eye staring at me, I can't even look at it.'

Neeve turned to Fionn. 'What is it, what does it mean?'

'No idea, it just reminds me of something I've seen before, but no idea how or why. Then again it could be something random that you just sort of dream up when you're in a bad state.' He immediately regretted being so blunt and contorted his face with embarrassment. 'I'm sorry,' he continued. 'I don't mean to... I wasn't saying...'

Neeve shot Fionn with an angry look and turned back to Joanna who seemed unaffected by the comment. 'Joanna, please tell us everything about this ring and this symbol. How long you looked at it for, how it makes you feel to remember it, what it reminds you of, OK?' She turned to Fionn. 'This might be the *tool* Adam was talking about.'

'Maybe.' Fionn pouted and hunched his shoulders. 'But I'm beginning to think the only tool around here is me.'

CHAPTER NINE

'You're clutching at straws,' proclaimed Tom Corcoran as he sat back in his leather swivel chair and raised his clasped hand underneath his chin. 'Actually, no, not even that, clutching at straws would actually be more useful than this because if you had a straw you could use it to suck up all the bullshit you just sprayed all over my desk. What you're telling me is borderline fantasy. My fourteen year old reads books about witches and wizards and vampires and magic and it's more believable than this nonsense.'

'Sir, I know it sounds a little out there right now,' Neeve conceded, 'but we really feel there is more going on here than there appears to be.'

'I'm failing to see what you want from me?'

'Sir?' Fionn began before receiving a pantomimed surprised look from Corcoran.

'Fagan? Out of the goodness of my heart I agreed to see you, I wasn't expecting to hear from you also.'

He continued regardless of the put down. 'Sir, we're asking for permission to look into this.'

'You obviously *are* looking into it, although I have no idea why.'

'No Sir, properly. Officially,' said Neeve.

Corcoran glanced around his desk aimlessly, picked up some sheets of paper and glanced over them intently as if there was something specific he was looking for. 'I don't see how. Bello, I'm thin on the ground so I need you on call. I can't spare you right now. And I technically don't even have you, Fagan. You're suspended, remember? Or had you assumed I'd forget? Perhaps you hoped your junkie murdering hypnotist had gotten to me this afternoon and used mind control to tell me to forget? Well guess what? He didn't.'

'Sir, I'm fully aware I'm suspended, I'm here to tell you that we've found something we think to be suspicious and we would like to look further into it, what do I have to do for you to reverse your suspension decision? What if I formally apologise to Det. Lyons?'

Corcoran gave a loud hearty laugh. Fionn and Neeve were taken aback by it, they had not often heard him laugh genuinely, it was usually fake and sarcastic.

'Good luck with that Det. Fagan, are you talking about the same Det. Lyons I think you are? Maybe this hypnotist of yours has gotten to you too? Jesus, this guy is running amuck.' Corcoran sat forward in his chair and leaned in towards Fionn. 'Wake up Fagan, when I click my fingers you will no longer act like a dumb shite.' Corcoran raised his right hand and clicked his fingers.

'Is that a no then, Sir?'

Corcoran thought for a brief few seconds. 'By all means, if you want to try and get Lyons to withdraw his grievance I'd be happy to have less paperwork to do. Be my guest but I best not hold my breath don't you think?'

'Thank you boss, that's all I'm asking, I'll let you know.'

'OK, but if your suspension is dropped and I do authorise an information hunt on this Frodo Baggins ring of yours I am by no means saying I'm letting you give your full attention to this investigation. As far as I'm concerned I only need enough information to be able to tell the media, "we looked into it, homeless people are mental, now shut up about it and let us get on with some real work." I'll need more than a junkie's confusion between her dreams and her reality and some hand sketched answer to a junior cert geometry question, got it?'

'Got it', replied Fionn and Neeve in unison as they stood up and headed for the door, knowing the conversation was over.

'Look, I also wanted to talk to you two about something else,' Corcoran said reluctantly.

The two colleagues stood silently to attention.

'I hate to blow smoke up asses, I am *not* a smoke blower, but as badly as the timing is for me to admit this, you are two of my best. This is absolutely on a need to know basis for now and should stay in this room until we're ready to progress, but I have it on good authority that there is a bad egg in the ranks, involved in drug dealing and goes by the name "Mr T".'

Fionn stood silently with an inquisitive expression waiting for more information while Neeve raised her hand enthusiastically and spoke. 'Are you checking all Guards with the surname T? I saw that in a show one time.'

'You're a bloody genius, Bello,' Corcoran said sarcastically. 'Right now I just want you both to keep those eyes and ears peeled and report to me immediately if you hear anything, OK? And once again, say nothing about it outside of this room, I know how you love to gossip when you're getting your hair and nails done.' He then stared intensely at Fionn and then turned back to Neeve. 'I hope I can also trust you to keep quiet too, Bello?'

Fionn let out a fake laugh. 'Good one Sir. And don't worry, message received. But can I ask one last quick question please? My partner, I wonder if and when you plan to let us work together again?'

'Budget says no I'm afraid. Anyway McGinty is on another project, I only need one man on it but he'll still be busy for the foreseeable future.'

'Ok Sir, understood,' conceded Fionn.

They both headed towards the stairs without saying anything to each other. Eventually Neeve broke the silence. 'Can I ask you something?'

'Uh-oh, what?'

'You do believe Joanna, don't you?'

'Why are you asking?'

'I suppose I thought maybe you don't and you're just going along with it to let Corcoran think he needs you?'

Fionn didn't answer but arched one of his eyebrows so as to look like a cartoon villain.

'You're a bastard, you are,' said Neeve.

'No, no, wait, I'm joking. I don't know if I completely believe her but I do believe there is something strange about the whole situation and I do want to find out what. Plus, I feel like I owe her one. I made a judgement on her before I knew the first thing about her and I was wrong.'

Neeve stared at Fionn sceptically.

'Look, of course I don't want to be suspended right now and yes I sort of did use this to argue my point but if I thought there was nothing whatsoever going on here then there is no way it would be worth apologising to Bagman.'

Neeve squinted and decided she read truthfulness in his eyes. 'OK, so what's the next move?'

'Here,' said Fionn, handing a piece of paper to Neeve. 'I photocopied my sketch of the symbol. I couldn't find anything in the database or online that even vaguely resembled the sketch, so maybe pin this up on our info board if you want to? If there's something in the symbol, maybe one of the others came across it in a different case. I put my number on it so if anyone recognises it they'll hopefully call me. The only lead I have is a homeless guy that goes by the name of 'Buzzer' and I don't trust him as far as I can throw him so I want to...'

'Just don't throw him into the Liffey,' Neeve interrupted.

Fionn just stared blankly at Neeve as she began to blush.

'Sorry,' she said.

'No, that was good, I just thought you were supposed to be the nice one?'

'Yeah, I suppose. So what are you going to do first?'

'I'll go find out where Lyons is, he's not here but he's definitely on duty so I'll track him down. I can't do much while off duty so I better swallow my pride and get this sorted.'

'OK, I better get back,' said Neeve as she checked her watch. 'I've just wasted my lunch on this. I'll talk to you later, good luck.'

'Thanks,' replied Fionn as he headed for the door.

'Oh hey, by the way,' shouted Neeve after him. 'If you do end up solving some murders, you better give me credit.'

'Of course', said Fionn offering a smug smile. 'Teamwork and all that.'

CHAPTER TEN

Born in Dublin city centre twenty-five years ago Aaron Doran grew up in a council flat with his mother. He never met his father and growing up, when he would ask about him, his mother had new information to tell him each time, some of which was contradictory to facts he previously had been told. As he got older he realised most, if not all of what his mother told him was untrue and he began to wonder if she even knew who his father was at all. Aaron had his first drink at eleven, he tried his first cigarette at twelve, he first pulled a knife on someone at thirteen, he started getting stoned at fourteen, he got arrested for the first time at fifteen, he made his first decent weeks wages selling drugs at sixteen and was thrown out of his house by his mother at the age of seventeen. When his mother died two years ago from bone cancer, which began as a neglected pain in her hip, he hadn't spoken to her for about eighteen months previously. Since he had been thrown out of the house, his mother and he hadn't been on good terms. She wanted him to clean up his act, which he had been unable to do. After narrowly escaping prison time for possession of cocaine and compounded with the loss of his mother he decided to finally do right by her and stop selling drugs. That decision lost him all that he thought were his friends and as his mother never owned her own house and his friends' sofas were his main source of accommodation, he found himself living in a hostel and relying on social welfare, which left him with barely enough to afford even the most basic of food. One sunny day Aaron had just collected his social welfare on Parnell Street and decided to treat himself to a luxury breakfast at McDonald's. After he ate his McMuffin, which he hoped would keep him full all day, he took his coffee outside to enjoy the morning sun. He sat down on the ground, coffee in hand, resting his back against the base of Jim Larkin's steadfast statue and fell asleep. When he woke up a while later he looked down at his coffee cup which was now empty, the original contents of which were now all over his old jeans. He had spilled the coffee as he fell asleep and it now looked like he had soiled himself. He realised the cup felt heavier than it had been before the spill so he looked into it to find a substantial amount of small change. He counted it up to be over €7. He realised that passers-by had mistaken him for a beggar and some had felt charitable. He was homeless, to an extent, as the roof over his head was a room in a hostel but he had over €100 in his pocket, he was clean and he had a short term goal of finding a job. Even though it was proving difficult, based on his address, appearance and general lack of experience in anything other than selling drugs, he was trying. He had kept a positive attitude of late and was feeling optimistic but at that moment he realised that the money making opportunity that lay in front of him required the same level of job skills and experience that he possessed. Little to none.

He had developed a routine that worked for him and found a good spot on O'Connell Street to position himself. He needed a place where he was less likely to be disturbed by addicts and the homeless that actually did on the street. He had been sitting at the same spot every day for several months collecting enough to be able to justify doing what he did rather than look for a job. He had no major trouble so far, the most heated situation he had been in was inside a Chinese restaurant where he was enjoying a nice meal and another customer recognised him from having given him money earlier. He accused Aaron of looking a lot healthier than he did earlier and having a fine taste in food for a starving homeless person. He inevitably received a light slap to the face for being an alleged faker. It certainly stung a little but that was the most trouble Aaron had found himself in since he started to collect money on O'Connell Street. Until today.

The city centre had been pretty quiet so far so Aaron's cup hadn't seen much money as of yet. He sat staring at it when all of a sudden out of the corner of his eye came a foot swinging in towards him and made contact with his cup as if it were a rugby ball being kicked upwards for the perfect conversion. He watched helplessly as the contents of his cup sprawled across the footpath and rolled under the southbound traffic. He looked up at the owner of the foot and back at his coins that were travelling further away from him in all directions. He tardily rolled sideways and stood into an upright position with the intention of diving under the cars that were temporarily stopped at a red light to retrieve his belongings. His movements were so slow that he barely moved a metre before he felt a pull on his collar that propelled him back to the ground.

'Get the hell back here you little weasel,' said the voice behind him.

Aaron lay on his back waiting for his vision to refocus and looked into the face of the person that had been giving him grief for reasons yet unknown. Although he was looking at the man's face upside down, after a few long blinks he finally recognised who it was looking down at him.

'Get the hell up, you waster,' demanded the man as he gently tapped Aaron's head with his foot.

Aaron squirmed back into his original sitting position. 'What the hell do you want? You just kicked away every penny I own.'

'Well unless you're planning a weekend city break up to Belfast, pennies won't get you very far, so no harm done.'

'You know what I mean,' responded Aaron. 'Bastard,' he added under his breath.

'What the hell did you call me?'

'Nothing.'

'I think it was something. What are you doing just sitting around like a lazy little shit, you had a job to do for me. Did you do it?'

'No,' replied Aaron.

'I bloody know you didn't, you little prick.'

'I can't help you anymore.' Aaron tried to speak with a confident tone but behind his words he felt his resolve waver as he stared into the pair of angry eyes before him that felt like they were burning into his soul. After several seconds of silence he was the first to break eye contact.

'Don't you even consider talking to me like that again or I'll end you,' said the menacing presence in front of Aaron. 'You owe me some major favours, dickhead. Do you want to end up in the same way as the others that I've gotten my hands on?'

'I can't do it. I won't. Some of these are good people, they can't help it. They have nothing else and because of me...' Aaron stopped as he felt himself well up with tears. He then composed himself by swallowing a mouthful of air and continued. 'People will start realising that I'm involved. You can't make me do this, I'll report you.'

'Oh you absolutely will not or you'll die, unless that's what you want?'

'No,' replied Aaron aggressively.

'Of course it's not,' said the man, calmly. 'So will you help me? The next job has to be soon.'

Aaron, who was on the verge of having his spirit broken, felt a sudden burst of determination explode in his gut and flow through him like a newly discovered energy no drug could ever deliver. Growing up as a teenager, he had always been the alpha male among his age group, however, he rarely hung out with the kids his own age. He had always ended up hanging out with an older crowd and although he was always accepted, it was rare when was not the butt of the jokes, the whipping boy of the gang and the one everyone took their aggression out on. He was always too small to fight back successfully but growing up in a gang where everyone was always five years older than him taught him how to take a beating like a man and to not fear confrontation. It was this nurtured attitude and approach to situations that led to him deciding to shift his weight to his left palm, straighten his elbow, push himself up on his hunkers and bring himself up with his weight in his knees. He stood steadily and upright and in a clear and defiant tone he spoke one word. 'No.'

He expected the next feeling to be that of self pride for standing up for himself but there was no time for that as the pain came quick and fast in the form of a hard punch to the diaphragm. It painfully winded Aaron, causing him to double over and hit the ground with a dull thud. He looked around to see if any onlookers had witnessed the assault and may be on their way over to come to his aid. The few people he could see from where he was lying seemed to either look down at him wearily or else awkwardly look away. All of them took an evasive route away from the altercation. The bystander effect. The theory that the more people that witness a crime the less likely anyone is to intervene. Next came a kick to the stomach. The crowd continued to put up no protest as a second and third kick came into his midsection. Finally on the fourth kick came a concerned voice that sounded to be getting closer.

'Hey, hey, hey stop that, what's going on, leave it out,' shouted a stout man in an oversized jacket as he approached the altercation with his palms out, as if to encourage peace.

As Aaron was trying to catch his breath he was beaten to an answer.

'Bloody junkie. Robbed my phone right out of my hand and legged it. I caught the bastard though, and now I'm just trying to make sure he doesn't do it again to someone else.'

The stout man blinked fast as he shifted his gaze from the man standing with a triumphant grin on his face to Aaron on the ground, who was practically coughing up his lower intestine.

'Ah I see', the stout man finally said. 'Well done, fair play to you.'

'No,' Aaron groaned and then realised it was all he could manage to say.

'Scumbag,' rasped the stout man as he gave Aaron a venomous look and returned back from the direction he came.

'Have a think about what you've done,' the voice above Aaron's head shouted loudly for all to hear. 'Or should I say, what you won't do,' said the same voice, this time quietly. Aaron stared at the expensive looking black shoes that were right at his face. He closed his eyes and tensed himself in anticipation of another inevitable blow from the hard rubber soles. When he reopened his eyes the shoes were gone.

David Lyons was crossing the street in front of stopped traffic on Parnell Square. As he got halfway across the pedestrian crossing, the car that was positioned first in line at the lights gave out a loud revving sound, by way of intimidating those on foot to move out of the way. The first thing to happen was that Lyons' natural reaction kicked in first. His basic human survival instinct caused him to flinch and pick up his pace as he made a dart across the dirty front grid of the red Nissan that was preparing to move off. Just as he passed the car he stopped and in a split second made three different observations. The light was still red for the car. He still had the right of way. The driver was taking the piss out of him. He walked back up in front of the bumper of the car and stared motionlessly in through the windshield observing the lone occupier sitting contently in the driver's seat. He decided that the man with the straight black fringe looked like he was probably something like a discontented tradesman and judging by the defiant smirk on his face probably used to be the kind of child that got a kick out of tearing the wings and legs off flies and watching them bounce around helplessly. The smile on the driver's face disappeared as soon as Lyons raised both fists high in the air and with a ferocious thump brought them down onto the car's bonnet, almost certainly causing a dent.

Seeing an expression of shock form on the face of the driver, Lyons began shouting with venom in his voice. 'Still think you're a smart prick now asshole?' Lyons gestured to the driver to come out of the car. 'Get out here I want to see if you're as enjoyable to punch as I think you are.'

The lights had turned green for the Nissan, so the cars behind started to beep their horns for him to drive on. In an effort to get out of his self-inflicted predicament the driver tried in vain to motion at Lyons to move out of the way.

'Oh, I'm sorry,' shouted Lyons loudly as if directed at someone on the other side of the city, not someone behind a windscreen a metre in front of him. 'Am I in your way? Oh come out here and let me apologise, it'll be such an unbelievably good apology it'll break your nose.'

Fionn had been sitting at a table outside The Old Music Shop, a Georgian building that used to sell musical equipment but was now a café. He had been waiting for Lyons who he believed to be in transit to the area so Fionn decided to have a coffee while he waited. He had almost finished a frothy cappuccino that had kept the leaf shape created by the Barista with the milk and was staring pensively at the incrusted inner rim of the cup. Suddenly the sound of car horns won his attention. He looked up to see Bagman across the street holding his ID high in the air and he seemed to be screaming at the car in front of him. He got out of his seat and walked in the direction of the apparent altercation. Crossing the four way junction was quick and easy as all of the cars were stopped. As he approached Lyons he was finally able to make out the words he was saying. They were mostly swear words to describe his mood, insults directed at the driver of the car in front of him and violent phrases to get across what was apparently going to happen next.

'Dave, what are you doing?' interrupted Fionn.

Lyons' head pivoted on his shoulders in the direction of the voice that had just addressed him. 'Fagan,' he proclaimed with surprise. 'What are you doing here?' After the initial interruption to his flow of colourful language he appeared no longer phased by Fionn's presence and turned back to the driver. 'Get the hell out of your car now you little shitty maggot. I'm arresting you and locking you up with the rapists. We'll see how far...'

'Dave,' Fionn said as he interrupted again. 'What has he done?' By now there were a couple of dozen cars behind the Nissan, all of which had horn noises blaring from them like an out of tune orchestra being conducted to play one note each.

'Piss off, Fagan and mind your own business,' replied Lyons with an adamant tone.

The driver rolled down his window just enough that he could be heard and shouted towards . 'Here, I didn't do anything wrong, this guy is a psycho, I think he wants to kill me, not arrest me. I don't even know if that's a real badge, where's his uniform?'

Fionn walked over to the window and produced his own badge. 'I'm afraid it's a real badge, this is a colleague of mine.' He then held up his own badge to the trailing cars and made a calming gesture with his other hand. He then turned to Lyons and spoke quietly. 'What the hell did he do? I was sitting over there this whole time and didn't notice anything.'

'What I arrest people for is my business and my business only, Fagan,' replied Lyons through gritted teeth.

'Eh, no it's not,' replied Fionn.

'He threatened a member of the Gardai.'

'With what? His high beam lights?'

'Disorderly conduct,' suggested Lyons, half-heartedly.

'Dave, he'll report you for harassment.'

Lyons looked from the car to and off into the middle distance. Fionn could see the manic glint in his eyes as they then looked down to the pavement and finally he nodded. Fionn shifted Lyons out of the way of the car with his outstretched right hand and gestured to the oncoming cars to proceed.

The Nissan which had already been in gear moved forward about a metre and stopped. The driver rolled his window down a little further and stuck his chin up to the gap. 'Can I get your names and badge numbers please, Guards?'

'Move along,' replied Fionn and Lyons in unison but with different levels of impatience in their tones. The car then continued through the green light which had come and gone three times in the interim. It was followed by the rest of the convoy that had finally stopped sounding their horns.

'What was that about, man?' asked Fionn.

'You've been an ache in my ball sack a lot this week Fagan, what are you doing here?'

'I want to talk to you.'

'Here? How did you know I'd be here?'

'I asked the station to get in contact with you, they said you were on the way here for lunch.'

'Ahh, I was wondering why those nosey bastards wanted to know,' stated Lyons as he scanned his surroundings. 'You know I was going to lie and say I was going somewhere south side because it's none of their business. Good job I didn't, you would be sitting in some dodgy shithole on your own all afternoon, for nothing. What do you want, anyway?'

'Can we go sit down, let me buy you lunch and we can talk inside? I want to sort this disagreement out so I can get back to what I'm supposed to be doing, solving crimes.'

Lyons laughed so loudly Fionn could smell his coffee and cigarette breath from three feet away. 'Ha. You're desperate aren't you? Have I got you at my mercy or what? I'm not hungry anymore so stick your lunch up your hole.'

Lyons' hostile tone suddenly caused Fionn to feel his temper rise up within him like a flame had just been ignited. Apart from feeling the warm glow of his own face flushing red with anger, he wasn't showing any other outward signs that he really wanted to punch Bagman, again.

'Look, Fagan, forget lunch you hungry bastard, I'm actually on my way to meet a contact to discuss a delicate situation. There was a failed take down last week on a fraud case I've put months of time into. I was working on information from an old snitch that turned out to be dodgy, so I need to pay him a visit. Either he fed me bullshit or he got fed bullshit. Either way I've got him by the bollox.' Lyons let out a hearty laugh. 'Well, no, I don't, you'll see, but anyway, a catch up is in order. I want to put the shits up him and usually only meet him alone, so if you come down with me and act like a bit of muscle, we can talk on the way and see if we can sort something out.'

'Why did you think the information was good to begin with?' asked Fionn.

'Me and Dennis go way back,' began Lyons as he started walking with Fionn in toe. 'I caught him in a sting about four years ago. He had ten balloons of heroin up his arse.'

Fionn grimaced and Lyons wasn't sure if he was puzzled or disgusted.

'Turns out this Dennis was well connected at the time and so, facing a jail term I highly exaggerated, he agreed to serve as an informant in return for the charges being dropped. Somewhat of an infamous go-to-girl, at the time he tipped me off on some serious deals. Remember the Coonan Brothers case last year? The knackers had been selling the same greyhounds to each other back and forth over a couple of months. They were using their drug money to pay, so the cheeky bastards were lodging their cash in the bank in broad daylight. When we arrested them they said they were running out of space to keep the cash in their flat and were worried they'd soon be robbed. So, some dodgy lawyer suggested a way they could legally declare it. They didn't think they'd have to explain where it came from in the first place. The idiots. Yeah, he got me some great catches in the past but he screwed me over on this one. Part of our arrangement is that our meetings stay off the books and that I meet him alone, so he'll be scared shitless to see you with me. You don't even have to say anything. If this goes well I might listen to whatever you came here to grovel to me about. What do you think?'

Fionn swallowed air as a means of staying calm and decided not to share his real thoughts with Lyons as it would likely ruin any chance of a reconciliation. He just nodded and followed Lyons in the direction of a council house off Dorset Street.

Lyons turned to Fionn with a sideways smirk. 'Oh and a heads up, he used to be Denise. And before that he used to be Dennis'

'What?' replied Fionn.

'He's always been Dennis I suppose, but he used to go by Denise for a while there. Now, what do you need to talk to me about?'

CHAPTER ELEVEN

'I swear I wasn't giving you any bullshit. They're on to me. You've got to believe me, I'm a dead man.' Dennis spoke in a soft effeminate voice and with a noticeable slur to his words as if he were on heavy medication. He peered out through his front door which was being held ajar with his foot, preventing it from opening any further. He had answered with caution, correctly assuming that whoever was calling was not bringing good news.

As soon as his wrinkled face filled the narrow gap, Fionn could see fear in his eyes.

An instantaneous wave of relief seemed to flicker across his face when he saw it was Lyons, which suggested he must be the lesser end of the potential threats that he had come to expect to his door. The relief soon transformed back into fear as his shiny-eyed gaze met Fionn.

Lyons had skipped formalities and introductions and got straight to the accusations. After he had his say he stood in silence looking menacingly at the part of Dennis' face that he could see.

'Look the info I gave you was solid. The McDonnell brothers came to me looking for an inside man for a job they had planned for Arnott's. They thought they had a foolproof plan to make off with some cash deposits on collection day. Seen as it's one of the biggest shops in the country they were sure the haul would be huge. They said if I could find someone suitable on the inside to work with, they would reward me handsomely, a one off fee before the job was even done.'

'I've heard all this already Dennis, what's your point?' asked Lyons irritably.

'My point is,' Dennis continued, 'I put him in touch with a friend of my cousins who works for security there. I'd only met him once but he seemed like a kind of "hate my job" sort of guy, so I figured he'd be open for discussion on the topic. That was months ago and I never heard any more about it so I thought it just never worked out. Until I was talking to my cousin last week. He said his friend told him in confidence when the job was happening. The bastards were actually doing it but I never got my fee for putting them in touch with this guy.'

Lyons folded his arms and was standing steadfast with his shoulder firmly pressed against the door. 'Oh you never mentioned that you sly little shit, you had me believe it was first-hand information, but you were actually using me. By putting me on to something that was based on three rounds of Chinese whispers you were getting your revenge for not getting a few quid for your funny pills, or whatever you spend your money on?'

'No, it's not like that I promise,' protested Dennis. 'It wasn't exactly first-hand information, I'll give you that, but it was the real deal. Everything about it that I told you is exactly what my cousin heard from his mate and I trust him completely. The next day I was as surprised as you when it didn't happen. I thought it would be in the news. I tried to ring my cousin to see if he knew anything. No answer. His phone is off every time I try. I've been over to his flat about four times since. No answer. No lights on or any sign of movement, he hasn't been home at all. I went to Arnott's to ask his mate if he's been talking to him but I was told his mate doesn't work there anymore. He wouldn't say why and wouldn't give me his contact details.' Dennis' voice was starting to croak with fear.

Lyons unfolded his arms and started to grimace through gritted teeth. 'And what, you're so paranoid from all the hash you smoke you think they're both up the Dublin Mountains one feet under?'

'Yes, and I'm next.'

'Oh come on you freak, who kidnapped them, the Arnott's management? That's certainly an autocratic style of disciplinary action. The job didn't work out, your cousin's mate was caught rotten beforehand and your cousin pissed off on holidays and didn't tell you. Snap out of it man.' Lyons turned to Fionn, raised an eyebrow and simultaneously rolled his eyes. He then turned back to Dennis. 'Are you not going to invite us in for a cup of Earl Grey?'

Dennis stared at Lyons blankly for a few seconds, looked at Fionn and back to Lyons. 'Who's he, anyway?' His slur seemed to be getting worse.

'This is Detective Fionn Fagan and he is even more pissed off about all this than I am,' Lyons lied as he introduced Fionn as the badder cop to his bad cop routine. 'He insisted on coming along because he believes the mutually beneficial professional relationship we have going on needs to cease and I need to report you to my superiors.'

Fionn didn't think the man's round thin face could be filled with any more fear than it already contained but he was proven wrong when Dennis then stared intensely at him. He looked almost childlike, as if the joys of life were being taken away from him in front of his eyes. Making no attempt to stay in character like he had agreed, he gave Dennis a calming smile and saw a glint of optimism creep back into his face.

'I can't just invite you in, they could be watching me right now, how is it going to look if I open my door to two men that are obviously Guards?'

'What if we force our way in,' suggested Lyons threateningly. 'Will we be helping you out then? Making it look better for you? Maybe do a bit of damage to your property just to make it look like the real deal?'

'What?' Dennis didn't have time to think any further about the question as suddenly Lyons took a step back and charged into the door shoulder first. The door popped back a few inches and the side of Dennis' foot that he was using as a stop got caught in the small gap between the bottom of the door and the surface of the floor. Dennis let out a shrill yelp of pain and hopped backwards three steps, bringing his foot up to his hand while doing so.

'For Christ sake, you've broken my toe,' shouted Dennis in a hoarse voice as he gingerly moved around his hall like a ballerina, slurring his words as if the whole scene was happening in slow motion.

Lyons walked through the threshold brushing the newly acquired dust off the sleeve of his jacket. 'You're welcome. Nothing suspicious about that was there? Now, where can I sit down in this dump?'

Fionn reluctantly followed Lyons through the dreary hallway and noticed he could now see Dennis a lot clearer. His face looked like that of a 50 year old with skin of a 40 year old due to decades of moisturising and perhaps having had some work done. His hair was dyed black, short and curly and he was wearing faded tracksuit bottoms and an old t-shirt. What caught Fionn's attention above anything else was Dennis' chest which was bouncing under his t-shirt as he hopped around in pain. His first thought was that Dennis has gynecomastia. An over development of breast tissue in men that gave them "man-boobs". He had never seen the condition in someone as slim as Dennis. He then quickly came to the realisation that there was no medical condition and Dennis had in fact a pair of breasts. He suspected Lyons was using dark humour earlier when describing Dennis but he now understood he was not. But with a masculine face and a feminine body, he wasn't sure if Dennis was living as a trans-man that kept his breasts or a trans-woman that kept her birth name.

Less than five minutes later all three were sitting around a coffee table with so many indentations, cracks and scratches that if it could talk it would have some interesting stories to tell. The open plan living area with a kitchenette in the corner was dark and grubby with a smell of stale food in the air.

Lyons had been doing all of the talking so far. All lies and all told solely to manipulate Dennis, just as he claimed he was going to do. 'So basically my hands are tied, Fagan was sent here with me because my bosses don't trust you anymore. They want you arrested and brought in for questioning. I don't know if I'll be able to keep you off the record after this, which of course means anyone and everyone will know you've been informing the police for a long time.'

'Oh Jesus,' Dennis squealed as he raised a shaky open palm to his forehead as if to test himself for a fever.

'The only way I'm going to save your tranny ass is if you give me something else. Something good. Information I can do something with.'

'Please, believe me, I don't have anything else that would be any good to you.'

'Fagan and I will go back to our boss and justify your existence but we need something good.'

'Give me some time to go ask some questions,' pleaded Dennis. 'I don't know anything right now.'

'Not good enough Dennis. Think.'

All three sat silently while Dennis appeared to retreat into himself in thought. Trying desperately to search for something in his head that was not there. Lyons sat staring at Dennis, fury radiating from his dark eyes. He was not going to leave until he got his way. Fionn looked at Dennis and felt pity for him. He had not played bad cop like he told Lyons he would, yet his purpose still seemed to have been served. He didn't approve of Lyons' bullying tactics and felt sorry for how Dennis was being manipulated. If he didn't need Lyons to drop the assault charge he would have intervened by now and put a stop to the charade. He wanted to tell Lyons to do one and tell Dennis the truth, that Lyons was using him. That no one else knew he was a contact. That so much time had passed, Lyons couldn't even hold the original charge against him anymore. Dennis owed Lyons nothing and Lyons was just using him to further his career. Fionn considered that he might come back on another occasion and tell him the truth. The poor man, he thought to himself. Or woman? Fionn looked down at Dennis' chest again. He thought to himself how it didn't seem to quite suit the rest of his body. At that moment Dennis looked over at Fionn. His eyes darted upwards to make direct eye contact but he knew Dennis had noticed him looking at his breasts.

'I identify as a non-binary, if that's what you're wondering,' said Dennis.

Fionn instantly sat up and blushed. Half due to the embarrassment of being caught staring and half due to the statement making him uncomfortable.

'Sorry?' He said, both as a question and an apology.

'You must be wondering about these?' said Dennis as he cupped his own breasts and pulled them up to emphasise their shape under his t-shirt. 'They're fake. I had them done when I was twenty-seven. After the pain went away, which didn't take too long, I was determined to get the whole operation done. I was making thousands a week back then doing what I did but the doctors insisted that I wait at least a year and take an array of hormone replacement medication, do all sorts of therapy and counselling, and take evaluation tests to make sure it was the right decision.'

'Oh, give it over Dennis, you're gay, simple as that, who cares?' sneered Lyons.

'Yes, I've known I was gay as long as I can remember,' continued Dennis unfazed by the interruption. 'When I was a child I used to take great pride in putting on a pair of my mother's tights and plastering on her lipstick. She thought it was a phase and blamed it on there being no father figure in my life. The first time I got a hard on I was about ten. There was a kissing scene on some TV show and something strange was happening to me. I remember it so well. I also remember it was because I thought the man was good looking and I wished I was the woman he was holding. I always wanted to be a girl. I was bullied in school, my family treated me badly, I only had two friends in my life, both girls. I lost my virginity when I was twenty-four to a gorgeous Brazilian escort with an amazing six pack and huge biceps. It was only after I got breasts that I felt even a little normal for the first time in my life. I knew I needed the full transgender operation. No tablets or therapy or tests were needed. I just wanted my penis gone. It didn't belong to me. It was in the way. I couldn't be my real self with it hanging off me. So an appointment with a doctor in Eastern Europe saw all the paperwork being skipped over and on my twenty-eight birthday I was 100% a woman. I was so happy, I felt the happiest I had ever been but what I didn't know was that soon I was to become more depressed than I had ever been.' Dennis sat forward, lifted a glass of water to his lips with a shaky hand, took a sip and continued without interruption. 'What I didn't realise could happen, or perhaps may have realised if I had done the preparation I was supposed to do, was that after the surgery I didn't feel female like I thought I would. I felt neutered.'

A few seconds of silence passed before Lyons started laughing loudly. It came so abruptly that Fionn and Dennis both jolted slightly in their seats.

'So then you wanted to go back to being a man didn't you Dennis? But it's too late now isn't it? You're a nutless nutter.' Lyons turned to Fionn and laughed expecting a supporting laugh that didn't come.'

'Yes, that's right', Dennis continued with a deflated tone but spoke solely to Fionn. 'I spent eight years living as Denise. I was getting more and more depressed every day and it took me that long to realise I was happier as a gay man than a straight woman. I stopped taking the tablets that stopped my body hair growing but I still like to wear makeup. Sometimes I wear women's clothes, sometimes men's. I can't afford to have the breast operation reversed but I'm not sure I even want to. And to add insult to injury I suffered a stroke. From alcohol abuse according to the doctors in the hospital. I spent years secretly drinking as a high functioning alcoholic and I was so good at it that no one ever knew I was plastered most hours of the day. Since my stroke I haven't touched a drop but because of the way I now walk and talk everyone thinks I'm constantly drunk. So maybe that's karma. Or my guardian angel giving me a kick up the arse. I don't know. But at this point in my life gender doesn't really matter to me. Most people call me "he". I'm OK with that. I don't actually mind what people say as long as they say it kindly.' Dennis stared solemnly at Fionn who had been listening intently in silence. He then turned to Lyons who had his arms crossed and was still projecting an amused expression on his face. 'Aaron Doran,' he said.

Lyons slipped around in his chair and then sat up. 'What?' he said.

'Aaron Doran. That's the only thing I can give you right now that may be of any use but even at that I don't know him all that well.'

'What about him', asked Lyons with a tone so serious all evidence he had laughed loudly seconds earlier had disappeared.

'He's in his twenties, sandy brown hair, you'll see him almost every day begging on O'Connell Street. I bought him a coffee one day and had a chat. I like to be nice to the poor and the homeless. He was suspicious at first but I stop and talk to him every so often. Once, he had a black eye and I asked him how it happened. He wouldn't tell me at first but eventually broke down and told me an undercover policeman did it to him. He was scared shitless to tell me anymore but what I gathered is that some guy who claims to be a Guard has him doing some shit that he is not comfortable doing. He is either very scared or very guilty about something, but the whole thing has him messed up. He wouldn't talk to me about it but if you talk to him he might tell you. There could be nothing to it either, I don't know but that's all I have for you, I swear there's nothing else happening that I know of or I would tell you.'

'I see,' said Lyons as he hummed to himself and got out of his chair. 'I should look into that all the same, but for now, and I bloody mean this, you say absolutely nothing to anyone else about this or I swear to God I'll rip your tits off, got it?'

'Yes of course, no I would never say anything,' asked Dennis, still sitting in his seat. 'Do you really think there could be something going on with the Guards and him?'

'What? No, I doubt it,' Lyons replied distantly as if his thoughts were now elsewhere. He walked swiftly towards the door without announcing he was leaving. Fionn gathered it was time to go and sat up slowly.

Fionn passed Dennis on his way out and looked ahead to make sure Lyons was out of earshot before he spoke. 'Nice to meet you Dennis, don't mind Det. Lyons, you're going to be OK. His bark is worse than his bite...'

'Lyons?' Dennis interrupted with surprise.

'Never mind,' Fionn replied, realising Lyons mustn't have used his real name with Dennis. 'See you later, take care.'

A hopeful smile appeared on Dennis' face which juxtaposed his youthful skin with his weathered eyes. 'Thank you Fionn. Oh, sorry, I should call you Det. Fagan.'

Fionn gently shook his head no, smiled, held up his hand to say goodbye and then increased his pace to catch up with Lyons. 'Jesus, that was intense.'

Lyons said nothing.

'Hey, does he know your full name?'

'God no', said Lyons.

'But you gave him my full name?'

Lyons shrugged.

Fionn grimaced and shook his head. 'I did you your favour, so are we square? You'll drop the assault charge?'

'You did a shit job, you were supposed to help me put the shits up him.'

Fionn looked at him blankly.

'But yeah, fine. I'll call Corcoran, tell him we sorted that thing out and it's all good. But you still owe me one.'

Fionn let out a long exhale. 'Cool. Thanks,' he finally said through gritted teeth and decided to change the subject before he said something to undo his efforts so far. 'So what do you think happened with the Arnott's job?'

'I don't know,' replied Lyons dismissing the question with a wave of his hand. 'Maybe one of their staff heard about the plan, reported the security guard and they fired him, so the job never went down even though we were there waiting for it with our trousers down around our ankles and our arses swinging in the air.'

'And the cousin?'

'Don't know, and I don't care.'

'Are you going to look for this Aaron guy, you think there's something in that?'

'What? No. It's bullshit, forget about it.' Lyons became visibly agitated by the question. 'I mean yes, leave it with me, don't stick your big snotty nose in, OK?'

Fionn held his hands up in surrender. 'OK. OK. Whatever, man. Hey, you know what might actually help...'

'Fagan,' Lyons interrupted. 'You can fuck off now.'

CHAPTER TWELVE

Due to recent department cutbacks, Fionn hadn't worked with his partner Billy in several weeks. Not needing two men to do a one man job had been a mantra Corcoran repeated on loop recently, even though having a partner in the field, as support and back up, was supposed to be a fundamental rule. Despite seldomly working together in recent times, Fionn and Billy had decided to sink their teeth into a project on their own time. There was something elusive out there that needed to be found and although they felt it was of the utmost importance to find it, it was certainly not the type of project that would get funding from the government, private or a third party to back it. It had caused argument and debate among society for centuries, so much so that most people believed it to be a myth. Like the Loch Ness monster, people had claimed to have discovered it but sadly it turned out to be a hoax. Fionn and Billy had put dozens of their own man hours and plenty of their own financial investment to find it but as of yet they had been unsuccessful. The search continued for the best pint of Guinness in the world.

It started a couple of months ago while drinking Guinness in The Old Storehouse in Temple Bar. They both agreed it was a surprisingly disappointing pint for one of the most popular and busiest pubs in Dublin. Having agreed that the tourists that made up 90% of the clientele wouldn't notice the difference, they decided that a popular pub and a good pint of Guinness could be mutually exclusive. They then discussed where they thought served the nicest pint, in their opinion. They named some spots they thought they remembered having a good pint in. Slattery's on Capel Street. Toners on Baggot Street. The Foggy Dew in Temple Bar. But they realised they had only ever categorised their pints into good and bad pints, never really taking note of what had been the best. They had made some calculations. Guinness doesn't travel well. Fact. Outside of Ireland you just can't get as good a pint. It could be the lines not receiving adequate upkeep. It could be the barmen not being appropriately skilled in the craft of pouring the perfect pint. Or it could be that the boat trip has a negative impact on the kegs, thus compromising them. But either way, the further from the brewery it gets the more the taste diminishes. They then deducted that logically the best pint ought to be in Dublin. Now, there was the Guinness Storehouse itself. They had been up there once before for a work function, and they agreed that it may have been the stunning panoramic view of the distinctively illustrious city from The Gravity Bar that made the Guinness taste so good but it would be a fair assumption that the Guinness factory itself would know how to serve the best pint. However as it's not open to the public and you need a tour ticket to access the bar, it doesn't count. They agreed that it shouldn't take too long to find the best pint and that together they could do it. The ground rules were that they both had to agree it was not just the nicest pint they have ever had but that it was perfect. Perfectly presented with the right amount of time left between pours. Perfect size head, not too thick, not too thin. Descends efficiently down the glass leaving perfect cloudy rings after each sup. The perfect level of creaminess. And of course, it must taste deliciously perfect. They decided to disqualify any place that stored its keg any more than one floor away, as the length of a line is believed to affect the taste. They also disqualified any pub that serves any less than fifty pints a day as a constant flow through the lines is also important.

They started with all the places that usually make the top 10 lists in travel blogs but none of the first few they tried made a lasting impression. By the time they got to Mulligans of Poolbeg Street, Billy was sure he had found the perfect pint but Fionn vetoed it because it didn't seem creamy enough. Two nights earlier Fionn thought he had found the perfect pint in Grogan's on South William Street but Billy disagreed because he thought it tasted off. A strange fizz to it as he had described. Tonight they agreed they would meet for one in The Stags Head, an inviting Victorian pub lined with chandeliers that look like they purposely haven't been altered in a hundred years. They met about fifteen minutes after both of their shifts had finished and sat in a corner of the Bar at an angle where they could see both doors, as well as everyone that was entering and exiting, a habit of their profession.

'Jesus Christ, that's bloody good,' Billy said after his first sip.

'You didn't even wait for yours to fully settle,' protested Fionn. 'But yeah this is definitely the best yet,' he agreed.

'Did you know the black stuff isn't actually black? It's ruby red.' Billy said in a tone you'd expect more from a guide on a tour bus.

'Yes,' replied Fionn. 'And when Ireland became a free state in 1922 we needed a national symbol so we took the Guinness harp, inverted it and stuck it on our passports. I know all the useless facts, thanks Billy.'

Billy threw his hands up in surrender. 'Ah alright, I'll spare you any more trivia. So anyway, that's mad about the girl that was rescued. Do you think there's something factual in what she's saying?'

'If you talk to Neeve she'll tell you there's a bogeyman on the loose running rampage on the bridges of Dublin. I think there's something strange going on alright but it's more than likely an inner gang feud type thing.'

'Are the homeless in gangs now?' asked Billy flippantly.

Fionn raised his glass to his lips and took another long sip. 'No. I don't know. But something along the lines of that sort of thing.'

'Are you going to head over to the crime scene tonight?' Billy asked as he in turn took another mouthful from his glass.

128

'Well, that's the plan. I was thinking two birds, one stone. Pint here and then have a swing by there on my way home, just to see who's about.'

Billy raised an eyebrow. 'Maybe even three birds?'

Fionn looked at Billy quizzically. 'What do you mean?'

'I'm sure you'll find a bookies or casino on the way home too?'

Fionn put his glass down and folded his arms. 'Ah Billy, come on.'

'Don't get all defensive on me chief, I don't think I'm wrong. Am I?'

Fionn then unfolded his arms. 'Defensive? Are you reading my body language, yeah?'

'75% of language is non-verbal,' Billy said with a smile.

'Yeah and 87.6% of statistics are incorrect. Body language is bullshit. I fold my arms and I'm being defensive. I put them behind my back and I've got something to hide. The only way to avoid analysis is to keep them in the air and do jazz hands,' he said as he started motioning over animated jazz hands and feigning a cheesy smile towards Billy, who just rolled his eyes. He then folded his arms again. 'I'm going to go ahead and keep them like this because it's comfortable. OK?'

Billy placed his palm under his chin and just smiled at Fionn.

'I'm sorry.' Fionn said. 'I'm just agitated. For a few reasons. One of them being I know what you're going to ask me next.'

'You know. I love ya buddy but a grand is a lot of cash for me and I kind of need it soon.'

'I know Billy, I know, I'm sorry. I thought I'd have it by now, I really did. Something I thought was going to come in but it never happened.'

'You mean a horse?' asked Billy.

'What? No, of course not. An, er, investment of sorts you could say.'

'Fionn, look. I know I've said it before and I don't want to fight over it but you might have been able to pay me back by now if you weren't in the bookies every night.'

'I'm not,' protested Fionn.

'Or online?'

'It's all small change Billy, you think I've some sort of a problem but it's just a hobby. Some people smoke, I play the lottery,'

'Do you actually play the lottery?' Billy asked.

'No. Chances of winning are far too slim. But you know what I mean,' said Fionn.

Billy looked at Fionn with a blank expression and slowly shook his head. 'Come on, we have time for another one,' he said, pivoting on his seat towards the bar man. 'I'll buy you that drink back.'

An hour and fifteen minutes later Fionn had brought the round buying ratio for the night back to 2:1 in his favour. They had spent the time discussing work issues, Guinness issues and agreed on a worst case payday deadline for Billy to get back his €1,000. At no point had he admitted that the money was squandered on a UFC match within an hour of getting it. The Irish guy was a sure thing, so much so everyone expected the American to go down in the first three rounds. It was so likely to happen that the bookmakers were only offering 2/1 on a KO before round three. It was a bet he had to make but had no money to do it. He had told Billy that before the night was out he'd turn his grand into two. €1,000 for giving his friend a loan of a grand for less than 24 hours. Billy's mouth watered a little as Fionn convinced him it was a no brainer. The Irishman had indeed won and the KO had come early but as it was in the fourth round it just wasn't early enough and there was no pay out. Billy's €1,000 became zero. Billy had forgiven the promise of interest and told Fionn to just get the grand back to him, which was a small relief for Fionn but he still had that to add to his other debts he was continuing to chase. Billy had overtaken Fionn's former friend Richie as the person he owes the third most amount of money to. He considered him a former friend because he had cut all ties with Fionn demanding the next time he saw him, also intending it to be the last, would be for the sole purpose of handing back the €800 he was owed. Despite Billy placing third in the rankings thanks to the four figure amount, his current bronze place position dwarfed in comparison to the twelve thousand he owed to his own mother and father. Some of it was a gift, some of it was a loan, and some of it was intended to pay for something that never arrived. Over time, the emotions of guilt, shame and frustration have intertwined themselves into a knot that lives indefinitely in Fionn's stomach. So too does the determination to turn it all around and fix everything. Deep down he knows for certain that someday he will.

Fionn's plan for the evening had been to meet Billy for one drink, grab some food he could eat on the go, patrol the vicinity of the recent cases and keep an eye out for anything suspicious. Then, and only if he had an hour free, he intended to place a couple of small bets on something before the bookmakers close. It was 9pm and he was feeling exhausted from two nights in a row of very little sleep so he decided he only had time to do one of those things after the one pint with Billy turned into three. As he was still deciding which one he should do he already found himself at the entrance to Dame's Dime, which was less than a hundred steps from The Stag's Head. He stood staring at the door for almost a minute weighing up what he should do. He should go down towards the Quays he told himself. He told himself he would. Then he took a deep breath, pushed the door open and stepped inside.

'I hope there hasn't been any trouble for you today?' He said walking towards the window.

'Fionn,' Jim said loudly with a smile. 'Great to see you.'

'Just checking in,' lied Fionn. 'I wasn't even sure if you'd be here but thought it no harm popping in seeing as I was just passing.'

'I think I already told you but I'm here almost every day. Almost all day every day. I have the life of a social entrepreneur I suppose you might say.

Between work and volunteering I hardly have time for anything else.'

'Tell me about it,' replied Fionn.

'Are you working too hard, Detective? Perhaps you need to take a break and enjoy some leisure time. Let me see if I can help.' Jim passed a slip of paper through the slit in the window. 'Here, your first €10 bet tonight is free.'

Fionn closed his eyes, took a deep breath and smiled internally. Despite already insisting such a gesture could be seen as bribery and accepting such things are strictly forbidden, he was off duty now and it was still music to his ears. He reached out and pulled the paper towards him in a brisk motion. He crouched down so he could see all of Jim's face through the divide. 'You know, that's the best news I've had all day.'

CHAPTER THIRTEEN

It was just after 8.30am when Neeve Bello arrived at work in the Harcourt Street headquarters. She had woken up naturally at 7am after a full eight hours of sleep, which she had badly needed after her night shift the previous night. She was hoping to sleep until her alarm went off at 8am but she had felt wide awake so decided to get up and go for a short run around Grand Canal Dock. She enjoyed running in that area as it was close to the house she rented with her two friends and she always found running close to water more fulfilling than around a park or in a gym. She also quite liked the area as it had a historical charm mixed with a modern vibe. She had nodded and smiled to several of her colleagues since she arrived but had not uttered a single word since she woke up. She passed through reception, took the stairs up to the canteen, took a tea bag from the communal stash and made herself tea in her reusable cup. She had managed to hold on to her cup since Christmas without it going AWOL, which was impressive by normal standards. Everything went missing from the canteen eventually, no matter how much people tried to hide their personal cups. Not through intentional thievery, just due to the need for an adequate drinking vessel when little else was available. The cup had been a Secret Santa gift but she knew full well it was from Fionn. Her name *Bello* written on a Christmas bell with holly and ivy interwoven through the design was a pun so bad only he could have come up with it. But it also explained why no one else had been tempted to take it so far.

She was walking past the locker rooms when she noticed David Lyons was about five paces in front of her walking in the same direction. She immediately blushed and her first reaction was to duck out of sight in case he turned and saw her. She dived behind an adjacent door and immediately swore at herself for doing so. She had said some things last night that she now realised she was embarrassed about. It started after a call from Fionn who had rang to let her know he sorted things with Lyons and that the grievance was being withdrawn. Soon after, Neeve had felt compelled to thank Lyons when she noticed he was online and so started a conversation with him. What started out as small talk quickly turned flirty due to some bold statements that Lyons initiated. Neeve was taken aback at first but then she realised his words had made her smile. She disliked Lyons as a person and always had but had objectively acknowledged to herself that she found his confidence and his handsome looks attractive. She never thought she was capable of flirting with him but as brash compliments started coming her way in typed form she found herself throwing caution to the wind with her phone as a shield against any embarrassment that having the conversation face to face would bring. As the topic of conversation became quite suggestive she became almost ashamed of herself for thinking of David Lyons in that way. She wondered if maybe because it had been so long since she had any action her standards had dropped. Then she wondered if he was her type after all. She wondered if maybe her type had changed and what she needed was a man that knows what he wants and will take control. She then shook her head vigorously while still typing recklessly and realised that she was not actually fantasising about making love to David Lyons. She was fantasising about having hate-sex with him. Hot, passionate hate-sex. After some things were already said that could never be unsaid she prematurely ended the conversation. Partly to finish with the upper hand but mainly because she needed to sleep. Ten hours later and here she was leering at her conversational partner from the night before through a 30mm square plane of glass. This was why she was cursing herself. She would never say those things she said last night to his face, let alone actually act them out and now a wave of schoolgirl shyness had come over her. She desperately didn't want to cross paths with David Lyons and have to look him in the eye.

She wanted to watch him until he got to the end of the corridor, he was bound to be heading for his desk on the first floor and there was no reason why they would meet each other over the course of the day. He was about half way down when Neeve saw him suddenly stop as something on the noticeboard to his left caught his attention. He spun around on the ball of his foot and looked at one specific spot intently. From her angle Neeve couldn't see what he was staring at but she concentrated hard and tried to search her photographic memory for what she had seen on that notice board the last time she walked by. She remembered a few pieces of information she had read but nothing she imagined Lyons would be interested in. She then saw him reach out and pull an A4 sheet off the wall. Two thumb tacks came with it and were sliding down the page but he caught them in his free left hand as they fell towards the ground. For almost a minute he stared at the sheet as if he was in a trance turning it several times to study it from different angles. Finally he looked up, glanced nonchalantly to his right and then to his left. Neeve ducked back further behind the door even though she was sure he wouldn't be able to see her standing in her discreet vantage point. She looked back out and saw Lyons begin to scrunch up the page like a frustrated artist would a piece of work he was unhappy with. After a split second he froze as if he was concentrating intently on listening for something so faint it needed absolute silence and stillness to be heard. He then seemed to have changed his mind about the demise of the page in his hand and started to straighten out the minor creases he had just caused and pinned the page back up on the wall. He looked at it one more time, shook his head dismissively and continued down the corridor, disappearing through the double doors at the end.

Neeve shimmied around the wooden door and walked over towards the notice board Lyons had been standing at. There were over a dozen notices on the wall, big and small, but she didn't need to scan them to find which one had caught Lyons' attention. There in the centre was an A4 page that looked like it had just been taken from a bin and pinned up. Neeve looked at the page. Studied every tiny detail. Took a step back and continued in the same direction Lyons had gone, taking her mobile out of her pocket as she walked.

'Good morning Buzzer, me old friend,' Fionn said insincerely.

Buzzer looked up at the silhouette that was blocking out the morning sun that despite being bright, wasn't bringing warmth to the day. He said nothing, just groaned to clearly indicate that Fionn's presence was an inconvenience to him.

'I see you're in your same old spot,' stated Fionn. 'I hope it wasn't too cold last night? Would you like a cup of tea?'

Buzzer looked up again quizzically. 'Ah yeah, give us the money for a cup of tea, so?'

'Hmmm,' Fionn said. 'I don't think it's supposed to work that way.'

'What do you want?' asked Buzzer.

'I just wanted to know if you've seen anything you think the Gardai should know about?'

'Like what?' replied Buzzer.

'There was another homeless person that ended up right here since I saw you last,' Fionn said pointing to the centre of the river behind him.

'Stupid bastards,' Buzzer said. 'Letting that happen to them.'

'Did you see anything?'

'No,' replied Buzzer adamantly.

'I didn't even tell you when it happened.'

'I don't care when it happened, I didn't see nothing at any time.' Buzzer looked away as if ignoring Fionn would make him go away.

'Where have you been the last few nights?' asked Fionn.

'Here, where do you think I've bleedin' been? Off having me dinner with the President of Amsterdam?'

'I don't think that The Netherlands... never mind...' Fionn said, surrendering the point. He stood and stared at Buzzer unsure if taking a friendly approach was working. He took a piece of paper from his inside pocket, unfolded it and handed it to Buzzer. 'Look at this page for me, do you recognise that symbol?'

Buzzer took the print of the image Joanna had described and looked at it. Fionn could see him squint his eyes as he concentrated on the page in front of him, holding it further away from his eyes with an outstretched arm and bringing it back up to right under his nose. After a short scrutinisation, Fionn could see Buzzer's face relax as a sign of recognition seemed to materialise in his eyes.

'No,' he finally said.

'No?' said Fionn. 'I think you're lying.'

'Never saw it before, don't know what you're talking about.' Buzzer put the page down on the bench beside him.

'You didn't even look at it for very long,' Fionn said as he picked the page up and handed it back to him. 'Here, look again.'

'I don't need to Guard, I don't know what that's supposed to be. Now, either arrest me for not being a bleedin' psychic or else leave me the hell alone.'

Fionn stood towering over Buzzer as a dark cloud of anger crept across his face. He was about to try to play hard ball when suddenly his mobile phone started to ring. He pulled it out of his pocket with one swift and heavy handed motion, at no point breaking eye contact with Buzzer. 'What?' he answered rudely.

'Fionn, it's Neeve.'

'Yeah, what?'

A few seconds of silence passed. 'Are you OK?' Neeve eventually asked. 'What's wrong?'

'Nothing, just the smell of bullshit in the air over here is making me feel sick,' said Fionn.

'What?' asked Neeve, bemused.

'Nothing, what's up?'

'You know the way you put a copy of your sketch of that symbol on the notice board here? The one Joanna saw on the guy's ring?'

'Yes, I'm looking at a copy of it right now,' said Fionn.

'Well the strangest thing just happened,' continued Neeve. 'I just saw Lyons staring at it. He didn't know I could see him but he took it off, was about to destroy it, but then put it back up.'

'Feck sake,' said Fionn. 'That doesn't surprise me, he's taking the piss out of it.' He abruptly grabbed the page back from Buzzer with his free hand and turned to continue the conversation out of ear shot. 'I actually thought we were starting to be civil to each other after yesterday.'

'No I don't think that was it,' replied Neeve. 'He was looking at it weird, like he was interested in it or something, I think it would be worth asking him about it.'

'It has my contact details on it. It says to contact me if anyone has any information on what the symbol means. If it meant anything to him he would have called me,' said Fionn.

Neeve let his statement sink in for a few seconds before she responded. 'You think?'

'No, I suppose not,' said Fionn. 'Could you ask him about it?'

'Me?' Neeve said with surprise. 'No, it's your case, you talk to him.'

'Please?' Fionn said, looking back at Buzzer. 'I'm miles away in the middle of something else, he's just upstairs from you.'

'I. But. I just....' Neeve searched for the right words to say she was too embarrassed to face him today without actually saying those words.

'Neeve? Please help me out here, I'll owe you one. I can't possibly go to him twice in two days for what he'll see as help. He'll think I want to shag him.'

Neeve let the awkward silence pass.

'Well?'

'OK fine,' Neeve conceded. 'I'll talk to him. But you owe me big time. He might think I want to shag him now.' Neeve gave a fake and nervous laugh.

'Legend, thank you.' Fionn said and then hung up. He turned back in the direction of Buzzer. 'Now Buzzer, where were we?'

David Lyons was at his desk reading over some notes, when he heard a soft voice from behind call his name. He looked back and saw Neeve awkwardly step sideways through the door and walk up to him.

Lyons swivelled on his chair to face Neeve, stretched his legs out, placed his hands behind his head like he was about to relax in front of the TV and gave a creepy smirk that immediately irked her.

'Can I have a quick word with you in private?' Neeve asked in a low tone so no one else in the open plan office would hear.

Lyons perked up in his chair. 'Bello, you randy minx,' he said loudly with an arched eyebrow and a smirk.

Neeve blushed, bowed her head slightly and walked back towards the door through which she entered. Lyons sprung off his chair and briskly followed her out to an alcove where they could talk privately.

'I just have a quick one for you,' Neeve began.

'I'm happy with a quick one Bello but I have loads of time, so why rush?' Lyons said while placing his hands on Neeve's slim waist.

Neeve immediately slapped his hands away. 'Dave,' she said quietly but firmly. 'That's not what I mean. I have a quick question about something.'

Lyons held out his hands in surrender. 'You already asked me so many questions last night, are you being shy with me now?' He slouched down to her 5ft 7 inches and looked intensely into her deep brown eyes.

Neeve gave a half smile. 'Let's keep last night's conversation exactly there and be professional here today, shall we?'

Lyons stood back up straight and perked his chest out.

'I saw you earlier looking at a sign Fionn put on the noticeboard,' said Neeve.

A more curious expression came into Lyons' face.

'Does the symbol on it mean anything to you?'

Lyons clasped his hands behind his back and seemed to stick his chest out even further. 'I'm not sure I know what you're talking about?'

'It's in the corridor downstairs after the locker rooms, on the general enquiries notice board. You were definitely looking at it earlier, I saw you.'

'Were you spying on me Bello? You creepy bitch, I love it.'

Neeve felt her face heat up like she was staring directly into an open fire. 'No, obviously not. I passed you earlier, I said hello but you didn't hear me, you were concentrating on Fionn's poster. I was wondering if you noticed anything familiar about it?'

Lyons raised an eyebrow and gave Neeve a suspicious look. His eyes shifted gently from side to side as he seemed to be deciding on how to answer. 'How about I buy you dinner later and we can discuss it then. And maybe other things?'

Neeve felt her face cool as she realised she now had the upper hand in the conversation. 'How about you tell me what it means to you and then based on how helpful you are I'll decide whether you deserve to buy me dinner or not.'

Fionn was almost finished eating the beef burrito he had ordered at his favourite Mexican restaurant when his phone rang. He hadn't enjoyed it as much as he hoped he would, mainly because he had gotten no further with Buzzer. He prided himself at being better than the average detective at picking up on when people are telling the truth and when they are lying but even a new recruit on their first day's training could have picked up on the fact that Buzzer was holding something back. He was positive the strange symbol was familiar to Buzzer and the fact that he wasn't saying anything made him suspicious. He had also had a carbon copy of the conversation from two days ago after Buzzer claimed he was once again in a bed in Lowes Hotel at the exact time Joanna had been rescued from the Liffey. He admitted to recognising Joanna from her photo but claimed to have never spoken to her before as he had only ever seen her around. Fionn was frustrated because he wanted to arrest Buzzer and bring him in for questioning but he knew that he didn't have a strong enough case for an arrest and that it would do no good as Buzzer would simply refuse to talk. He made a mental note to himself to call into Dame's Dime later and ask Jim a few more questions about Buzzer. And to do an accumulator on the Premiership matches at the weekend.

'Hello?' mumbled Fionn, spitting crumbs onto his phone as he strained to swallow the last bite and talk at the same time.

'Fionn, it's Neeve again. I was talking to David, I think I might have got something on the symbol.'

'David?' exclaimed Fionn, thrown by the unusual use of his first name.

'Lyons, Bagman, whatever, you know who I mean,' responded Neeve boldly.

'Sure, sure. I'm listening,' said Fionn, resting his phone between his ear and his shoulder while he wiped his hands and sucked in a long breath to combat the spicy tingle on his tongue.

'What do you know about The Freemasons?' asked Neeve.

'The Freemasons?' repeated Fionn. 'Not a lot. Secret society. New world order. I heard my mother complaining about them once. Something about making a mockery of Mass and that it's all a front for an evil plot against the church.' Fionn blew loudly into the mic.

Neeve laughed. 'I don't know much about it either but Lyons is a Freemason. He didn't go into any great detail about it but he said that he goes to the Dublin Lodge every week and he recognised the symbol on your sign because it's on the wall where he hangs his coat every week.'

'That slippery bastard. A Freemason, eh?' Fionn gave out a forced chuckle. 'Must be a dodgy set up if he's a part of it. Where is this Lodge anyway?'

'Molesworth Street,' replied Neeve. 'Everyone knows that, Fionn.'

'Oh yeah that big old building, never knew what it was exactly. Never needed to know. It always gave me the creeps though, walking by. Looks like a haunted house. What are its opening times, do you know?' he asked while still breathing loudly into his phone.

'I don't think it has opening times, Fionn. It's not exactly a museum.'

'It's not? I'll head over that way now. Thanks so much for your help,' said Fionn.

'Pleasure as always, let me know how you get on,' said Neeve before hanging up.

Fionn blew air in and out of his mouth really fast. The burrito was too spicy after all. He shouldn't have asked for extra jalapeños. He would need to stop for ice cream along the way to neutralise the temperature in his mouth.

CHAPTER FOURTEEN

The Grand Masonic Lodge of Ireland stands between Georgian houses linking the historic buildings of Dawson Street to the home of the Irish Parliament on Kildare Street. Fionn drove past St. Anne's Church and took a sharp right, finding a space just outside a neglected looking art deco building he assumed housed mostly offices. As he approached the Lodge he watched for movement in or out of the front door and noticed none. He wasn't even sure if anyone was going to be inside the large three story building on a quiet weekday afternoon.

He walked up a few short steps to a set of large double doors, pushed the handle and wasn't surprised to find that it wouldn't open. He did a quick scan for a doorbell or knocker and after not finding any, gently tapped three times on a glass window that had a colourful Celtic design weaving through it. Seeing no movement behind the frosted glass he tapped three more times and within five seconds saw a silhouette coming towards the door. The door opened and he was greeted by an attractive woman who stood at the same height as him with blonde hair that was glamorously styled in a short bob. She wore smart attire that was offset by a dainty stud in her left nostril and looked so fashionable that it made her appear like she could be a celebrity. She offered him a friendly smile that extended to her eyes, which were the lightest shade of blue he had ever seen, so much so they almost looked to have a tint of silver.

'Hello, can I help you?' she said with a helpful beam.

Her sheer presence was so stunning he needed a few seconds to gather his thoughts and had to concentrate on not stuttering over his words.

'Hello. Hi. Hi there,' he said as he clasped his hands awkwardly in front of him. 'My name is Fionn Fagan. I'm with the Guards.'

'Oh?' she said with a sudden tone of concern.

'Oh, don't worry,' Fionn said in his most macho voice. 'No one is in trouble, I just have a few questions I was hoping you could help me with?'

'Oh thank goodness,' she said with the brightness back in her smile, 'I'll do whatever I can, come, you better step in.'

She opened the door fully and moved to the side gesturing for him to enter. As he passed her he realised she might have half an inch on him height wise and noticed she was wearing a perfume he did not recognise but it reminded him of a mix between grapefruit and leather. Despite its unusual muskiness he found it pleasant. He looked around, saw a door to a reception area he assumed she had come from and a long dark corridor that looked old and stately. There was a smell of wealth and history in the air, the same you get in ancient churches and historical buildings.

'My name is Stephanie, how can I help you Guard?'

'Please, call me Fionn,' he said in a self-assured tone while swatting away an invisible fly. 'Thank you for letting me in, it's lovely to meet you, Stephanie. I hope this is not a bad time?'

'Not at all,' she said, her beaming smile and sparkling eyes not wavering.

Fionn just stood grinning childishly at her as she smiled back.

'I suppose I should ask to see your badge?' she said.

'Oh, of course,' he said as he fumbled around in his pocket, producing his wallet which contained his badge and ID. He held it up at eye level but she barely looked at it.

'Nice mug shot,' she joked. 'I hope you're not always that serious?' she said in reference to the facial expression on his photo I.D. Without waiting for a response she turned and walked towards a door that led to a reception area. 'Would you like to sit down? Can I get you tea or coffee?'

'No need at all thanks, I won't keep you long. I'm investigating a case, the details of which I won't bore you with but there is a symbol I have a rough drawing of here and after getting nowhere with searching for it online it's been brought to my attention there might be a plaque or something to that description somewhere inside that may look like this?' Fionn took the page out, unfolded it and handed it to Stephanie. 'Possibly near a coat stand?'

She stared pensively at it for several seconds and made a humming sound. 'It's not a very good drawing is it? You guys need to sack your sketch artist,' she said with a smile.

'I suppose. I actually drew it myself,' he said in an attempted macho tone but sounding deflated. 'I'm not much of a drawer, I suppose I was only going by what was being described,' he continued.

'Oh my God, I'm sorry I didn't mean to offend you,' she said as she placed her palm on Fionn's lapel, instantly sending an electrical jolt through him and making him blush.

After an awkward moment's silence the redness subsided from Fionn's face and he smiled back at her. 'I don't think I could be offended by anything you say, Stephanie, no matter how mean you tried to be,'

Stephanie gave a loud chuckle as the whites of her big eyes expanded with what she found to be a cheesy compliment. 'Is it not unprofessional to flirt with people you interview Garda Fionn?'

'Oh not at all,' he replied. 'In fact it's encouraged.'

'Oh yeah,' she said as her smile expanded, showing off her perfectly straight white teeth.

'Yes, it's one of the first things we learn in Garda college, how to flirt to get answers,' said Fionn, feigning a serious tone. 'In fact, do you have any idea of the amount of hardened criminals I've caught through simply giving them a cheeky wink and complementing their tattoos?'

Stephanie let out a hearty laugh. 'I'm sure I have no idea.'

150

'No, you certainly don't, so if I flirt with you, your best course of action is to flirt back I'm afraid.'

'Is that right?,' she said as she tucked her hair behind her ear, tilted her head and gave him a quizzical smile before turning her gaze back to the page. 'Despite the sheer brilliance of your creative endeavours I'm afraid I don't recognise it. But you said something about a coat rack? There's a row of them just down here, perhaps they might have something you're looking for?'

Stephanie led Fionn about ten metres down the corridor to a row of hooks on the wall protruding from an assortment of carved wooden plaques, each made up of different symbolic contours. 'These are all Masonic imagery as far as I know but what they all mean I'm not sure, you'll have to ask the expert on that.'

'So what do you do here Stephanie?' Fionn asked as she then led him through a door into a large hall. 'Are you a Freemason?'

'Oh no of course I'm not, there are no women in the Freemasons, I'm the Lodge secretary.'

'There aren't?' said Fionn. 'That's highly sexist isn't it?'

'Nah, I don't really see it like that. It was set up by men for men. It's a fraternity. That means brotherhood, I'm told. You can't have women in a brotherhood by definition,' she said with a smile. 'I just work in the office, I'm doing a night course in criminal psychology and hope to get into that line of work, but for now this is my job and I actually quite enjoy it,' she said defensively.

'Oh I could tell you a thing or two about the psychology of a criminal, believe me,' Fionn boasted.

'Oh yeah? Like what?'

'Well,' Fionn began and then paused for thought. 'They tend to commit crimes for one.'

Stephanie giggled. 'How interesting.'

Fionn stood grinning at Stephanie, enjoying her smile and feeling proud of himself for being able to make her laugh. 'So you said something about asking the expert, is there somebody here that might be a little less useless than you?

'Hey,' she said, smiling. She gave him a light slap on his forearm. 'I'm reporting you for cheekiness.'

He smiled back but had nothing else to say.

'Hang on there, I'll call someone that might be able to help you. If that symbol exists here, this guy will know.'

Stephanie walked back to the office and Fionn could hear her lift a phone, push four numbers and tap her finger on wood as she waited for an answer.

'Hi Frank, is Brian there? Could I have a quick word with him? Thank you.'

In the silence that followed Fionn considered the level to which he had instantly been smitten. He thought about how it was a horribly inappropriate time and place to meet Stephanie and how, because of this fact he had to stay as professional as he could, he was not in a position to be able to do anything about the fact that he wanted to meet her again under more suitable circumstances. He considered how on most occasions the reaction he gets from women while on duty is far more attentive than when he's off duty and in a social environment. He could usually see through the fakery of people acting on their best behaviour in front of a badge but he couldn't help but think that Stephanie seemed different. More genuine. He felt like what he saw was what he got. He knew that he wanted to see her again beyond this conversation. He figured that there was only one way to do that and that it could either go very right or go horribly wrong. So wrong there was no coming back from such a gamble. So, he asked himself, should he take the gamble?

'Hi Brian, there's a Garda Fionn Fagan here to ask about a drawing that might be like something we have here, could you pop down and see if you can help?

Fionn felt a flutter rise from the pit of his stomach as she said his name.

'There is someone on the way down to meet you now,' Stephanie said as she walked back towards him. Brian is a long-time member of the Lodge, if he doesn't know what this drawing might be, no one will.'

'Thanks so much for your help, you're bloody amazing,' Fionn said, noticing the confidence had gone from his voice.

Stephanie just gave an unsure smile and a half nod.

'While we're waiting, I have one more question you can help me with. I was just wondering, and this is purely hypothetical because I'm on duty at the moment so this would obviously never happen in real life, but if I was to ask you for coffee because, I don't know, let's pretend I found you really interesting and I wanted to get to know you more, would you have said yes or no? In this hypothetical situation.'

Stephanie blushed a little and although her body language became awkward as she turned away from him, her sky blue eyes were smiling. 'Gosh, I don't know,' she finally said. 'It's hard to know what I would say. It's just such an unlikely situation to be in. You have a great imagination, Fionn.'

Fionn wondered if her not answering was a way of letting him down gently. Then again, the way she said his first name was overly tender, so maybe she was just playing along and making him work harder. 'Try hard to picture the situation,' he said and raised his eyebrows in preparation for an answer.

'What would happen if I said no?' Stephanie asked in a serious tone.

Fionn exhaled and bowed his head in defeat feeling the pendulum had swung the wrong way. 'I suppose I'd have to arrest you and throw you in a cell until Stockholm Syndrome kicked in and you fell in love with me,' he said in a deadpan tone.

Stephanie laughed loudly and harder than before. 'You've got a weird sense of humour Fionn, but I like it. I think it's a little more complicated than just yes or no but I think it's pointless talking about it, it is all hypothetical, don't forget.

Fionn did one more scan of her left hand to confirm there were no rings on the finger that he hoped would not have any rings on it. 'Of course, you must have a boyfriend? Good job I didn't ask you out, that would have been both unprofessional and embarrassing.'

'No actually, I don't,' said Stephanie.

Fionn stood smiling awkwardly knowing not to push the issue any further but hoping she would volunteer more information. He was about to change the subject when his attention suddenly turned to a booming sound coming down the set of stairs in front of them. They both looked up to see a tall burly man descending with an awkward efficiency to his steps. He was heavy footed and overweight but smartly dressed and clean shaven. He had a neat haircut that suited his middle aged face. The tall man spoke in a loud commanding voice as he approached Fionn, offering a handshake that had been prematurely outstretched before he even reached the bottom step. 'Good afternoon Guard, Brian Johnson is my name, how may I be of assistance to you today?'

Fionn held out his hand which was dwarfed in comparison to the shovel sized palm that gripped his and squeezed uncomfortably tight. 'Det. Fionn Fagan, nice to meet you, Sir.'

Before Fionn could continue, Brain turned to Stephanie. 'Stephanie, dear, did you offer the Detective a tea or a coffee?'

Stephanie just smiled and gave a slow nod.

'Yes, we were just talking about coffee actually,' Fionn said and gave Stephanie a wink.

Stephanie's face went rigid, losing all expression and he realised how she was far more professional at her job than he was at his.

'But I'm fine for now, thank you,' he continued. He took the page back out of his pocket and showed it to Brian. 'I was wondering if you could tell me if you recognise this symbol? Please excuse its sub-standard artistry, it's just a rough sketch,' he said as he smiled towards Stephanie who returned it with a roll of her shoulders.

Brian studied it pensively.

'I understand from one of your members it may be similar to a symbol on a wall somewhere inside? I think he may have seen it when he was hanging up his coat, if that helps?' Fionn said.

Brian peered up from the drawing. 'And who told you this?'

'One of our Detectives that came here told a colleague it looked familiar. David Lyons.'

'Ah Brethren Lyons? He's a friend of yours?'

'More like one of the team, I suppose you could say,' said Fionn.

'Does he often talk about the Lodge?'

'Not to me anyway, I only found out today that he's a Freemason,' Fionn said with a flippant tone, purposely showing apathy towards Lyons' personal life.

'Do you know much about what we do?' asked Brian defensively, incorrectly reading his tone and taking it personally.

'No, not much actually. You're a secret society right?'

As Brian looked on expressionless Stephanie shook her head with a smile.

'We're not a secret society,' Brian responded. 'We're a society, with secrets.'

'Ah I see, the secret handshake, of course,' said Fionn.

'We have a secret handshake and a secret word. I won't tell you what either of those are, but ask me any other question and I'll answer you honestly.'

'OK,' Fionn said, looking around. He took the page back off Brian and held it up again. 'Do you recognise this?'

'Yes,' Brian said, without hesitation.

'Yes?' Fionn replied, sounding surprised.

'Yes. Come with me and I'll show you this symbol. Would you like a tour of the Lodge while you're here? The public rarely gets to see inside this building.'

'That would be great, if you have time,' Fionn said politely. He gave Stephanie a nod goodbye and followed Brian up the stairs he had come down.

Brian led Fionn up to the first floor and down another corridor, offering no conversation along the way.

'Stephine is great, we could do with someone like her working for us you know?' Fionn said, by way of breaking the silence.

Brian stopped at a door and turned to Fionn. 'What do you mean?'

Fionn's tendency to act without thinking often paid off. Colleagues considered it a keen intuition and it was what made him a good detective. However, his tendency to speak without thinking rarely paid off and this was no exception as he realised his attempt to make small talk had been taken up the wrong way. 'I mean, because she's so helpful,' he said. 'You should try and ask some of our office staff for a favour sometime. They wouldn't even spell the word for you.'

'I see,' muttered Brian in an unconvinced tone. 'She certainly is a great young woman, with a bright future ahead of her. Anyway,' he continued without pause. 'This here is the balloting room.' He opened the door in front of them and held it for Fionn to walk ahead of him.

Fionn entered and looked around in awe at the badly lit room, the likes of which he had never seen before. There was a unique smell of incense mixed with old wood and the acoustics made the room feel larger than it was. An obnoxiously bright red carpet that was thick and pristine covered the room. In the centre stood a solitary wooden table and chair. On the small triangle shaped chair was a type of wooden jewellery box. Surrounding the perimeter of the room were seats built into individual wooden compartments that reminded Fionn of church confession boxes without doors. They each had a gothic style roof above them that jutted out from the wall like the hood of a villain in a fairytale. Across the roofs were mediaeval style spears and above them dangled worn flags made up of crosses, circles and stripes. In the centre back of the room was a large chair that could be described more as a throne. It was high and wooden with intricate carvings along the edge and luxurious upholstered cushioning.

'Before a prospective new Brethren of the Lodge becomes a member they must first be voted in. This all happens here,' Brian spoke with an outstretched arm that he propelled around the room. He walked over to the single chair in the middle of the room, opened the wooden box on the adjacent table and pointed.

Fionn followed him over and peered inside. Sitting on a miniature shelf inside the wooden box were a mixture of black and white coffee beans.

'This is a secret ballot,' Brian began. 'When it comes to the voting the prospective Mason will come in here and take a seat in the centre of the room. Our members sit around the room and one by one come up here and place their vote into this box in the form of either a black or a white bean. White if they want to accept this man as a fellow Brethren, black if they do not. Once each member has cast their vote the box is opened and if there is even just one single black bean in there, the person will not be accepted in. You've heard of the term "to be black balled?" This is where it originates from.'

'Wow, tough crowd for the last guy,' said Fionn pointing to the several black beans in the drawer.

'Indeed,' replied Brian.

They exited and went further down the corridor on the same floor. The next room Brian led Fionn into had the same old smell, dim lighting and booming echo as the previous one but the décor was much different. He looked around and saw lights fixed to the wall with lamp shades in the shape of the heads of ancient Samurai, small statues sculpted in the shape of the Egyptian sphinx and furniture that could have been props from the set of any movie set in Biblical times.

'This is the induction room', Brian said, leading Fionn across the carpet that was so dark purple it almost looked blood soaked. In the centre of the room was a pit about two feet deep. They both walked down the three steps that descended into it. 'Where we stand now is where our new Brethren would stand for the ceremony during which we initiate him into our Lodge. The floor we stand on is lowered during the ceremony and the ritual will be delivered to him from here.

A cold shiver ran up Fionn's spine. He wasn't sure if it was the imagery of what was being described or the dramatic way Brian was describing it that had caused it. 'So what do people do around here once they join?'

'For one, we are heavily involved in charity work.' replied Brian. 'We raise a lot of money for hospitals around the country through different initiatives. We used to run an orphanage for years up until the middle of the last century. Thankfully the state's standard of care for orphaned children finally got to an acceptable level so it no longer operates but today we still have our own internally run charity that raises money to support the care of sick children.'

160

Fionn hummed a low sound in response and looked around. 'The first thing I pictured when I walked in was you all sitting around in a circle here with a naked virgin being sacrificed in your moving pit.'

Brian gave Fionn a cold stare and Fionn nervously laughed away the remark.

'What do you talk about when you all meet up and when there's not a new member to welcome?' Fionn asked in an attempt to change the subject.

'Oh, anything really. It's a great place for like-minded people to meet and discuss topics of interest. We do not discuss Religion or Politics once inside the Lodge but anything else can and is discussed during our weekly meetings. Often we just socialise.'

'So, you don't plot the roll out of your new world order then?' Fionn tried his best to adjust his tone so Brian knew the question was meant in jest.

'Hard to discuss taking over the world without bringing up politics,' Brian replied with a smile.

'So why no talk of Politics or Religion?' asked Fionn.

'They are private and personal beliefs,' replied Brian. 'Disagreements can develop from a difference in individual convictions but we want to have an environment of harmony and unity, so they are simply off the cards. Come, I have one more room to show you before we reach what you're looking for.'

As they stepped inside it was as if they had entered a church. The walls were made of stone and an oak ceiling had metal beams running across it. There were stained glass windows with crests paying tribute to family names and territories. There was a mixture of religious and regal ornaments scattered across the room with seemingly no theme or purpose to its arrangement. At the top of the room stood an altar with a space marked to stand in front of it with your back to the rest of the room, similar to where a priest would stand to say Latin Mass.

Fionn stood looking around, unsure how to compliment the room.

Brian stood proudly with his arms folded and followed Fionn's gaze as he took in the view. 'This is the liturgy hall. This is where we come to reflect and to worship. The phrase we have among ourselves is that this is the place we come to hang our coats. To shut off from the world and to pray to whatever it is that means something to us. This is where your colleague Det. Lyons was talking about.'

'I don't understand,' Fionn said. 'You're not supposed to talk about Religion yet this room is full of religious iconography. There is an altar over here with The Quran placed on it and a crucifix either side of it. There is a skull and bones on the wall, a statue of Buddha over here and a sculpture of a Hindu temple on that table. I thought you said you don't have Religion in here?'

Brian gave a hearty laugh. 'On the contrary, I said you cannot *talk* about Religion. It does however play an important part in being a Freemason. It is in fact the first piece of criteria needed in order to become a Freemason. You must believe in a supreme being.'

'A supreme being?' asked Fionn. 'You mean God?'

'Yes, or whatever God is to you. Allah, Buddha, Thor, it doesn't matter, you just have to believe that there is a higher power out there.'

'So an atheist can't be a Freemason?'

'No, they cannot.'

'What if you believe that God is a vampire and to get to heaven you must murder people and drink their blood?' asked Fionn with the flippant tone back in his voice.

Brian's mannerly smile turned into a grimace. 'Oh no, it can't be anything diabolical. You must be an upstanding member of society to become a Mason.'

Fionn just pursed his lips and nodded.

'Let me show you this window here,' Brian said, leading Fionn towards the back of the room. 'See anything here you recognise?'

Fionn glanced around the stained glass window that was much like the others in that it had the same layout but different shapes of flags, crests and symbols. Almost immediately his eye caught a shape that seemed familiar. On the bottom left of the window was a crest that was in the shape of a battlefield shield. On it was a series of triangles within circles with colours of red yellow and blue like the colours of the Romanian flag, one of the few flags in the world made up only of primary colours. He took out the page from his pocket once again and compared the two.

'Quite similar isn't it?' said Brian.

'It is,' said Fionn. 'Do you know what the meaning behind this crest is?'

Brian laughed. 'Of course I do. I know the origin of just about every symbol in this whole Lodge. This is DeWolf's Crest.'

'The wolf's crest? Like the animal?' asked Fionn.

'No, DeWolf, as in the name. Arthur DeWolf. Successful English architect in the 19th century. Moved to Dublin in the mid 1800's at the height of his career and was a long time member of this very Lodge. In 1887 he designed this whole wing of the building and of course included a crest he created for himself in the windows that were installed. The shield above that is the DeWolf family crest and on the other side of the window is his wife's family crest, and underneath that is the shield and colours of his home town in Devon, England. So he very much dedicated this whole window to himself.

As Brian was speaking Fionn had taken his phone out and was speedily typing while listening to his insight. 'I'm not getting any hits online for him, he mustn't be too famous?'

'You're correct, although he was highly successful at the time and built half of the southwest of England, most of what he built I expect is half demolished by now. Good at designing buildings that could be made quickly and cheaply, unfortunately they weren't built well and didn't stand the test of time.'

'He seemed to do a good job here?'

'Quite true, although I'm sure no expense was spared in the construction of the oldest documented continuously running Lodge in the world,' said Brian.

'How do you know all this if there's nothing online about him?' said Fionn.

'We keep full biographies on all our members, past and present and we're not inclined to publish this information online I'm afraid,' replied Brian.

'So tell me the significance of this crest?'

'There is none,' said Brian. 'DeWolf designed this himself for himself and it has served as nothing more than a shape in a window for over a hundred years. May I ask where this drawing of yours popped up?'

'We have a murder suspect that we cannot identify. All we have is this symbol to go on, that's about all I can tell you I'm afraid.'

'Oh,' said Brian, as a look of surprise and confusion came over his face.

'Was this DeWolf guy a particularly celebrated Mason?'

'Not really,' responded Brian. 'In fact, quite the opposite. He was expelled from the Masons somewhere around the time of the 1916 rising.'

'Oh I see,' said Fionn as he took out his pen and notepad to jot down everything he learned so far, afraid he might forget something. 'Any idea why?'

'According to our records he became an outspoken atheist in his later years. Despite building this wonderful room he ended up rejecting its purpose.'

'And of course you need to believe in a higher power to be a Mason,' said Fionn as he continued writing.

'Supreme being,' said Brian correcting Fionn. 'That's right. He was also reported to have had strong views against the Nationalist Rebels at the time. I suppose you could say he was into ethnic cleansing. He believed Dublin and Ireland belonged under British rule and that if the Catholic working class gained control of the city the whole country would go into turmoil.'

'So he was an economist?' quipped Fionn. 'And he wasn't far off. A period of unrest follows any country's independence. I'm sure there were loads of like-minded people at the time?'

'Maybe, but it's said he was encouraging the banishing of the working class Catholics that supported independence. I read that he was openly offering financial reward for the execution of those he believed to be detrimental to the development of the society he believed.'

Fionn stopped writing and looked up. 'Sounds like an absolute bastard.'

'I agree,' said Brian. 'Hence why he was expelled. Like I said, nothing diabolical allowed. I don't know why someone would want to use his symbol today. Perhaps this symbol of yours is coincidental and has nothing to do with DeWolf's crest?'

'Perhaps,' said Fionn. 'But it's unique. It has an interesting backstory and right now it's all I have to go on. Who else could have seen this crest and knows the story behind it?'

Brian laughed disingenuously. 'Many people,' he said before continuing his fake chuckle. 'Anybody from our own Brethren to prospective Masons, to guests, to members of the public. We host many tours a year and I have given the history behind every inch of this room many times.'

Fionn thought to himself. He didn't think that the window would leave a lasting impression on a visitor who saw it just once. He believed that somewhere among the members of the Lodge was the best place to find a lead. 'Have you ever noticed a member with a ring containing this crest?'

'A ring? No,' said Brian immediately.

'Anyone that seemed unusually interested in it?'

'No,' said Brian again, just as quickly.

'Right,' said Fionn. He then paused in thought for a few seconds. 'You've been incredibly helpful Mr. Johnson. Thank you.'

'Glad to hear,' said Brian.

'Just one more thing I'll need for my investigation. Can you give me a full list of all current members of this Lodge?'

'Absolutely not,' said Brian curtly.

Fionn scowled at Brian. It wasn't as easy as he hoped it would be. Usually people don't think twice about data protection when it comes to assisting the Guards. The public always assumes law enforcement trump personal information.

'That is private and confidential data,' continued Brian, 'and not something I am just going to hand over to you for no reason.'

'There is a suspect...' began Fionn.

'Come back to me with a name,' interrupted Brian. 'Until you have one there is no suspect that is a member of this Lodge. Unless you have a court order on you right now that allows you to seize our computers?'

Fionn realised Brian not only knew full well he hadn't got a court order for the information but was unlikely to ever get one based solely on a bad sketch, a one hundred year old stained glass window and a hunch. 'I never asked you what you do for a living yourself, Mr. Johnson?'

'I'm a semi-retired solicitor, Det. Fagan,' replied Brian.

'Of course you are,' mumbled Fionn. 'I thought I could ask you anything except about the handshake and the secret word?'

'You can ask me anything, I'm not necessarily going to give you the answer.'

'Ok then, can I ask you to help a member of the Gardai with an investigation into murder?'

The use of the word murder seemed to unsettle Brian momentarily but he soon saw through Fionn's attempt of manipulation. 'I will help in any way I think I can help. But I don't think handing over private information to you based on the likeness between a ring and an old window is going to get you anywhere. Come back to me with a name and I might be able to help.'

'I can't get a name without first cross checking a list, Brian,' said Fionn with an air of desperation in his voice.

Brian shook his head and gave Fionn a regretful grin. 'I'm sorry Son, I can't help you there.'

Two minutes later Fionn was standing alone outside the office on the ground floor where his tour had begun. He tapped lightly on the open door as Stephanie looked up from her small desk that was awkwardly positioned up against the back wall, probably due to lack of space. 'I'm off,' he said with a wave. 'Thank you so much for everything, I can't tell you how helpful you've been and how wonderful it is to meet you.'

Stephanie put her pen down and tilted her head to the side with a smile. 'You're more than welcome,' she said. 'I hope you found what you're looking for?'

'I did,' he said. 'Sort of. Hey, by the way, I'm sorry about earlier,' he said, 'I speak without thinking sometimes. It's actually kind of my thing.'

Stephanie gave Fionn a reassuring look and waved her hand away. 'Oh don't worry it's fine. Besides, it was all hypothetical,' she said.

'Indeed it was,' he said in a deflated tone as he backed out of the door.

Stephanie got off her chair and walked towards Fionn. 'I'll see you out,' she said.

As he stepped out into the fresh air he shuffled awkwardly, placing both hands in his pockets and then immediately removed them. He shuffled from one foot to the other, unable to to find a comfortable position to stand in. 'Actually I do have one more question for you.'

'Oh yeah?' she said as she formed a crescent shape with her mouth.

'But I need to make a quick call first,' Fionn said while taking out his mobile. 'Can you wait there for two seconds?'

'Of course,' said Stephanie as the smile disappeared in confusion.

Fionn dialled a number stored in his phone and held it to his ear. It took five rings before the phone was answered on the other side.

'Corcoran,' said the voice on the other end.

'Boss, it's Fagan.'

'Fagan,' exclaimed Corcoran. 'This better be important, I'm very busy.'

'OK, sorry Boss, I'm getting a little further on this case but not a lot. I can brief you soon but it's nothing that can't wait until tomorrow. Right now I have a last minute request. Something has just popped up that I need to deal with. Something personal.' He looked up at Stephanie as he spoke, noting the confused look in her face. He realised she must be feeling a chill as she was standing rigid with her arms folded and she was kicking the ground with her ankle boots.

'Oh yeah? Is it serious?'

'No not at all, everything is fine, I just need to take the rest of the day off, can you please authorise personal time off so I can attend to it? I can be in your office early tomorrow to make up for lost time.'

'Oh yeah, sure, no problem,' replied Corcoran sarcastically. 'Will I organise a limo to come pick you up and drop you home? Maybe a voucher for some spa treatment for good measure?' A few seconds of silence passed and Corcoran considered the possibility something serious had occurred. He finally let out a sign and changed to a placid tone. 'Ok, fine. But I expect you to work it back by staying on later tomorrow.'

Fionn gulped silently at the prospect of such a long day. 'Absolutely.'

'Then, fine,' continued Corcoran. 'Take the rest of the day off and mind yourself.'

'Thank you very much, Sir,' Fionn said before hanging up, all the while grinning at a perplexed Stephanie.

'I'm not one to take such a gamble,' he said as he considered the inaccuracy of the statement. 'But I need to risk embarrassment and ask you a non-hypothetical question.' He saw her eyes widen and her body language tense up even more than before but continued undeterred. 'I am now officially off duty. I am a Garda Detective, with the afternoon off, standing in the street and I'm asking the most beautiful woman I've ever met if she would be interested in allowing me to take her for dinner.'

Stephanie exhaled slowly and a blank look came over her face. She looked as though she had been transported onto a stage in front of a live audience and had forgotten her lines.

Fionn's heart instantly sank as he read the apprehension on her face. They both stood in silence with seagulls circling overhead offering their squawk as the only soundtrack to the scene. Fionn had said all he wanted to say and was giving her as long as she needed to phrase her rejection.

'I'd like to,' she finally said as softly and sadly as if it were a break up.

'But?' replied Fionn. He stared deep into her penetrating blue eyes and noted how truly striking they were. Beauty beamed out of them. It was like looking at a tropical sea that had frozen over. Clear with a crystal sparkle yet they also had an icy haze.

'It's just, I don't know you. Dinner might be a bit full on, what if we realise we don't like each other after twenty minutes? It'd be so awkward.'

'Fair enough,' replied Fionn as he pursed his lips. He turned on his heels and stared up the shaded street in the direction of his car. He noticed a black town car turning into Leinster House as many do each day and in a momentary trail of thought considered how life still goes on no matter what the outcome of a choice results in. He was pretty certain he wasn't going to decide after twenty minutes that he didn't like her but he couldn't be sure the opposite would be true.'.

'Ok,' he said again, directing his words towards Stephanie as he turned back to her. 'How about this? I meet you here after work and we walk to get coffee. On that walk we can tell each other all about ourselves and by the time we get there if you think you'd be happy to keep talking maybe you would take my number and we can chat over text?'

Stephanie smiled and her eyes glinted. 'OK,' she said and nodded gently a couple of times.

'That would be something different. You're a strange one, but I think I like it.'

'Being strange is actually my best quality. I got a first in strangeness at college.'

Stephanie laughed.

'Is that a yes?'

'Perhaps it is,' she said. 'But I might ask my Dad if he would approve of you.'

'Why would you need to...' Fionn wasn't able to finish the question before a surge of realisation emanated across his face. 'Brian?'

'Yep,' she said with a smile.

'But you referred to him as Brian on the phone?'

'I can't call him Dad at work, that's unprofessional,' she said.

Fionn scratched his head. 'So your name is Stephanie Johnson?'

'It is,' she replied.

'See, we're getting to know each other so well already.' Fionn said as confidently as he could, trying to hide the internal pang of cringe he felt as he recalled his earlier conversation with Brian when he chose his words badly.

'Today?' Stephanie asked.

'I just took the rest of the day off so I'm free. But if it doesn't suit you don't worry I'll get stuck into some train watching' Fionn said.

She looked at him sceptically.

'That was a joke,' he clarified.

She nodded her head with a grin by way of acknowledging that's what she figured. 'Fine,' she

173

said. 'You're on. See you back here at five o'clock. You can walk me to college.'

Fionn exhaled loudly, perked up and smiled at her. 'Great,' he said. 'So where do you study?'

'Trinity College,' she said.

Fionn thought about the distance on foot and figured it as a slow ten minute walk. 'That doesn't give me much time at all,' he said.

'Don't give up on yourself,' she said with a wink. 'Just make every minute count.' She turned back to the door, stepped inside and stood behind it, leaving it open wide enough to talk through. 'I might be done by a quarter to. And I feel like walking slowly today.' She closed the door with a curious grin and without saying goodbye.

Fionn was left standing alone, leaning on the gold plated handrail for support as the swirl in his head began to dissipate. He was tempted to do a triumphant jump off the step but instead performed a slight shuffle of glee. It wasn't much; it wasn't even really a date. It was merely walking with and talking to someone between two points of close proximity in broad daylight. He had more intimate moments leading criminals up the steps of the Four Courts. On paper it was far from a win, but he felt on top of the world. He sensed chemistry between the two of them and he was glad that his gamble had paid off. He now had a couple of hours to kill. He had to be back there for 4.45pm. He considered going back to the office but decided he'd take the afternoon off, considering it to be unlikely he'd be granted last minute time off like that again anytime soon. He probably had enough time to go home and change into one of the two suits he owned but decided not to. If he came back wearing his best clothes and smelling of freshly sprayed cologne he would be coming across like he's trying too hard. If that wasn't already evident. The upper hand was with Stephanie but going to that much effort would raise it even higher. Fionn had played this game many times and both loved the excitement and loathed the monotony of it. Two people meet, sparks fly, they like each other, they want the other person to like them back so they pretend to be a person that they are not. A more fun, outgoing, kinder, selfless loveable version of themselves with no issues whatsoever. When the fake niceties get stripped away and the warts are finally revealed the only hope is that the other person has just gotten so fond of them that they accept them for who they really are. That had been Fionn's cynical view on relationships for quite some time and yet one has never evolved like that for him. Something has always prevented his previous relationships from reaching the status of long-term. Sometimes it was him. He wasn't in the right place, he didn't feel there was a future there, or the relationship simply ran its course. But more often than not Fionn was the one being dumped. *You're too immature.* He'd been told that several times. *You're too selfish and you only want to do what you want to do.* Or the thing that really hit hard was when he was accused of being *too fond of gambling.* He'd been accused a couple of times of being a gambling addict and that always caused a big argument. First of all he would point out if anything it would be a disorder, not an addiction. Not that he had either. Yes, he liked gambling, he would even admit to being obsessed with gambling but it wasn't an addiction. He had a few colleagues, who by their own admission would play computer games a couple of hours a night. Was anyone getting on their case telling them they had an addiction? No. Probably not anyway. They liked to spend their free time playing computer games and he liked to spend his gambling. It was a psychological state of mind, not a disease that needed treatment. He would point out that if it was a problem he would be in debt but he only ever gambled with what he could afford. OK, so he does owe money to some family and friends, but they didn't know that. It's the nature of the game, you have to speculate to accumulate. Sometimes he won, sometimes he lost. He had failed at the dating game several times too but he was sure there was at least one person out there that was willing to take him as he was. In the meantime he would have to play the game one more time with Stephanie. Show her all his positive traits, show her some that don't exist. Hide some that do. Get her number and text her but wait the appropriate amount of time before replying. It would be a long process but for now the first step was to walk with her from one point to another. He had about ten minutes to convince her to see him again. And he had two hours to go until that time came.

 His first thought was to nip into a bookies but he quickly dismissed that for two reasons. If he came out at a loss it would put him in a bad mood and he wouldn't be in the right frame of mind for Stephanie. More importantly however, was that he didn't feel like it. Rarely would something come along to divert his attention from the fun of gambling and right now the excitement of meeting Stephanie again was doing just that.

He pulled out his earphones, found Modest Mouse on his phone, hit play and walked with a shuffle to his step as the opening riff of 'Float On' began reverberating loudly in his ears. He decided to grab a coffee. He hadn't been able to finish one all day. And this one would be no exception.

CHAPTER FIFTEEN

Fionn had bought a take-away coffee from Coffee Angel and was walking up the narrow footpath of Wicklow Street intending to spend the remainder of his time browsing around Tower Records. As he approached the music store he spotted Luke O'Loughlin on duty, a Guard he had known for a long time but not that well. Luke had been in Templemore at the same time as Fionn when they were both doing their training. He had been known to have barely made the cut and the general consensus was that progressing any further than the lowest rank of Garda was beyond his capabilities. Many were surprised that he even completed his training at all. A tall thin man with hunched shoulders and a beak shaped nose, he was often nicknamed "the flamingo" or "the walking stick". He was not well liked because of his cold and confrontational personality and his creepy and inappropriate sense of humour. He had poor social awareness and as much as people tried to include him he was always like that guy at a party everyone rolled their eyes at when they walked in. On one occasion in a pub during an afterwork drinks he started meandering jovially through the crowd of colleagues with a tray full of Sambuca shots he had bought. No one really wanted one. It was only about 6pm and it wasn't that kind of night but not wanting to be rude, most people took one. He then spent the rest of the night using it as a talking point, expecting a barrage of gratitude for the kind thought. Over the following weeks he regularly held people to ransom with the gesture and would suggest to people they should go for a pint, as they owed him one. The request was usually at the worst possible time such as lunch time on a Monday or Valentine's Day or at the funeral of a retired Chief Superintendent. He also had a reputation for reporting fellow Guards for petty reasons and seemed to enjoy the dramatics that ensued. Any attention at all seemed to suit him.

Fionn could see that O'Loughlin was being heavy handed with a young man wearing a tracksuit and a crew cut hair style. He had him up against a shop window and was holding him tightly by his collar. Fionn considered crossing the road and avoiding the incident but decided he better interject to see if his help was needed.

'O'Loughlin, what's happening?' Fionn gently said as he approached.

O'Loughlin looked around searching for the voice he had just heard say his name. His eyes quickly found Fionn approaching. 'Fagan, how are you doing?' he said nonchalantly as if he was merely leaning against a window doing nothing in particular.

'Do you need help?'

The man in the tracksuit interjected. 'Get this bleedin' sap off me will ya Pal?'

'You shut the hell up, no one is talking to you,' replied O'Loughlin as he pulled on the collar a little more.

'What's going on, what did he do?' asked Fionn.

'I saw this muppet selling a bag of something in broad daylight. He was standing right in front of the Molly Malone statue. Didn't care who was looking, tourists taking photos with him in the background dealing drugs and him not giving a shit.'

Fionn shook his head judgingly and looked at the man in the tracksuit. 'Keep an eye online, if the photos go up you can tag yourself in them.'

'It's not funny,' snapped O'Loughlin. 'He nearly crushed an old lady on the footpath as I chased after him. Didn't get far though, did you?'

'Lanky prick', said the man in the tracksuit.

As he spoke Fionn could see the man only had about half of his teeth and those he did have were a dark brown colour as if he had just eaten a bar of chocolate. 'Keep cool,' he said to O'Loughlin who was getting noticeably more agitated. 'So what does he have on him?'

'That's the problem,' replied O'Loughlin. He hadn't handed anything over when I started chasing after him. I was watching to see if he'd drop what he had but I'm sure he didn't. He's got something on him, I know it.'

'Did you check his pockets?' advised Fionn.

'Of course I checked his bloody pockets, don't patronise me.'

'I've got nothing on me, you're seeing things, Guard, you may let me go and head off there to Specsavers,' said the man.

'Did you pat him down? Could be in his underwear,' said Fionn calmly, trying not to further irritate O'Loughlin.

'The scumbag isn't wearing any. He showed me what was underneath his trousers before I'd even asked. And I'll tell you what, it wasn't pretty.'

'You loved it,' said the man. 'You're trying to ride me now and all.'

O'Loughlin pulled back his arm behind his head and clenched his fist.

Fionn grabbed it before he could swing it forward. 'Careful now,' he said. 'Did you give him a cavity search?'

'A what?' shouted O'Loughlin in horror. 'I would have noticed if he shoved it up his arse for feck sake.'

'Not that kind of cavity,' responded Fionn. 'I mean a tooth cavity. This guy looks perfectly equipped to be able to hide things in his mouth.'

O'Loughlin paused momentarily to process the information and then grabbed the man's chin with one hand and placing the palm of his other hand on the man's forehead he pushed his head back. 'Open wide,' said O'Loughlin.

The Guard and the Garda Detective were standing side by side with a perfect view inside the man's mouth. If they were asked to instantly decide how many teeth they were looking at, both would have agreed on nine. They both immediately saw it. A miniscule bag wedged into a crevice in his lower gum, like it was precious brown sand wrapped in plastic and buried in grimy terra cotta clay. They could see the ghosts of the teeth that used to sit upright and sturdily should be. But after a cocktail of time and mistreatment caused them to decay and deteriorate they had given way to the deep and grotesque crater that stared back at them.

'Say "awwww... busted",' said O'Loughlin as he pulled out the bag, holding it delicately between his thumb and forefinger so as to touch as little of it as possible. 'Heroine,' he said as he dropped it into a pocket in his jacket.

The man made a sudden knee-jerk bolt to get away as O'Loughlin wiped his fingers. Fionn grabbed him by the arm before he could take off. 'I'll hold him while you cuff him and call it in.'

O'Loughlin turned and looked over Fionn's shoulder and seemed to drift away deep in thought as he stared blankly into oncoming traffic. 'I couldn't be arsed,' he said as he suddenly grabbed the man firmly by the chest forcing Fionn to release his grip. He swung the man around in a semi-circle until his feet were slipping off the footpath. The man looked around and saw the side mirror of a bus come straight towards his face and he could feel himself about to abseil off the footpath right under the bus.

'You messed with the wrong guy today you piece of shit,' said O'Loughlin as he loosened his grip.

'Luke,' shouted Fionn loudly in a moment of helpless panic.

Suddenly O'Loughlin pulled the man back towards him and out of the way of the oncoming bus that was breaking and blowing its horn in equally forceful measures. He pushed the man up against the wall as he removed his hand cuffs from his belt. He then started to laugh menacingly. 'Wouldn't you just love to do it sometimes, Fagan? Just chuck them all right under the bus.' He continued to laugh as pedestrians were beginning to stop in their tracks to observe the scene.

Fionn didn't respond. He just looked at O'Loughlin as he cuffed the man. The distorted and tormented expression on his face made him look like a different person. Like a person possessed. He thought about how, despite knowing him for years, he wasn't sure who the real Luke O'Loughlin was. Was he the type of person who wouldn't throw someone under a bus? Or the type of person who pretends he wouldn't.

After offering a sheepish farewell Fionn continued back on his way towards Tower Records.

'Scumbags, Fionn,' O'Loughlin shouted after him. Fionn turned back and could see him pulling on the sleeve of the drug dealer who all of a sudden had a solemn darkness washed over his face that made him look ten years older. 'They're scabby infections in our city and it's our job to keep the streets clean, don't you think?'

Fionn gave a reluctant wave as he turned his back.

CHAPTER SIXTEEN

Fionn was back at the Freemason's Hall ten minutes early but waited slightly further down the street so that when he saw Stephanie come out he would walk towards her making it look like he was just arriving. It was 4.46pm when she finished work. He had already lost one minute. Fionn started walking towards her in what he believed to be a cool strut.

'Oh hello there, Mister,' she said with a smile. 'You're just in time.'

One minute late, Fionn thought. 'I sure am,' he said.

They turned and started walking back in the direction Fionn had come from.

Fionn started the conversation immediately. 'So how was work?'

'Work was OK thank you, not too busy. Yes, the weather has been nice for this time of year. No, I didn't see the match and yes, I do come here often,' replied Stephanie.

'What?' Fionn asked, taken aback.

'That's all the small talk out of the way now, start asking me some real questions,' she said with a grin. You don't have much time here and I'm rooting for you.'

Fionn sighed silently in relief. He felt no matter what he did now, everything would go OK. Maybe there was no need to play the game. He could just be himself. 'OK, great, so tell me everything. I know your name, what you study, where you study, where you work, your Dads name and what he does. Tell me everything else about you.'

'No way,' she replied. 'You first.'

'Fine,' he replied and then took a deep breath before talking at a pace faster than he had ever spoken before. 'Born 33 years ago and raised in Co. Kildare. Only son to John and Sheila. Totally different people but still happily married after 35 years. No brothers and one sister. Yvonne, my twin and twenty minutes younger than me. Looks nothing like me anymore. Acts nothing like me either. I was a relatively good student in school and always wanted to be a Guard. Did a year of Business in college but took a place in the Guards the first chance I got. I was made Garda Detective after just three years mainly due to a good case record and excellent ability to complete paperwork correctly. Due to a freeze on promotions for the last five years I haven't progressed much further but I hope to be a Detective Sergeant within three years. I rent a one bedroom apartment on Foley St. It's plastered with modern art prints and framed posters of my favourite bands. I love music and prefer to walk everywhere so I can spend the time listening to it. I carry my earphones everywhere. I play piano but I'm a bit rusty. I always wanted to be in a band but none of the cool bands ever wanted a keyboard player. I don't own a car but borrow an unmarked work car if I need to travel for work. I watch football and I support Tottenham Hotspur. I enjoy watching football at the weekend. Other hobbies are reading, when I have time. Going to the cinema, when I have time. Travelling, when I have time. Going to the gym, when I have time. Stopping to breathe, when I have time.'

This was going well, he hadn't had to lie once. He thought he should throw some in for good measure. 'I enjoy heading out with friends but only once a week. I've had three serious relationships and we broke up because they didn't want to commit. I love kids and hope to have my own some day.

'Do you like dogs or cats?' asked Stephanie.

Damn it, he thought. A 50/50 chance of saying the wrong thing. He went with the truth. 'Definitely dogs but I don't have one because...'

'You don't have time?' Stephanie interrupted.

'You know me so well,' he quipped.

'Are you close to your twin sister?'

She's not talking to me because I owe my parents money and she thinks I'm an asshole, he thought to himself. 'Very close, always have been,' he lied.

'You say you don't have time to do all the things you enjoy. Why not?'

Because I spend all my spare time in bookies, casinos and playing online poker, he thought to himself. 'Work,' he replied. 'I put in a lot of hours because I'm ambitious and I want to progress sooner rather than later.'

'Except when you ask to take the afternoon off for no good reason?' Stephanie had an air of defiance in her voice.

'That never happened,' he protested. 'I did take an afternoon off recently but it was for a very good reason.'

'Good save,' she replied, the friendly air still gone. Maybe she wasn't making this easy for him after all.

They came to a stop in front of pedestrian lights at a busy junction with cars moving steadily in both directions.

'Now your turn,' said Fionn in an inquisitive tone.

'I'm from Sandymount. Three older brothers, all bigger than me. Very protective.'
I hope they like to talk about football, thought Fionn.
'I want to work in the area of criminal rehabilitation, which is why I'm doing this course. I only got 440 points in my Leaving cert so I have to go about getting onto the course the long way.'

Only 440, he thought to himself. Not exactly a feeble result. He had only got three hundred and seventy and was proud of that.

'I hate football but I watch rugby, as my brothers all play.'

Damn it, Fionn thought.

I love modern art too and I can't stand when people say they think modern art is pretentious bullshit. I've had a car since I was seventeen. She's a red mini and I love her. She's ten years old now but still going strong.'

A clue to her age, thought Fionn. *She's no older than twenty-seven*. 'You haven't mentioned how old you are,' said Fionn, too curious to bite his tongue knowing full well he should have bitten right down. 'While we're on the subject, I mean.'

'How old do you think I am?' Stephanie seems mischievous as she asked.

'Do you want my honest guess? Or do you want me to aim low to flatter you?'

Stephanie's jaw dropped but she seemed to be enjoying stringing Fionn along. 'I'll give you one guess and if you're out by more than one year it's an automatic fail, so best tell me how old you think I am.'

'Twenty-seven?'

'How did you know? Did you check up on me before you came back to collect me?'

Fionn punched the air in victory. 'No, of course not, besides, unless you've been arrested I wouldn't be able to find out anything about you. Although that's a good idea for the next convict I want to ask out on a date.'

Stephanie smiled but still had a serious glint in her eyes as she looked at Fionn waiting for him to answer the question.

'Your Dad,' he replied.

'He told you? Why?' She had a look of disdain on her face.

'No no,' he continued. 'I know he's a semi-retired solicitor, but he's not that old. He can afford to semi-retire, so he was probably successful as a younger man. He had three boys and then finally, a girl. So I'm betting you are his pride and joy. If you got a car when you were seventeen you hardly bought it yourself, so it was probably a gift from your parents. And I'd imagine only the best is good enough for Mr. Johnson's little girl so he bought you a brand new mini.

Which is ten years old now, so that makes you twenty-seven.'

Stephanie was impressed but tried not to show it. 'Anyway,' she continued. 'I like to travel too but unlike you I make time to do so. The world is too beautiful and we only have one lifetime to see as much of it as we can. I like to cook and to be cooked for, which you never mentioned. I don't mind the gym but I prefer to go out cycling. I just find the gym a bit of an artificial environment and feel like I'm wasting my time if I'm not watching the world go around while I exercise.'

Fionn had never thought about gyms like that but found himself agreeing with her point of view.

'I love going to the cinema. Who doesn't? But pouring your chocolate sweets into your bag of popcorn and eating them together is a must and if you can't get down with that then you need to speak up now because it'll be a deal breaker.'

Fionn smiled. 'It's not, I like that too.'

'Having said that,' she continued like she was going to announce a revelation. 'Give me a movie on TV and a glass of wine and I'll be just as happy.'

'Me too,' he replied. 'Except maybe a beer instead of wine. You didn't mention if you like music or not?'

'Oh what sort of weirdo doesn't like music?' she replied. 'That's a no-brainer. But what kind of music are you into?'

'Oh most types,' he replied.

'Me too, but what is your favourite?'

'Oh I don't know. Depends on the mood, but alternative rock is probably my favourite.'

'Same', she replied. 'Do you like "The National"?'

'Are you joking me, I've seen them live three times.'

'Same,' she replied with a grin that formed a crescent shape under her nose. 'They're one of my favourites too.'

Fionn smiled back and they walked along for a few moments in silence as they let all the information digest in their minds. 'Wow,' he finally said. 'I think we've touched on just about everything except politics and religion.'

'And where do you stand on those?' Stephanie asked.

'I don't believe those subjects should be brought up on a first date,' he replied. 'Your Dad has the right idea, best to leave them topics out for now.'

'This could be your only chance,' she said. 'Don't you want to know?'

'OK you tell me your views then,' said Fionn, threading the subject matter lightly and giving her the opportunity to show her cards first. Not that it mattered what she said, she'll still seem even more beautiful than ever.

'Politically, I suppose I'm liberal. Equal rights for all, help those who need it, progressive taxing, care for the environment. What about you?'

Fionn's initial thought to lie and automatically agree with her suddenly seemed like a bad idea so he told the truth. That would make him feel more comfortable.

'I don't really have any political convictions. Whoever will invest more in the Department of Justice, I'll vote for them. Although no one ever seems to, they only ever cut spending. It must be frustrating being liberal in a country where the two biggest political parties are both conservative?'

'That's not necessarily true,' she replied.

'Aren't our government told what to do by Europe anyway?'

'Of course not,' she replied.

'OK, maybe you can explain it to me some time. What about religion then? Is there a God?'

'Of course there is,' she replied.

'Oh yeah? I think you're in the minority these days aren't you?'

'Perhaps,' she said, pausing in thought while she considered the statement. 'But that doesn't affect my own faith.'

'Do you go to mass every Sunday, yeah?'

'Most of the time, yeah. Not as much as I should, probably. My uncle is a Jesuit priest and a college professor so I was brought up with it being an important part of family life and the tradition has never waivered. My faith is actually very important to me. What about you, are you religious?'

Once again Fionn decided there was no point in lying. 'I suppose I'd consider myself a lapsed Catholic.'

Stephanie nodded and smiled.

It made Fionn feel reassured that she wasn't rejecting him if he wasn't as religious as her. 'I was an altar boy when I was younger, I went with my parents every week and I prayed all the time. My Mother is super religious. A typical family loving and God fearing country woman. She talked to me about religion a lot when I was younger. I don't think my Dad was particularly interested in it, he never spoke about it. I think he might just go along with it for her sake. Anyway, I left it all behind as soon as I moved away from home. It's not that I've stopped believing in a God, I guess I just don't really think about it.'

'Sounds more like an agnostic to me,' replied Stephanie. 'What do your parents do?'

'My Dad has done lots of things. He's had a new job every couple of years. A Jack of all trades but a master of none. He would find a balance between decent pay and a job that kept him interested enough not to get depressed. When he'd get bored he'd leave and work somewhere else that paid more.'

'Well it's often times better than a master of one,' replied Stephanie.

'What do you mean?' replied Fionn.

'That's the full "Jack of all trades" saying. It means that it's actually better to be reasonably good at lots of things than to be an expert at just one thing. You're underestimating your Dad.

Fionn made a humming sound as he pensively considered what he had just learned.

'What about your Mother,' she asked to break the silence.

'My mother worked as a receptionist when she was younger but gave it up to raise me and my sister. She never went back to work. Never needed to I suppose. Or wanted to.'

Stephanie had a smile on her face but her eyes were sad. 'It sounds like we come from completely different backgrounds. But it's interesting.'

Interesting? Fionn thought to himself. That's not necessarily a good thing. This wasn't going bad but it wasn't going brilliantly.

They continued to ask each other questions as the journey got into its final leg. It felt like she was asking half hearted questions about things she had no significant interest in just to fill dead air. Fionn was feeling deflated about this but also increasingly frustrated as the more she told him about herself the more fascinating she became.

They approached the jet black gates of Trinity College that always seem to look like they've had a fresh coat of gloss paint applied. Fionn knew this was possibly the last couple of minutes he would spend in Stephanie Johnson's company. He had been fooling himself, he was nowhere near good enough for this woman. She was way out of his league and she had just shown him that with great gentility and sweetness. He was about to be rejected in the kindest way imaginable. They stopped under the Romanesque door to the college's courtyard. It would be impossible to calculate the sheer number of scholars and nobility that had passed through this same entrance over the centuries. Fionn looked around as he searched for something witty to say. Drawing a blank he reverted to simply saying what he saw.

'Oliver Smith and Edmund Burke,' he said.

'Who?' Stephanie asked, confused.

'The two statues here on either side of us, that's who they are.'

She looked up and acknowledged the statues with a nod. 'I never knew that. I pass them so often but never knew who they were supposed to be.'

'Don't ask me anything about them though,' said Fionn. 'I only remember their names, the fact that they are past students of the college and that the guy who sculpted them was not that good at sculpting legs, so both statues are identical from the waist down.'

Stephanie walked back towards the exit of the college and turned around to get a panoramic view of both statues. She then grinned widely.

'Once again, I never noticed that. I doubt many have,' she said as Fionn approached her. 'Where did you learn that?'

'I don't have a clue,' he said. 'Someone told me once, I tend to retain useless information, but where I get it from is never important.'

They looked at each other and smiled. Several seconds of silence went by. Fionn wondered if it would be better to admit defeat before Stephanie stated the obvious. Jump before he was pushed.

'So that was an interesting walk,' she said, breaking the silence.

'It really was,' he said. *I think I love you*, he thought to himself. 'So...'

'So are you going to ask me for my number or what?'

Fionn's jaw dropped with the way the question came so unexpectedly. 'Seriously?'

'Don't you want it anymore?' she asked as she scrunched up her face.

'Of course,' he replied. 'But I just assumed, I don't know, I'm not your type?'

'Ah we differ in certain ways, that's true. But none of that is important. I like dogs too. That's all that matters.' She took a pen from her bag, tore a piece of paper from her notepad and wrote a phone number on it. 'Text me,' she said as she gave him an affectionate wink, turned and walked through the open courtyard door, once again disappearing through a threshold without waiting for a response and looking as if she was radiating a majestic flutter of lights and colours as she disappeared from view.

CHAPTER SEVENTEEN

Aaron was sitting on a concrete bench in Wolfe Tone Park. The seats were first installed to encourage people to use the otherwise derelict area as a community space, but it soon became a hangout area for drunks, rebels and deadbeats. Topless burley men with an array of faded tattoos across their arms and chest. Rugged women with sleepy eyes and skeletal faces. Angsty teenagers dressed all in black with shaggy fringes protruding from under their hoods. Despite these being examples of some of the usual clientele it didn't deter anyone from using the area. People would often sit down for a rest while shopping around Henry Street or eat their lunch in the fresh air while on a break from work, because the groups of lairy drunks and mischievous youths mostly kept to themselves. He was finishing the end of a fizzy drink that he had bought earlier and he was quietly observing the people around him. There was a child riding a statue of the cow. There was a toddler chasing the pigeons. There were a couple of backpackers sitting and looking around. They wouldn't be there long, there wasn't much to see. One particular couple that were high on meth and were screaming gibberish to each other was interesting enough to keep them entertained for the time being. They may not have seen local addicts fight with each other before. One young lady that looked like a student was texting on her phone and pretending not to notice the argument in case they asked her what they were looking at. As much as it seemed to be attracting the attention of those around him, the argument between the couple was of no interest to Aaron. He was trying to blank out the screams of the man demanding his tenner back for reasons unbeknown to anyone. He couldn't help but notice the subtle murmur of sniggers from the other onlookers when the woman put her hand into her dirty bra, pulled out a rolled up bank note, threw it on the ground, spat on it and then stormed off. By the time the man caught up to her with the €10 waving in his hand Aaron had finally zoned out and heard none of the grovelling he was doing while declaring his love for her. Aaron had enough on his mind to care about other people's problems. "Your name came up", he had been told earlier that day. He had apparently said something he shouldn't have to some guy he shouldn't have been speaking to and now there were Guards out looking for him. What the two of them had done together was going to be all pinned on him and there was nothing he was going to be able to do about it. He had messed up and he only had himself to blame. It was true that the Guard had saved him from spending a long time in prison and it was true that he owed him a debt, but he felt that at this stage his debts were paid back to the point that he was going to end up in prison either way. The Guard had turned a blind eye on his crime and then forced his hand into committing many more. Crimes that were far worse. He regretted accepting the deal in the first place. It was enticing at the time but now he realised he should have just taken the punishment for his actions. At least he would have atoned by now.

At the time it happened he had already given up selling drugs but an old contact of his had offered him a job and because he was broke, he agreed to it. He wouldn't have to sell anything, just transport some items. He reasoned to himself that someone had to move the packages from here to there, so why not him. It was a rucksack full of cannabis and a guitar case full of cash. He was to pick it up from a container in Dublin Port and just walk it into town like he was a busking musician just off the boat. The organisers had been fully aware that the chances of getting the product out were slim. He realised afterwards he was being watched by the authorities who had set it as a trap. His employer knew this but wanted to make one last attempt to retrieve it before the cops stepped in and locked it up in evidence forever. Aaron had been the dispensable pawn sacrificed in an end game that was impossible to win.

He hadn't got five hundred metres before two undercover cops waving their guns and badges were on top of him. They had arrested him, brought him to one of the stations on the south side of the city and interrogated him. Aaron had buckled under the pressure. He felt no loyalty towards those that had just sent him out to sail a sinking ship without a life jacket so he gave up each name and every detail he knew. He had asked for a deal in return for giving the others up but that was rejected. Eventually, one of the Guards got him alone and told him that he knew a way of letting him off without charge but that he would have to agree to assist him going forward. It seemed like a no brainer and later that same night he was back in his hostel feeling like he had dodged a bullet. Maybe not dodged it. More like he'd been shot but the bullet had missed all the important stuff, the doctor stitched him up and he was now indebted to the doctor. Stitched up was right. The Guard didn't wait long to call in a favour. Together they had targeted what the Guard was calling the scum of the earth that deserved everything that happened to them. In the beginning Aaron had convinced himself it was true but after he saw that people who were only trying to make ends meet were losing their lives, he realised that he was not on the side of good. This Guard owned him. He had him trapped in a web and he felt helpless. He had tried several times to do something about it. He tried to report it but it was intercepted. He tried to refuse but he was beaten and threatened. He once even sought advice from a friendly stranger who seemed helpful at the time but even that conversation had gotten back to the Guard. He couldn't even warn people as to what he was doing as to work with the Guards and be a rat is the worst crime of all, if any of his old friends ever found out he'd be dead. But not before having to endure the worst type of torture imaginable. He had no choice but to be a slave to this one man's sick quest. These people he was after, he knew where they were coming from. He had been one of them not too long ago.

As he sat staring at the walls and windows of the Jervis shopping centre and thought about the fresh warning he had just received he decided he needed to try a different tactic. He would try to escape. He would get a bus to somewhere else in Ireland and live there. He would prefer to leave the country but he didn't own a passport. Maybe if he went to Belfast he wouldn't be easily found. The Guard knew his name so if he changed it he wouldn't be able to find him. He smiled to himself with no hint of humour whatsoever. *My name*, he thought to himself. He was worried about his own name but had forgotten he didn't know the Guards name. He must have heard it several times the night he was arrested but he wasn't listening and couldn't remember. It's difficult to report a Guard when you don't even know his name. He had asked him once but the Guard just laughed. He knew it gave him an even higher upper hand. He then thought about the instructions he had just been given. Maybe he would disobey and not follow through. He suddenly shuddered at the thoughts of another beating. *There must be a way out*, he thought to himself. He was sure he'd think of something. But for now he'd better do what he needed to. Continue to pay back his debts.

CHAPTER EIGHTEEN

Morrissey was being interrupted from telling William it was really nothing when the tone of an incoming call sounded in Fionn's ear in place of The Smith's album he was listening to. He didn't bother checking the display to see who it was and just answered using the button on his earphones. 'Hello,' he said in a detached tone.

'Well?' said the voice on the other end which he instantly recognised as his father.

'Oh, hi Dad,' he responded.

'Haven't got you at a bad time have I?'

'Not at all, I'm just defusing a bomb at the moment, but I have you on hands free so keep talking.'

'Are you serious?' There was a tone of panic in his father's voice.

Fionn laughed heartily. The closer his father approached to seventy the more gullible he seemed to be getting. 'Of course not. That's not actually my job, I'm a member of An Garda Síochána. You know that right?'

It was John Fagan's turn to laugh. 'Yes, I suppose there's a section in the army for that isn't there? I've seen enough films about it, you'd think I wouldn't be so easily fooled. How are you doing, son?'

'Fine thanks Dad, how's all at home?' Fionn knew the call was just for salutation purposes. His father only ever calls to check in and say hello. His mother only ever rang with bad news and lectures.

'All good here, thanks.' His father remained silent as if waiting for Fionn to do the talking.

'Is Mam OK?' he asked cautiously.

'Oh yes,' his father replied. 'Not a bother.' A further awkward silence hung in the air. Fionn decided to wait it out until his father finally continued. 'Your sister was down with us yesterday. She said you two still aren't talking. It breaks your Mothers heart, you know?'

Fionn sighed down the phone. 'I know Dad but it's no big deal, we're like chalk and cheese, that's all. It's nothing to worry about.'

'She said you owe her quite a bit of money.'

Fionn's heart sank. Yvonne had promised not to bring their parents into it. It wasn't even that much. Not compared to what he owed others.

'And that she really needs it back right now but you haven't returned a cent yet.'

He could feel his cheeks burn as anger started to build up inside him.

John's voice was starting to crackle with emotion as he continued. 'You know your mother and I always tried to instil in both of you from an early age that you should never fall out over money. Looks like we've failed on that. You were always so close growing up, you remember? You were best friends.'

'We'll be fine Dad, don't worry.' It suddenly occurred to Fionn why his sister broke her promise not to tell their parents about the money he owed her. 'Wait, did she ask you for help?'

'She needs help, we had to.'

'Ah Dad, this is between me and her, you can't afford it.'

'You owe her money, you owe us money. Now you just owe us the money. There's no rush in paying us back if you make talking to your sister again the priority.'

'Thanks Dad but that's easier said than done, she still has issues with what I owe you.'

'It's a lot of money, son,' John said ruefully before adopting a more stern tone. 'You haven't paid any of it back yet, are you still not able to save? Rent in Dublin can't be that high, or can it?'

'It is Dad, but I'm sorry. I thought I'd have been able to get you a couple of grand back by now.' A knot was forming in Fionn's stomach as a wave of guilt was beginning to engulf him. 'I'm planning on moving into a two bed flat and getting a housemate again, to split the rent.'

'You should have your own mortgage by now,' John replied.

'I've no savings whatsoever Dad, if I did I'd be paying you back before I buy a house.'

Another bout of silence came and went before John spoke again. 'Look, your mother and I are OK. We don't get up to much these days, we can get by on just our pensions for now. We don't want you giving us any money you don't have, we just want to see you back on your feet but we're just worried that it's taking so long. Do you owe any money to anyone else?'

'No, absolutely not,' Fionn lied.

'You don't have a loan with the banks?'

'No and I never will.' He was telling the truth but only because the banks rejected his loan application.

'You know your mother prays for you every day. For both of you.'

'I assume Mam is standing right beside you,' said Fionn. 'Can I say hello?'

'Of course,' replied John. 'Look after yourself, son.'

Fionn heard an inaudible whisper before his mother's voice blared into his ear.

'Hello, son,' said Sheila with a loud bellow as if she were speaking to a room full of people. 'How are you doing?'

'Fine thanks, Mam. Any news with you?'

'Yvonne was down,' she began.

'I've just been over this with Dad, you don't have to repeat it. I'm doing the best I can.'

Sheila waited in silence for several seconds, giving her son time to calm down before she changed the subject. 'Are you going to mass every week, son?'

'Yes of course I am,' Fionn lied.

'And are you praying for God's help?' she asked.

'Not sure if I deserve his help,' replied Fionn.

'Nonsense,' replied Sheila. 'The good lord won't help us unless we ask for it, you know?'

Fionn was trying to choose his next words carefully so as to move on without hurting his Mother's feelings. 'Honestly Mam, I've had enough God talk for today.'

'Oh really?' Sheila said, perking up. 'What do you mean?'

'I had a tour of a Freemason's Lodge earlier and they went on about their superior beings the whole time. Have you ever heard of the Freemasons?'

'What were you doing there?' she said with a cocktail of shock, concern and disappointment in her voice.

'A case brought me there, I was investigating a symbol on a window.'

'Oh thank God,' she said with a deep breath. 'I was worried you were going to tell me you were thinking of joining.'

'Well, no. But why would that be so bad? They do a lot of charitable work. And you have to believe in God to be a member, I thought you'd approve?'

'Yes, but what God?'

'Any God I suppose?'

'Exactly', said Sheila.

Fionn was confused and waited for his mother to continue. 'What do you mean?' he asked after realising she had obviously felt her point had been made.

'I've actually read a lot about this. God doesn't have any real meaning for the Freemasons. They believe in religious indifference. They say it themselves that all religions are the same and that they are all in darkness.' Sheila not only had a strong belief in her faith but also an intense passion for theology in general. Every book she read typically had a religious theme of some kind.

'But is that not a good thing?' challenged Fionn. To suggest that we should be able to co-exist and be tolerable and respectful of each other's religions? What is important to one person means nothing to another but the way in which they practise their faith, whatever that faith may be, might be right for them?'

'Tolerable, yes. Respectful, yes. But religious indifference suggests that no one religion is correct. That means that Jesus' life was pointless and that there was no reason for him to ever have lived on earth.'

Fionn said nothing. He enjoyed playing devil's advocate when discussing religion with his mother but couldn't find the right words to counter argue.

'Freemasonry is an attack on Christianity. It was founded during the enlightenment period which was hundreds of years ago. Illuminism is big in freemasonry and part of it is the destruction of religion. When joining you have to recite a blasphemous oath. Part of the initiation is that you have to remove all personal belongings. That includes any religious symbols such as a wedding ring or a crucifix from around your neck. You can't be wearing anything that can be offensive or defensive during your initiation. Think about that, offensive as in it offends the people that are there? Defensive as in it defends you against what? They were trying to destroy the church for years but they realised they were failing so they changed their plan. They decided to infiltrate the church instead.'

'Ah Mam, come on,' scoffed Fionn. 'You're starting to get into conspiracy theories now.'

'I am not. It's a known fact that past Popes were Freemasons.'

'Let me guess, the ones that wanted to modernise the church?'

'Exactly. And not just the church. Governments that were founded on their faith in God have had masons rise to the top and we now live in a world that is accepting of all sorts of evil things.'

'And what, you believe this to be true just because you heard it during a Sunday morning sermon? Do you always listen to everything the priest says? They are only human too, they can't always be right.'

'Of course I listen to my priest. But it doesn't end there. Like everyone should do when they hear about something, I go and read into it. I listen to both sides of the argument, I pray for guidance and I make my own mind up about it.'

'And what reading on the freemasons have you done?' asked . 'You seem to know an awful lot about a society that is known to be quite secretive.'

'The Principles of Masonic Law is a good read,' replied Sheila, without missing a beat. 'One thing was crystal clear to me from reading that. Their grand architect of the universe is not the loving God I pray to. The whole thing is based on secrets, interpretation and separation of the truth. That's exactly how evil operates. It hides, confuses, divides and conquers.'

'I see,' said Fionn, unsure of what else he could say. His mother clearly felt strongly about the matter. He saw little point or reason to argue.

'Look son, I can't make you do anything, I can only advise you, but I advise you to stay well clear of the Freemasons. Do not associate with them. I understand there are many Guards a part of it.'

'I wasn't planning to,' he replied with reservation in his voice. 'And there's none in it that I know of.'

'Good,' Sheila said. 'So what other news have you got for me? I was hoping you were ringing to tell me that you've met a nice girl?'

Fionn was thankful that his mother was not able to see him blush, although he was suspicious she could still sense it. He also wondered what she'd say if she knew he was about to enter a bookmakers. 'Look Mam, I have to go, I'm about to meet someone,' he lied as he approached the door of Dame's Dime.

'OK Son, take care of yourself, and don't lose your faith, OK? Once you have that, everything else will follow.'

'I won't,' said Fionn. 'Bye.'

Sheila returned a goodbye and hung up her phone. What she didn't realise was that even before her handset was placed back on the switch hook of her telephone Fionn had received a heavy blow to the back of the head.

CHAPTER NINETEEN

At first Fionn wasn't sure what had just hit him. He slowly stumbled down to his side trying to soften his impact with the hard ground while simultaneously blinking rapidly to prevent his vision from clouding over. It was only when he turned and was faced with a man wearing a Spider-man mask did he realise he had been struck intentionally. Feeling quite disoriented, Fionn just lay staring at the man in confusion while rubbing the back of his head. People were beginning to stop and stare.

The man with the mask spoke in a husky voice that he was exaggerating in order to disguise it. 'I need you to start minding your own fucking business,' he said.

Fionn continued to look on in confusion. He realised he might have concussion. He looked the man up and down. He was wearing a blue unbranded tracksuit and what looked like brand new unbranded runners. He was holding an old police baton. The mask looked so out of place it was almost laughable. 'Nice mask,' he finally said as he lunged himself upright into a standing position.

'Shut the fuck up, asshole,' the man said in return, his voice still purposely distorted. 'And listen carefully. You're beginning to stick your nose into business you should stay out of. So butt out. For your own sake.'

'What business is that?'

'You know very fucking well.'

'I really don't,' Fionn replied, his voice remaining calm and collected. It was not the first time he received a blow to the head from someone decidedly standing on the wrong side of the law. 'I'm a Guard you know. It's my job to stick my nose into business I should stay out of. Like how I plan to stick my nose into your business to find out who the hell you are so I can have you crucified, you psychopathic bastard.'

His calm deadpan tone seemed to infuriate the man in the mask. He raised his baton intending to make contact with Fionn's skull. As the baton came down Fionn side stepped, narrowly dodging contact with the baton. He reached out with a quick jab to the man's elbow, causing him to instantly drop the weapon. Fionn followed this with a dive to the ground and reached out to grab the baton but his attacker was steadfast in his position and outstretched his foot, kicking Fionn over onto his back before reaching for the baton himself. Fionn rolled away from his attacker and jumped back up to his feet.

One onlooker, deciding from what he saw so far that Fionn was the victim, tried to get involved. 'Break it up,' he shouted at the masked man as he approached him with his hands outstretched.

'Sir, I'm a Guard, please stand back or you might get injured,' Fionn said while simultaneously trying to catch his breath and plan his next manoeuvre.

The onlooker stared at Fionn with intense concern but then took heed of the advice and retreated. Fionn was edging closer and closer to his attacker and was willing him to strike again with the baton so he could successfully execute his next move. He was crouching and holding his hands out in front of his face, ready to intercept anything that was coming his way. The masked man was standing steady with the baton raised behind him. As Fionn got to within striking distance the man lashed out with a heavy swipe aiming for the side of Fionn's head. He reached out with quick reflexes and caught the baton with both hands as it came for him. With both men holding either end of the baton they proceeded to make circular motions around the pavement like they were reluctantly learning to dance a ceilidh. They both tried desperately to break the other one's grip. With a powerful lunge the masked man suddenly pulled in the other direction taking Fionn off the pavement and out onto the road in front of an oncoming taxi. Seeing the altercation the driver suddenly hit the brakes but the momentum caused Fionn to hit the front wing of the car and slide directly over the bonnet, disappearing down the other side. With a quick reaction he took advantage of being out of sight and briskly crawled around to the back of the car like a wild cat escaping its prey. He peered out from the back of the car to see the masked man still scrutinising the front of the car like he was expecting him to gingerly arise from the far side of the bonnet. As Fionn pounced towards the man from the side he realised the mask must restrict his peripheral vision as he seemed to be completely unaware of the oncoming attack to his flank. A millisecond before Fionn made contact his attacker glanced sideways to see him approaching like a runaway truck, but it was too late to react. The rugby tackle took the wind out of him like a plastic bottle being crushed under a tire. The only possible destination for him next was the ground. A three foot metal bollard broke the masked man's fall as he was rammed, rib cage first, into the flat top of the black cylinder that was cemented into the ground. The masked man lay on the ground in pain, breathing heavy and holding his ribcage. He had fallen onto his right foot with his left outstretched perpendicular to the bollard he had just fallen into. With sudden brute force Fionn stepped back and kicked the man's left foot like it was a football and he was a player about to score the most important goal of his career. He heard a crack as he followed through. The bollard held the man's shin in place as Fionn's kick thrust his ankle around the bollard. The man let out a loud shriek of pain that sounded like a primitive call to war. Satisfied he had been adequately disarmed, Fionn walked around to the baton and kicked it onto the road. As he approached the man who was still lying on the ground clutching his left ankle in pain, Fionn felt a sudden tug from behind. With a sturdy pull he found himself travelling backwards through the threshold of Dame's Dime. He saw Jim Rogers step in front of him with a key and lock the door from the inside. He then turned and gave him a slight smile.

'You're safe now,' said Jim as he shook the door to show it was safely locked. 'I already called 112 and told them a Guard was being attacked.'

'Open this door immediately,' demanded Fionn. 'Before he gets away.'

Jim turned and looked out the clear glass panel of the door, then turned back to Fionn. 'Are you joking? He was about to kill you.'

'I had it under control,' Fionn said. 'He's no longer a threat. I need to find out who he is.' Fionn lunged at Jim to retrieve the bunch of keys from his hands.

He firmly held out his arm to prevent Fionn from moving forward. 'He could be still out there waiting to get in,' he said. 'I don't want him coming in here. I don't want to get hurt.'

Fionn continued to argue with Jim, however he held steady and would not relent.

'After what happened here the other day I'm not taking any more risks,' Jim reasoned.

'You're absolutely right,' agreed Fionn. 'Your own safety is paramount, but this is my job, there is a violent criminal out there, possibly a psychopath that will hurt others, and he's getting away.'

As a shadow came over the entrance they were standing in, the two men turned and looked towards the door. Through the glass they could see Spider-Man staring back at them. The profile of the figure was as still as a statue and although it was the face of a universally loved superhero, it somehow seemed to be staring at them menacingly. Fionn couldn't see the face of the person underneath the mask, but he imagined them to have dark dead evil eyes and he couldn't help but feel he was grinning mockingly beneath the black web. All three men stood staring at the masked man silently when suddenly, in a brisk swooping movement, the face was gone from the doorway and daylight filled the room again. Fionn ran to the window and stared out in helpless frustration as his attacker limped across the street in front of a late breaking, furiously honking car, and out of sight down a dark Temple Bar alley.

'You've let him escape,' Fionn said while still staring out the window. 'You just let him go.'

'Come inside my office and sit down, you're in shock.' reasoned Jim, leading him through the bookmakers and into his office. He offered him a glass of water which he took and drank with shaky hands.

'Thank you,' Fionn finally conceded. He was frustrated the man in the mask escaped but understood that Jim meant well. 'I'm sorry you had to be in that position, putting yourself in danger to help me.'

'No problem at all, replied Jim.' I don't have anyone in this world I'm responsible for apart from my customers and those I meet during my charity work, so it's nice to be there for someone when they need me.'

'What about your wife?' asked Fionn. 'Aren't you there for her?'

'I'm not married,' replied Jim with a surprised expression.

Fionn looked at him sceptically. 'Did you not tell me you were married?'

'Certainly not', Jim replied reassuringly.

'Why did I think you were married?' Fionn asked rhetorically in a confused tone, turning and looking at the ground as if to find the answer there. 'I'm sorry I hope I didn't offend you?'

Jim smiled politely. 'I'm a bachelor and wouldn't have it any other way. I think the knock on the head may have given you a concussion. Make sure and have that looked at, you could end up collapsing in a few hours.'

'I will,' replied Fionn just as he heard the sirens approaching.

CHAPTER TWENTY

'You look like you're not doing so well,' said Neeve to one of the two Guards standing across from her. 'Are you OK?'

'It's my first, er, you know. I suppose I'm just a bit shocked,' replied the Guard with a pale sickly looking face. 'I'm sorry Detective. How unprofessional.'

'Not at all,' Neeve replied. 'You're grand, don't worry. It doesn't get any easier if I'm being honest, you just learn to detach yourself from it.' She looked sympathetically at the baby faced Guard that had introduced himself as Aidan Traynor. He looked to be getting queasy. His breathing was shallow and he was holding his stomach. It could have been the sight of congealed blood. It could have been the fact that a dead body lay in front of him. It was probably due to both. He was clearly not long out of training. As was common practice he had been teamed up with an experienced and more seasoned Guard and sent to his first murder scene. His partner was a woman by the name of Paula O'Donnell that Neeve had first met several years earlier at the scene of a murder when a middle class professional had killed his girlfriend during a drug fuelled rampage. She liked dealing with O'Donnell. She was thorough and professional and did not let her short stature be a reason for people to talk down to her.

O'Donnell nodded in agreement. 'Go out and get some air if you want Aidan, I'll talk to Detective Bello.'

Traynor looked to Neeve as if to clarify that he was authorised to do so and after sensing no protest he apologised, excused himself and walked back out of the Bath Avenue apartment that was situated down a narrow lane and was shadowed by the neighbouring stadium.

'Talk me through what you have so far Paula,' requested Neeve in a professional but informal tone.

'The body belongs to Peter McGee,' began O'Donnell in a matter-of-fact tone. 'Death appears to be an apparent suicide. His elderly mother called us an hour ago, at 6am. She lives directly across the road.'

'Does the family own multiple properties on the block?'

'No, his mother said he started renting the apartment several years ago because it had good space for a workshop and he wanted somewhere close to his mother so that he could look after her.'

Neeve frowned. 'That's so sad.'

'I know,' replied O'Donnell. 'She says she wakes up every morning at that time and comes over to clean his house before he gets up. He was a jewellery maker and apparently worked long hours. He was constantly coming in and out of his workshop making a mess so early in the morning was the only opportunity his mother had to give the place a clean. She claims she opened her curtains and knew straight away something was wrong because when she looked across at his house she could see most lights still turned on. Apparently the victim was big into conserving energy so leaving lights on overnight would be extremely out of character.'

'Did she call us straight away?' asked Neeve.

'Yes,' replied O'Donnell. 'She was too scared to enter by herself. Traynor and I arrived within 15 minutes and using the mother's key we entered and searched the place. This bedroom door was locked and after searching the rest of the house we knocked several times and eventually broke in to find the body. The mother is inconsolable, she's back over in her own house with members of the ambulance service.'

'Any sign of a break in? Does it look like they were searching for anything in particular? Does it look like anything was taken?' She glanced down at the body. She noted how the victim's dreadlocks had soaked up a lot of the blood. It looked like a discarded mop that had been used to clean up tar. Her eyes ran across the victim's arm to the unusual looking gun that was still clasped in his hand. It was silver in colour and covered in gaudy jewels. It looked like something a stereotypical Mexican drug lord might have owned in a Hollywood action film.

'It's a suicide,' O'Donnell replied. 'Why would we check for missing items?'

Neeve surveyed the rest of the room and then looked over to the large window on the other side of the room. She carefully walked up to it and slid the glass across. The window opened sideways, not outwards and was large enough for an average sized adult to fit through. 'It's unusual that he would lock himself into the room if he wanted to kill himself isn't it? Have you checked out here yet?' She glanced out the window, at the flat roof that jutted out just below her and the adjacent wall separating the back yard from the main road.

'Fair point,' conceded O'Donnell. 'But it could have been a force of habit? God knows what goes through a person's mind when they're in that state.'

'If that was the only unusual thing in the room you'd be right. But all things considered I think this was a murder made to look like a suicide.' Neeve paused, waiting to be asked what else she saw. The question never came, so she continued. 'The bloodstain on the wall is at about chest height. The victim was in a sitting position on the bed when the trigger was pulled and then he fell backwards. But look at how outstretched his arm holding the gun is. The arm would have immediately gone limp and fallen straight down by his side. Physics doesn't work like this.' She motioned shooting herself in the head with her finger and then made an exaggerated windmill motion as she outstretched her arm.

O'Donnell looked on and nodded reluctantly without comment.

'And also, he's left-handed. So it's unlikely he'd shoot himself with his right hand.'

'How do you know he's left handed?' responded O'Donnell immediately.

Neeve thought for a second. 'His watch,' she finally said.

'His watch?'

'It's on his right hand. Right handed people wear it on their left hand.'

O'Donnell took her walkie-talkie off her belt as she spoke. 'I'll get the guys to ask his mother, but it could be as simple as him having a sore on his left wrist.'

'Yes do that,' replied Neeve to O'Donnell as she left the room to contact the ambulance crew. She noted that O'Donnell seemed frustrated with her observations. When she surveyed the room she had also noticed that the computer mouse was on the left side of the keyboard and that the guitar in the corner of the room was stringed upside down. She decided it would look more impressive if it seemed she deducted that the victim was left handed based solely on the watch.

While waiting for O'Donnell to return she walked around the room examining every square inch before finally returning again to the body. As she began to look over the deceased man for the second time her eyes were drawn back to the gun. It looked so unusual, yet, despite the gruesome environment surrounding it and the way in which it had just been used, it was strangely beautiful. Almost like someone had taken a Glock, painted it white and then attached a kaleidoscope of jewels to it. Remembering the victim's profession was a jewellery maker, she considered that the gun may have been his own work. The gun was pointing to the far wall and her natural eye line followed it. It led her to an array of assorted jewellery and ornaments that had been mounted neatly in a glass display case. She walked a few short steps towards it to study the items more closely. It appeared to be an expensive collection and varied from necklaces and rings to paper weights and letter openers. Suddenly her eyes stopped on something that stood out like the blinding beam of a lighthouse. She focused and concentrated for about five seconds before the significance of the small object hit her like a ten tonne truck into a concrete wall.

'Holy shit,' she said out loud to no one in particular. Then she took her mobile phone out of her pocket.

The south-side traffic was flowing at a brisk and steady pace so Fionn decided there was no need to attach his siren, it wasn't going to get him down Mount Street and over the Grand Canal any faster. For the second time this week Neeve had rang him at an unsociable hour, however, this time she did actually wake him up. He had leaped from his bed, ran the shower hose over his sore head, brushed his teeth, got dressed and left his flat in seven minutes flat. When he finally arrived at the scene it was exactly thirty minutes after Neeve had called him. As he got out of his car he saw her exiting the house and upon seeing him she turned on her heels and gestured with her head for him to follow her back into the building.

'Holy crap, you look like you just woke up from a bender,' she said upon laying eyes on him, making no attempt to soften the bluntness of her observation. 'How many drinks did you have last night?'

'None,' he replied. 'But I did catch my reflection in the rear view mirror alright, you're not wrong. I was attacked last night.'

'What the hell. When? Where?' replied Neeve. 'Why?' she asked in a louder voice, elongating the word.

'I don't know yet, but I have my suspicions. I have a feeling it'll all come clear soon.'

'Are you OK?' she asked?

'You know me, I'm a trooper,' he replied. 'Don't worry I've seen worse, tell me what we have here?

'I'm pretty positive I've found our symbol,' she said as they ascended the stairs to the room.

'Pretty positive is not positive enough for my liking,' said Fionn. 'You seemed adamant when you woke me up. Only being pretty positive shouldn't be enough to interrupt my beauty sleep. God knows I need it.'

'Just come and take a look for yourself.' Neeve led him through the creepily dark hall and into the bedroom.

'What happened here exactly?' he asked.

'The guy was shot in the head with what is probably his own illegally owned gun and the murderer made it look like suicide.'

'Jesus. How Hollywood. How do you know it definitely wasn't suicide?'

'Take a look around and tell me what you think yourself,' said Neeve as she gestured widely around the room with her outstretched arm like she was a magician unveiling an amazing trick.

Fionn looked around pensively and hummed as if he was sucking on a sweet he wasn't enjoying. He walked around the room studying everything Neeve had already seen. He turned back to the door, put his fingers on the handle, shook it a little and looked at Neeve asking his question with just a raised eyebrow.

'Yes, it was locked,' Neeve said, answering the question that wasn't asked. 'First response broke it down.'

Fionn nodded in agreement. 'Weird, alright.'

With experience they had both come to learn how to not just read a crime scene but feel it. No two crime scenes are ever the same but each one needs to be understood in the same way. Even if not all the facts are there, what is evident can be mixed with experience and instinct to form patterns and tell a story of its own. They could both read the same unwritten account of what had happened in the room and in this case the premise was murder.

'I need you to look at this glass case,' Neeve said, leading him across the room. 'There,' she said as she pointed.

It took Fionn a few seconds to find which piece of jewellery she was specifically pointing at but finally his eyes focused on a ring that was on a shelf with several other items but was unlike any of them. It stood out like a rotten tooth in an otherwise perfect smile. It had an ugly shape to it that seemed all too familiar to Fionn and yet he had never seen it in this form before. Only in his mind, on paper and in the design of a window. The triangles within circles seemed to have a new dimension to them as they were set layered on top of each other on such a dainty item. 'DeWolf's crest,' he finally said, after staring at the ring for some time.

'What?' asked Neeve. 'What wolf?' Sheer confusion washed over her face and for a brief moment she considered if the ring was having a hypnotic effect on Fionn. 'This could be the ring Joanna was talking about, right?'

'I'll explain in a minute but yes, I think so. Great find. Help me lift the victim's trousers legs up, I need to see his ankle. Chances are it might look bruised.'

They both approached the body and gently lifted the left trouser leg. There was no evidence of bruising, swelling or damage. They then examined the right ankle, in case Fionn had remembered last night's incident incorrectly.

'Damn it,' he finally said. 'I was sure this was going to be him.' He slowly walked around the room examining everything for a second time and then repeated it a third time, remaining silent while in thought as if Neeve were no longer there. He then walked to the window and opened it wide, looking out onto the flat roof. 'The murderer obviously left through here, have you found his escape route yet?'

'Not yet,' replied Neeve. 'The yard is completely empty apart from a bin so they must have scaled the ivy walls at some point. There's no specific tares in the ivy at any one place to indicate specifically where. It's as if they just disappeared.'

Fionn jumped out of the window and stood on the flat roof looking down into the modest and neatly kept back yard. It was a fully concrete slabbed ground with not a single weed sprouting through the cracks. There were no flowers, plants or bushes and the only shade of green came from the thick hefty ivy that was covering all three surrounding walls. The walls were twelve feet high and looked almost impossible to scale without a ladder to climb on. He was disappointed when he laid eyes on the bin. He thought Neeve may have overlooked the bin as a possible aid in climbing over the wall, but on seeing it he realised his error was assuming it was going to be a typical waste bin most Dublin houses use. The standard size of a city council bin would add significant height to a person standing on it. Instead, what he saw was a small plastic household bin. He expected it would only come up to his knee if he stood beside it. Apart from that had not been exaggerating, there was not a single other thing in the backyard. Not so much as a hose pipe. Fionn exhaled loudly and turned around. He came face to face with two windows. The large one he had just climbed out of and a small one he could see the hall of the house through.

'I know what you're thinking,' Neeve said as her eyeline followed his. 'We already looked at that, the window is completely sealed shut. It looks like it has been for several years. No one can get through it.'

Fionn said nothing but continued to examine the window and area around it. He could see the height from the first floor flat roof to the peak of the house was only a couple of metres, albeit not a straightforward route. 'Maybe we're not seeing the whole picture,' he said before placing one foot on the sill of the window and another on the drain pipe that ran a metre alongside it. He repeated the process finding his footing between the window and the drain pipe and began ascending the wall.

'What are you doing?' Neeve exclaimed. 'Are you nuts? Jesus, be careful.'

It took just a couple of awkward manoeuvres before Fionn had reached the top of the house. He began examining the area from his new viewpoint while carefully managing his footing so as not to disturb or damage any of the delicate moss infused tiles. He gingerly crept to all four corners of the roof before returning to his original position. He then suddenly let out a hearty laugh.

The sudden outburst startled Neeve who felt a slight tinge of pain in her neck as she craned it swiftly to look back up towards the roof. 'What is it? Have you found the route down?'

Fionn continued to laugh through his explanation. 'I was way off with my theory that the murderer escaped by coming up here anyway. Way off. There is no way down from here, not a chance.'

'Why are you laughing?' Neeve asked in a frustrated tone. 'Are you alright in the head today?'

Fionn suddenly stopped laughing and looked at Neeve with a serious expression on his face. 'It's all about perspective Neeve. The eye of the beholder.'

Neeve became concerned for Fionn's state of mind as she tried to make sense of what he had just said. She had never known him to speak so enigmatically before, it was certainly out of character. As she considered this he just stood with his arms outstretched and palms pointing upwards as if he were a prophecy appearing to his believers on the roof of a Dublin house. 'What do you mean?' she finally asked.

'Coming up here has given me a new perspective on things. I have seen the light. I am a believer. I know how the murderer found his way out.'

'Has it come to you in a vision or something? Tell me. And stop freaking me out.'

Fionn dropped his hands and took out his phone from his pocket. He started taking pictures of the back yard. 'There was a ladder in the yard and he used that to climb up.'

'Where's the ladder now?'

Fionn jumped back onto the flat roof with an ungraceful thud. He handed his phone to Neeve. She looked at the screen of the phone and saw the same yard she had been looking at all morning. It looked exactly the same in the picture except from a higher angle. It only took her a second to notice the silver glint coming from within the ivy. Lying straight across the top of the wall that divided the back yard with a side alley was a ladder no shorter than ten feet long.

'There it is,' Fionn said. 'This has been the easiest case to crack I've ever seen. I won't be surprised if the murder's fingerprints are all over the house and there's a text from him on the victim's phone telling him he's going to kill him.'

When they returned downstairs O'Donnell was waiting for them in front of a pile of paperwork and a DNA kit. 'Detective, we've collected several hairs from around the room. We'll be able to compare them to his DNA to see if any come from anyone beyond his direct family. We also scraped under his nails, that's the easiest place to find other people's skin particles.'

'Great work,' replied Neeve, keep us posted. She gestured to a stack of folders. 'Fionn look, I found a folder with printed photos of all this guy's work, going back years. Your ring is among them. No reference to anything else about it, just several angles of the ring taken by what I would call an expert jewellery maker but what I'd consider an amateur photographer. Also, I cross checked serial numbers and I'm confident this is the one,' she said handing a page to Neeve.

'What's this?' Fionn asked.

Neeve scrutinised the page before answering Fionn. 'I had the guys cross check the serial number on the ring with all his paperwork to see if they could find anything. It could have just been part of his collection but a person that makes and sells jewellery for a living is likely to keep receipts for everything.' She handed the paper to Fionn with her finger placed on one specific part of the page. 'Anyway, it looks like he definitely made this ring. This is a copy of an invoice and the serial numbers etched into the inside match the reference number here.'

'Why would he have an invoice if he still owns it?'

'Just read it,' snapped Neeve.

Fionn looked over the invoice. 'Ah I see, this invoice is for two rings.'

'Exactly, and the other ring?'

'This invoice is addressed to a Michael Behan. I bet he'll shed some light on where the other ring is.'

'I'll bet,' agreed Neeve. 'Judging by the fact the ring was only €60, I'll bet Behan is either poor or a cheapskate. The ring must be made of tin.'

'Easiest case, ever,' said Fionn as he handed the sheet back to Neeve, following it up with an animated shuffle of his feet to display his excitement. Neeve stood smiling but didn't join in with the theatrics. She remained still and rigid. As motionless as the lifeless body of Peter McGee that lay on the bed upstairs.

CHAPTER TWENTY ONE

The office seemed to be darker than it had ever been despite the Indian summer sun shining brightly outside. Dust particles could be seen floating and dancing through the light filled cracks in the blinds and the air smelled of sweat and frustration. As Fionn spoke and began hearing his own words out loud a sudden wave of doubt in his own story washed over him. There was always something about Superintendent Corcoran's deadpan stare that could crack the most steadfast of foundations. When Fionn had finished speaking Corcoran turned in his chair and faced the window, clasping his hands above his chin. He was either contemplating what he had just heard or else he was praying. The silence had become unbearably uncomfortable by the time he finally spoke.

'I'll tell you what everything you've just told me sounds like to me, shall I Fagan?' He continued without waiting for a response. 'It sounds like you're getting up in the morning, coming to work and doing a good job. You have uncovered some interesting facts regarding the homeless deaths situation. It's worrying and we need to look into this a little more, and I think you're doing great. All good so far. But then, it's lunch time and whereas most people take the opportunity to go downstairs to the deli or out to a shop for a soup and a sandwich you have decided instead to drop some acid and trip your absolute balls off. Then, the next day you come to me with information that you have acquired from nosing in on Det. Bello's case. Don't get me wrong here, I understand you were using your initiative and were off duty doing so, so once again good work here. The problem I have is that because of the LSD trip you took to Strawberry Fields with Colonel Mustard, your mashed up brain is connecting both of these cases with a single bloody ring that has been locked in a glass case for years and your theory is that the bloody Freemasons that are behind everything?'

Fionn waited until he was sure Corcoran was finished before speaking. 'No, not exactly Sir. I know I don't have enough solid evidence yet but I'm willing to bet anything there is a connection, I just have to find it. I need you to let me find it, Sir.'

'Yes,' muttered Corcoran while slowly shaking his head no. 'I understand you would be willing to bet anything alright.'

Fionn suddenly became rigid and a jab of anger hit the pit of his stomach. 'What's that supposed to mean?' he said with conviction.

'Don't have a hissy fit Fagan, I'm just stating a fact and so far I don't think I've said anything you don't already know. I know people, I can read them like a book. I can see beyond the bravado and the peacocking and the hard man exteriors. I've had people scream at me for making a decision they didn't like. I've had people try to punch me for telling them something they didn't want to hear. I've seen it a hundred times. They all stand up to me the exact same way. The words they say and the way they say it, all identical. Defensive.

Overconfident. Arrogant. They walk out of here with their heads held as high as the previous person, believing they stand on the higher moral ground. But I know which ones will move past it quickly and right on to the next challenge and which ones go straight to the bathroom, ring their mothers and have a cry about it. I make it my business to know who the people I work with really are. It makes it easier to manage them.' He swung in his chair making several quick jutting motions from side to side and studied Fionn's face as he looked on inquisitively. 'You, for instance. What you see is what you get, I'll give you that. But you have an obsessive personality. It causes you to mindlessly and irresponsibly act on your impulse. Sometimes it gets you somewhere, sometimes it doesn't. But the thrill you get from the win far outweighs the risk of failure. It's true that because of this attitude you'll go places others wouldn't even consider and find things that otherwise would have missed, but can you see from my point of view how I'm the one that has to think sensibly about whether or not there's a risk involved?' He turned in his chair and looked away, letting his words sink into the silence. 'Fagan, what I'm trying to say is that you're one of my strongest assets, but you're equally one of my biggest liabilities.'

Unable to make eye contact and finding the mixed emotions of feeling both proud and ashamed hard to balance, he let several moments go by before responding. 'I don't know whether to shout at you and move on or shout at you and go cry,' he finally said.

Corcoran let a crooked smile wash briefly over his face. 'You'll do neither. You'll tell me you understand my position and you'll tell me again what you think I should do next and you'll listen to yourself talk this time.'

Fionn nodded while he gathered his thoughts. 'Ok,' he agreed. 'We have a suspected murderer among the homeless community. You have already assigned me to this case and I'm still on it. We also have the murder of a jewellery maker earlier this morning. I expect you haven't assigned anyone to that investigation yet. I'm coming to you with a theory that they are related although my evidence linking the two of them is admittedly fairly weak. What I'm asking you is that you let me trust my gut instinct and assign me to investigate both cases. I won't officially investigate them as related but if I happen to find a link then so be it. Give me both cases separately. I'll give them both my equal attention and if I'm wrong I'll deliver two different outcomes and I won't have put you in an awkward position.'

'But you're going into these assuming there's a link,' replied Corcoran. 'When you don't find what's not there you miss what is.'

'I've got one route I want to go. These rings you scoff at were made for and paid for by a person named Michael Behan. A quick check tells me he's a well respected dentist in Glasnevin and curiously he has a gun licence. What that has to do with fixing teeth I don't know. He has no previous record but I want to find out why he had these rings made, what they mean to him, his relationship with the victim and where he was last night. If I find no connection to the homeless deaths I'll leave it and treat them separately, you have my word.'

Corcoran once again paused in silence as he considered his decision. 'You fully expect to find a connection with this Behan guy don't you?'

'Absolutely.'

'OK, fine.'

'Yes?'

'Yes. I'm giving you both cases. *Separately.* You have seventy-two hours to give me a detailed report on both, no matter how they progress. Do not come back to me with a bunch of dead ends. Follow logic, got it?'

'Yes, got it Sir, thank you Sir.' Fionn didn't want to wait for any more conditions so he turned and headed straight for the door.

'Oh and one more thing,' Corcoran said before he reached it.

Fionn said a curse word in his mind and slowly turned back around expecting an unreasonable caveat.

'Two cases need two people. You should have your partner back for this. I'll free McGinty up, I'll let you give him the good news that you can be bum chums again. For now.'

'Yes, Sir,' Fionn said, almost singing the words as he exited the office.

Things were starting to go well. He had a lead, he had resources and he had his partner back. The outlook was turning positive and momentum was building. However, he also considered the fact that sometimes the faster you build up momentum, the harder you hit the wall.

CHAPTER TWENTY TWO

'The last time we were talking you weren't impressed with my Guinness facts,' Billy said as he went in for the third sip of his pint. He inhaled a mouthful of the black stuff, or more factually, the ruby red stuff, and continued. 'But do you know how many children Arthur Guinness had?'

'No I don't,' replied Fionn with a tone of disinterest. 'But if I could be bothered taking my phone out of my pocket I could find out in two seconds flat.'

'Twenty-one,' said Billy, triumphantly.

'I don't care,' said Fionn.

'So, I guess Guinness really is good for you,' Billy said with a loud laugh as he dug his elbow into his gut and formed a stiff fist.

Fionn stared disapprovingly with his own fist resting under his chin.

'So how was your weekend anyway?' asked Billy.

'Pretty good actually. Friday ended on a high with a break in the case and of course the fact we've been put back on duty together to work on it was a bonus. I've been checking in quite a lot with the forensic guys and even though they've not come up with anything new, at least they confirmed it was definitely a murder. Actually, are you sure you're fully caught up on everything?'

'Ah yeah, I got everything this morning, we are officially on the same page, chief. Let's get this

Behan fella,' Billy said as he raised his glass with a wink.

'Yes, I think we have him. The guys have checked thoroughly on that ring, he definitely paid for it. Two in fact, although one was found at the scene of the crime. I'm excited to see what this Behan guy has to say about the whereabouts of the other one. We showed Joanna, the girl that nearly drowned, a photo of both the victim and our suspect but unfortunately neither meant anything to her. She's adamant she's never seen either McGee or Behan before. She previously said she'd be sure she'd recognise the guy with the ring if she saw him again. I think maybe we need to get him in person and then it might come back to her. Either way there is someone going around wearing a ring that this Behan guy bought and he's bound to shed some light on the whole issue.'

'And more importantly, the murder of this McGee guy?'

'Yes of course, especially that. Definitely.'

'If he's guilty, he's bound to have a story concocted already,' suggested Billy.

'Absolutely, but it's our job to cut through that isn't it?'

'Do you think he did it? Killed the guy?'

'Innocent until proven guilty, my friend. But I'm gunning for him. He doesn't know we know about the ring you see. He might not even know that Joanna is still alive. We need to catch him off guard. He won't be expecting us so soon.'

'You think it all hinges on this ring, don't you?'

'Yes. Yes, I suppose I do.'

'My precious,' Billy said in a croaky voice.

'What?' asked Fionn, not understanding the Lord of the Rings reference.

'Never mind,' replied Billy. 'So was that all you did over the weekend? Work on this case and get your facts in order?'

'No actually. I had time for pleasure too.'

'Oh yeah? Any luck?'

'Definitely.'

'Oh yeah? How much did you win?'

'What do you mean?' Fionn was about to take a sip of his pint but stopped and put his glass down.

'I take it you mean you had a bet come through for you?'

'What? No. I had a date.'

'Ahhh,' said Billy as he realised he had misunderstood what was meant by pleasure. 'Who's the unlucky lady?'

'Stephanie,' replied Fionn with a glow of confidence in his voice. 'She is stunning. I met her last week. We went for coffee.' A smile started to form slowly on Fionn's face. Partly because of the exaggeration of *going* for coffee and partly because he enjoyed talking about her. 'We've been texting non-stop ever since. We'll be meeting for dinner next.'

'Dinner? Jesus Christ. What's next, a proposal?' Billy mocked.

'Don't tempt me,' replied Fionn.

'Where will you take her?'

'I'm not sure yet, probably for something ethnic in one of those places on Capel St.'

'The north side?' Billy shouted in jest. 'You're a mad man. I hope living so dangerously will pay off.' He gave a slight wink.

'Don't be creepy, Billy,' Fionn responded. 'I'm sure the closest you'll get to a girl anytime soon will be sitting near me when I tell you what happens next but I'm saying nothing. I'm a gentleman.'

'C'mon,' said Billy with a smirk, not attempting to defend himself. 'Finish your pint and tell me all about her on the way to see this Behan guy.'

Fionn drank a couple of large mouthfuls to catch up with Billy's already empty glass.

'What's the verdict on the Guinness in McDaid's anyway?'

'Meh,' said Fionn as he finished his glass.

'Yeah I agree. Not bad but not the best. But hey, what do you think Corcoran would think if he knew that four hours into our first day back working together we were having a pint?'

Fionn put €10 on the counter and stood up. 'Meh,' he repeated.

Michael Behan's office was housed within his nineteenth century red brick home. It lay in the middle of half a dozen other terraced houses that looked identical to each other apart from the wooden sign hanging from the patio indicating that number 64 is a dental surgery. Fionn had parked up in a designated parking spot and he and Billy slowly approached the front door so they could observe as much of their surroundings as possible. So far nothing was standing out for either of them.

The door opened with a push and they entered a narrow but rustically decorated hallway. At the far end was an oversized reception desk that dwarfed the thin wooden seats that were placed around it.

'Hello Gentlemen, how can I help you?' the young girl behind the desk asked with a bright smile. She had tanned skin dotted with acne and a button nose that looked like it hadn't grown with the rest of her face. She spoke perfect English but with a heavy South American accent.

Fionn decided she couldn't be more than sixteen years old and wondered why she wasn't in school. He wondered if Billy was thinking the same thing.

'Good afternoon my dear and how might you be on this fine day? Billy said with a distinct flirtatious tone.

Fionn realised either he or Billy were a bad judge of age. 'Could we please speak to Michael Behan,' he interrupted as he produced his badge from his pocket.

Between the surprise of seeing the badge and the serious tone in his voice, the girl became nervous. 'Oh, er, Dr. Behan is with a patient. Should I interrupt him?'

'No, no, not at all. It can wait,' Fionn said, immediately realising he had unsettled the teenager. He offered a smile in an attempt to counteract startling her. 'My name is Fionn, by the way, and this is Billy. We have some questions we hope the Doctor can help us with. When will he be free next?'

240

The girl looked across to the computer monitor and scrolled for a few seconds. 'His next appointment is with Mrs Barry at 3pm and she's already here. So he should be done by then at least.

Fionn looked at his watch. That was 20 minutes away. He was feeling impatient and that was too long of a wait for his liking. 'That's not long to wait, now is it?' he said. 'We'll pop into the waiting room here and then you might give us a shout when he's free next?'

'Of course I will,' she replied.

Fionn stepped sideways and put his hand on the handle of the waiting room door before turning back. 'Oh, but maybe you should let him know now that there are two Garda Detectives here to see him?' He figured that when Behan became aware they were there he would cut the appointment short and want to deal with them as soon as possible.

'Of course,' the girl said with a smile as she arose from her chair.

Twenty-five minutes later the girl popped her head into the waiting room. 'Hi Sirs, Dr. Behan's appointment ran a little late. He apologises and says you can go into his office now.'

An old lady sitting across from Fionn and Billy gave a loud tut and shook her head. They assumed she was Mrs Barry. As they were already frustrated from being kept waiting for twenty-five minutes they got up ignoring the disgruntled woman and omitting an apology for skipping the queue.

There were only two chairs in his office and Michael Behan was already sitting in one of them. His desk was shoved up against the back wall so he was sitting with his back to the door filling out some paperwork, failing to offer a greeting as they entered. Fionn took the vacant chair and Billy stood leaning assertively against the door, overlooking the whole office.

'What do you want, Guards? I'm a very busy man,' Behan said with disdain, showing no sign of helpfulness.

Fionn stared at him for several seconds as he tried to figure out why Behan was going on the offence right from the start. He turned and looked at Billy who just raised his eyebrows at him.

'Do you know why we're here today Mr. Behan?' Fionn finally said.

'*Doctor* Behan,' he replied.

Fionn made no attempt to apologise or correct himself and waited silently for an answer.

The tension hung thick in the air for several seconds before Behan finally gave in and continued. 'No, I have no bloody idea but I know I haven't done anything wrong so I don't particularly care.'

'You appear to be quite stressed Mr Behan', Billy said from the door. 'Are you feeling OK?'

'*Doctor* Behan,' he replied again, putting a louder and longer emphasis on his title.

'I have to agree with my partner,' Fionn said. 'If you have no idea why we're here then why are you acting so anxiously? Have you got something to hide?'

'I can assure you I am not in the slightest bit anxious or stressed. Annoyed, perhaps. Can you please state your business and be on your way?'

Neither Fionn nor Billy spoke. They stared at Behan like they were conducting an interrogation on him and were waiting for him to break. As he continued to stare back with the same level of contempt in his eyes they were beginning to realise he was going to deal with being caught the hard way and wasn't going down easily.'

Behan picked up the phone on his desk and proceeded to dial a number.

'Excuse me Mr Behan, we're not finished talking to you,' Fionn said.

Behan turned his back to the Guards as if they were no longer there and sat pensively with his phone to his ear. Fionn turned and looked at Billy with a look of wonderment like he had never seen a person react like that before. Billy just rolled his shoulders.

'Hello, Vincent,' Behan finally said. 'Sorry to disturb you on your mobile, it's Mickey here. *Doctor* Behan, yeah.'

Fionn and Billy knew the emphasis on the word Doctor was for their benefit.

'Listen, I have a couple of Guards in my office giving me hassle when I'm just trying to help them. What should I do?'

Fionn looked around at Billy once more, his expression becoming one of disconcertment. Billy just stared at Behan, impatience building in his eyes. Fionn turned back to Behan. 'Mr Behan, we are not hassling you, we haven't even told you why we're here.'

'Hmm, aww-haw, I see,' Behan said down the phone, ignoring Fionn.

'Doctor Behan,' he almost shouted, frustration showing in his voice.

After a further minute of mumbles down the phone Behan finished the conversation by saying; 'OK that's fine, thanks for the advice. I'll call you back later,' and hung up the phone. 'That was my solicitor. I felt I just needed his advice before we continued this conversation.'

'But Mr. Behan, what makes you assume you would need to speak to your solicitor, unless you know full well why we're here?' Fionn felt he had made progress with this question and would start backing him into a corner, legal advice or not.

'Because you think I'm guilty of something,' he replied with authority. 'And as I know that I have done nothing illegal in my life and I am in fact an upstanding member of society, I think I have the right to legal advice.'

A quick thought occurred to Fionn. Something about that sentence seemed familiar. 'What makes you think we believe you've done something illegal?' he replied.

'You have me pegged as being guilty of something before you even saw me. I could tell by your cocky swagger as you walked into my office and the stinking attitude you had when you spoke to me. You look at me like I've just murdered your family and yet you stand there with a desperate stench about you like a couple of dogs that have just found their buried bone. You're not here because you need my help with something, because if you did you would have been more respectful to the intern at reception. You're not here to gather information on something other than me, because you wouldn't have been so brazen from the second you met me. The look of contempt in both your faces is unnerving and the sooner the better that you ask me so I can quash your mission, whatever that may be, and show you for the unprofessional amateurs that you both are.'

Both Fionn and Billy blushed due to both anger and embarrassment. Anger for the way they were being spoken to and embarrassment for the truth in what Behan had just called them out on. Having no counter-argument, neither of them responded.

'Why are you here, Guards?'

Fionn coughed gently to clear his throat. 'Can you please tell us where you were from last Thursday at 9pm until the following Friday morning at 6am?'

Behan looked up to the ceiling and started playfully swinging his chair. 'Last Thursday, was it? Let's see…' He exhaled loudly which gave the impression of relief and didn't appear to be phased by the question. 'Let me think for a second. It was only a few days ago but at my age the days blend into one.'

As Behan began to grin for the first time since they arrived, Fionn's heart sank as he realised Behan could not be this confident if he had murdered someone at the exact time he had just asked about. He considered to himself that either he's innocent and has an alibi or he is completely insane.

As he continued to search his memory banks for his whereabouts four nights ago he subtly reached behind him and pulled open a small drawer on his desk. He removed two rings from the drawer and proceeded to place them on his fingers, so casually it was as if he was doing it out of habit as opposed to for a specific reason. The first one went on his ring finger. A gold wedding band. The second ring went on his middle finger on the same hand. He raised his hand to rub his chin and Fionn stared intently at the second ring, completely certain it was the same one found in Peter McGee's house. He looked back at Billy who hadn't picked up on the ring at all. He felt his heartbeat start to race and tried his best to control his breathing as adrenaline started to course through his body. He was sure Behan was playing a game with him but knew the arrogant dentist was also highly intelligent and so he needed to play along to get the upper hand.

'I was out for dinner that night with my wife,' he finally answered. 'It was booked for 8.30pm but as women traditionally do, my wife had us running a little late so I would have been sitting down at the table around 9pm. I had a perfectly cooked rare fillet steak with an amazing bottle of Malbec. We had a nightcap after dinner, if I remember correctly I specifically had a Gin and tonic and I guess we called it a night approximately midnight. So I would have been fast asleep from then until 6am the following morning.'

A burst of excitement hit Fionn like a wave on a choppy shoreline. That was a weak alibi. He could have been anywhere between midnight and 6am if his wife was asleep. That's assuming she wouldn't just be lying for him if she corroborated his account of the evening's events. He was beginning to believe the confident front was just an act. 'So strictly speaking, Mr. Behan, you could have been anywhere between midnight and 6am, if your wife was asleep she technically can't say for sure that you were there the entire time. Isn't it possible you could have left the house for a couple of hours while your wife was asleep and she wouldn't know?' He had him. This was becoming a fun game of cool cat and cocky mouse.

Behan sat back in his chair and slightly loosened his tie. 'You got me there, Guard.'

Fionn looked back at Billy who dared not smile but gave him a victorious look.

'Except,' Behan continued. 'My wife is a light sleeper. Annoyingly so. I can't take a piss in the night without her waking up and wondering if there's something wrong. No matter how quietly I try to thread.'

That's a pathetic alibi, Fionn thought to himself.

'But I'm sure you think that's not a great excuse,' Behan continued. 'I must ask you, where do you suspect I was between these hours? It must have been within walking distance of the bed because I was in no fit state to drive, I tell you that. My wife doesn't drink you see so I had the whole bottle to myself. Put that with the gin and tonic and I must admit I was fit for a deep sleep.'

Fionn thought for a moment before replying. 'I'm not in a position to divulge any information right now. I only need information from you at the moment. But let's assume you weren't fit to drive, it's not inconceivable that you left and got a taxi somewhere, is it?'

'Oh, absolutely. That is something I could have done. But either way reception could have video recorded me if I left.'

'Reception?' Fionn replied.

'Yeah, there are cameras there, they'll show I never left my room all night. As far as I recall they have a camera outside the main entrance too in case you think I may have snuck out a back exit, or climbed out my window, or flew up the chimney with an umbrella.'

Fionn started to look around the room confused. 'The only way to leave your house is through the reception of your practice?'

Behan let out a hearty laugh. 'No, of course not Guard. But I'm talking about the hotel reception.'

'Hotel?' Fionn replied even more confused.

'Yes. Hotel. Oh, had I not mentioned that part?' Behan laughed again, this time for longer. 'See, this is why my wife won't let me tell stories. She insists on telling them herself, she says I leave out all the important parts.'

'Where the hell were you,' Billy said brazenly from the door.

Behan stopped laughing immediately and a stern look came over his face. 'Valley House

Hotel, in Wicklow. An hour and a half drive from Dublin. I took last Thursday and Friday off work to celebrate my wife's birthday and made a long weekend out of it. We checked out at 1pm the next day. Please check their cameras as soon as you can, some places wipe their saved footage weekly. I'd like you to verify my whereabouts as soon as you can. So you can fuck off.'

The rug had just been pulled out from under Fionn's feet. He felt deflated. He realised why Behan was being so coy. He had a rock solid alibi. But he was sure Behan knew something. He decided all he could do was press on and hope he slipped up. 'That ring you appear to be showing off. It's very interesting. Where did you get that?'

Behan instinctively covered his left hand with his right and realising the gesture to be a defensive tell immediately pulled his hands apart almost as quickly. For the first time Fionn sensed the dentist had been taken off guard. He wasn't expecting his ring to be brought into question. Fionn considered that maybe he wasn't putting the ring on to antagonise him but perhaps removed his rings while in surgery and was replacing them when he sat back down.

'Excuse me?' Behan finally said.

'That ring. Where did you get it?' Fionn firmly repeated.

Behan looked rapidly from Fionn to Billy. They both noticed that despite the serene expression on his face his jugular was hopping from his neck like a parasite fighting for air was trying to frantically break free through his skin.

'It's my wedding ring. You usually wear one after you get married.'

'Very good Mr. Behan, I think you know I mean the other ring.'

'Answer the bloody question,' Billy chimed in unnecessarily.

Behan gave Billy a long contemptuous look and then turned to Fionn. 'This is getting pathetic now lads. What does a ring have to do with anything? I'd like you to leave now, I think I've given you enough of my time.'

Billy perked up and shook his shoulders. 'You can answer the question now or you can answer it down at the station, the choice is yours but either way you're answering it.'

'Where are we, downtown L.A? I don't have to answer shit. Piss off.'

'Oh, Mister Behan,' Billy said mockingly. 'I think we've touched a nerve.'

'You touched a nerve the minute you walked in,' he replied.

'What is it about the ring you don't want to tell us?' asked Fionn.

Behan sat silently, fury building in his face.

Fionn knew he had to keep asking questions to get a reaction. 'De Wolf's crest, right?'

Behan's eyes widened to two white circles. But he continued not to speak.

'Are you a Freemason Dr. Behan?' asked Billy, trying to keep the pressure on him.

Behan continued his silence.

'No, nothing?' Fionn continued. 'Let me tell you this then. We have a witness that puts this ring at the scene of a crime and we know this is a unique ring. In fact we know only two were ever made. We found one with the person that made it. Now we know you wear the other one. You see why we need some questions answered?'

Behan shook his head slowly for a few moments before finally speaking. 'I saw the design once. I liked it. I wanted it made into a ring. I paid for two as I wanted a spare should I ever damage it but I'm yet to receive it. The maker needed more time but it should be ready for collection any day. Now, I'm sure if you contact him he'll corroborate my story and you'll realise you have nothing on me because I have done nothing wrong.

'Actually Dr. Behan,' Billy said. 'The jewellery maker has been found dead.'

Behan's shoulders became limp and his jaw dropped. 'My God. What happened?'

Fionn and Billy just stared at him.

'On Thursday night I assume? That's why you want to know where I was? Why? Just because I bought a ring from him?'

'No,' replied Fionn. 'The ring is an issue from a different crime.'

'I see,' said Behan sitting deep in thought through several seconds of silence. 'Maybe the second ring is out there somewhere? Could that be a possibility? What if the other ring is already complete and had been in his possession, did you check that?'

'Yes, we did,' replied Fionn.

'And?'

'And nothing, that's not relevant right now.'

'Excuse me, of course it is.' Behan stared Fionn down like a lion does its prey. He then turned to Billy and did the same. 'It bloody was there, wasn't it? You're avoiding the question because the penny just dropped that this is a wild goose chase, didn't it?'

Fionn and Billy both stood silently as they tried to search for the right words to counter-argue.

'You're about to leave my office now gentlemen. I'm sorry that you have to go with less than what you came with but I can assure you that is your problem and I'd appreciate it if you never bothered me again.'

Fionn turned to Billy who looked as disheartened as he felt. They said nothing and made their way back out the way they came in, walking with a posture that resembled cave men leaving for the village empty handed after a day of hunting.

Back at the car Fionn and Billy sat glumly for several minutes dissecting and replaying the entire interview in their own heads before either of them spoke.

'Let's just list out what we know,' suggested Billy.

'Yeah, OK.'

'Tell me if I'm missing anything.' Billy began. 'Guy with a weird ring is throwing people in the river. Guy who made the ring turns up dead. Guy who bought the ring did not kill the guy who made the ring. We know there are two rings in existence as the ring maker created them bespoke and all the jewellers we asked had never seen anything like that before. Woman who survived does not recognise either the ring maker or the ring wearer from their photos. And then throw a Freemason reference in there for good measure too.'

'That's about right,' replied Fionn.

'It's like we have a few decent pieces to the puzzle but no idea how they all link together,' remarked Billy.

'Yeah, that's for sure. But I feel like we're getting closer. Grilling Behan did not work out as I hoped it would but I still feel like things are starting to unravel. One thing is for sure, we need to keep an eye on this guy. We need to take turns following him, see where he goes, who he talks to.'

Billy turned the ignition on. 'Are you doing this because you don't trust him and expect to find something on him or because you don't like him and you *hope* to find something?'

'Maybe a little of both. Anyway, any plans after work?'

'None actually, fancy a pint? I think Slattery's on Capel St is next on the list?'

'Nah, I have that date with Stephanie, so if you've no plans can you keep tabs on Behan? If he's going to slip up it'll be tonight, he'll be on edge after our visit.'

'You're a prick', said Billy.

CHAPTER TWENTY THREE

Aaron shuffled along the boardwalk slowly with his hood pulled up so high even the street lights couldn't illuminate his face. He stopped and looked down at a homeless man lying as still as a mannequin under an old torn sleeping blanket. He looked to be dead. The skin on his face was a pasty white and the blanket covering his chest wasn't expanding and compressing like you'd expect when a human breathes.

'Hey, pal?' said Aaron.

The man stirred abruptly and sat up stiffly, like he had just received an electric shock but in slow motion. He looked around and on seeing Aaron he scowled at him in disgust. 'What do you want? Piss off.'

'Ah now Pal, c'mon, don't be like that,' replied Aaron. 'I'm a friend.'

'You're not my friend,' the homeless man replied venomously.

'I *could* be your friend,' he then said.

'I don't need a friend, I have a friend right here.' From under his blanket he produced a can of cheap cider and then took a sip. 'Four friends in fact,' he said, producing three unopened cans, the same type as the first, joined together with plastic rings.

'Ah, I see,' said Aaron. 'But is that all you've got?'

'It's all I need,' he said and then gave Aaron a condescending wink.

'Do you not have anything stronger? The nights are starting to get a lot colder, you know.'

'Piss off back to your house will ya?'

'I'm homeless too, Pal.'

'No you're bleedin' not, I can tell by the smug head on ya, you go home to a roof over your head every night. Feckin' gobshite. What are you, a do-gooder? Bleedin' faker, feck off.'

'Jesus,' said Aaron and just stood silently as the man lying on the bench seemed to be attempting to prove the belief that looks can kill. 'Look, you're right. I'm not homeless. But my home is barely what you'd call a home and I beg every day to be able to afford it. I don't want to start a row, Pal, I just wanted help with something. What's your name?'

'Piss off.'

'My name is Aaron. What's yours?'

The man lay silent for several seconds and eventually spoke sheepishly. 'Ignatius.'

'Ah come on, what's your name?'

Suddenly the man's tone became loud and aggressive. 'Ignatius is me bleedin' name, is there something wrong with that?'

'No no, of course not,' said Aaron, slightly backing away. 'Nice to meet you Ignatius. It's a grand name, pal.'

The homeless man then erupted in a sharp exhale of laughter. His lungs seemed to rattle like a faulty lawnmower engine as he coughed out some fluid along with the laughs. His face went red and his eyes watered up. 'Ignatius? What do I look like, a bleedin' African missionary or something?

Of course me name isn't bleedin' Ignatius, ya feckin' eejit.'

Aaron just stood still and waited for the laughing and name calling to stop. His mouth formed a grin but his eyes portrayed frustration and contempt.

'Me name's Buzzer. You're alright kid. You're a bit of a gobshite but you're alright. You wouldn't give me the price of a can would you?'

'Are your four friends not enough?' replied Aaron.

'Ah come on, don't get upset kid, I'm just buzzin' with ya.'

'Am I buzzing with Buzzer?'

'That you are my friend, that you are. What do you want anyway? Cause you're not getting any of me bleedin' cans I tell ya that. This is me dinner right here.'

'Nah, you're OK, thanks. I was actually hoping you could point me towards something stronger. My usual dealer got arrested a few days ago and I'm desperate. Do you know where I could get my hands on something? Any mates selling?

Buzzer looked Aaron up and down. 'You're no junkie,' he said.

Aaron jolted. 'What?'

'I know an addict when I see one. You're not one.'

Aaron cursed himself for underestimating the perceptiveness of this so-called Buzzer. 'I never said it was for me.'

'You said you were desperate,' said Buzzer.

'I am. To get some. But not for me, for me missus, she's really sick. She needs some H.'

'Oh yeah?'

'Yeah.'

'Doesn't matter who it's for I don't know anyone anyway, I don't associate with anything to do with that stuff.'

'But you must know where I could go to find someone?' pleaded Aaron, feigning a tone of anxiety in his voice.

'If I know then you must know too,' said Buzzer.

'If I did, then I wouldn't need to be asking you, would I? I only ever had one guy. Never thought to pay attention beyond that.'

'I don't be paying attention either,' proclaimed Buzzer with open arms.

'Look, if you can help me there'll be something in it for you. Something I have that will, let's just say, help you sleep like a baby during the rough nights.'

Buzzer thought about the offer as he perched up into a more attentive sitting position. He thought back to several nights earlier when he had been lying in his usual place trying to get to sleep. His head had been spinning from the many cans he had drank throughout that day and the cutting breeze that drifted forebodingly in from Dublin Bay and up the river added to the difficulty he was having in getting some shut-eye. It felt like he had only managed five minutes when he was awoken to a feeling of being crushed. In a second of sheer panic he thought he had been loaded into a garbage truck by accident and began squirming frantically. He turned his head around as far as he could and taking in his surroundings as quickly as possible, realised that a man with an even tan and foreign accent was pointing an expensive looking camera at him. He was chuckling ecstatically and saying words in a different language. Another man just as tanned and with the same accent was lying on top of him, simulating a humping motion. He was grunting with his tongue out, his boozy breath in Buzzer's face and his eyes looking towards the camera and waiting for a flash. Judging by how the man with the camera was fidgeting there was a problem with it and he wasn't able to capture the photo properly. As the man continued to hold his facial expression and continue his body movement Buzzer was able to free his hand, the same hand that he was holding his Stanley knife. He instinctively always kept a grip on it each night while he slept. He wielded his arm out in as quick a motion as he could manage. It was a wide circular swipe and his whole body rotated with the swing as if he were a pig on a spit. The blade made contact with the face of the man that was on top of him, giving him a red moustache across the top of his lip. The man let out a high pitched yelp and propelled himself off of Buzzer. The other man instinctively dropped his camera and both men ran away, along the boardwalk as if it was about to disappear from under them. Buzzer felt infuriated as he threw the knife and the camera into the river, knowing it was best to destroy anything that might become incriminating at a later time. He still hadn't found a new weapon to protect himself.

It was because of that incident he decided that although he had never taken drugs out of principle, he would definitely never resort to them now, for his own safety. He didn't ever want to be so knocked out that he would sleep through obnoxious messers dry humping him at 4am. He needed to always have his wits about him. 'I'll tell you what,' he finally said as he presented an antique silver letter opener from his pocket, the closest thing to a self-defence weapon he could get his hands on since he threw his knife in the river. 'Why don't you hang around and annoy the shite out of me for just one more minute so I can stick this up your bleedin' hole.'

Aaron looked on as Buzzer's lips tightened and formed into a crescent shaped sinister pout. He was going to have to try a different approach.

CHAPTER TWENTY FOUR

'This has certainly been an unusual choice,' said Stephanie as she scanned the décor of the Capel St restaurant that Fionn had taken her to. 'It's gorgeous here but I don't think I've ever tried Moroccan food before tonight.'

'Yeah I was in Marrakech once,' replied Fionn. 'I hated it. The place is insane. All the locals act friendly but constantly send you the wrong way when offering directions. One of the few things I did like was the food and so I thought of here.'

'It definitely was delicious and it kind of makes me want to visit Morocco now.'

Fionn slammed his fork down on the plate of cinnamon orange they were sharing for dessert. 'No, you can't,' he shouted in jest. 'I command it.'

Stephanie shushed Fionn through bursts of gentle laughter. 'OK, OK I won't go. Where am I allowed to go?'

Fionn folded his arms. 'Wherever I feel like taking you.'

'Oh really now? You're bossy, aren't you? You don't think I can decide for myself, no?'

'I - am - man,' said Fionn as he puffed out his chest and sat square shouldered with his nose in the air.

Stephanie offered a smirk.

'Oh dear, you're not finding this casual chauvinism funny are you? Quick, change the subject, how was your day, did I even ask you that yet?'

'No, you actually didn't, how rude.'

'Sorry, but there just wasn't time. We still have our whole lives to catch up on. I barely know anything about what you did when you were ten through to twenty-five, never mind what happened today.'

Stephanie smiled. 'But I'd rather talk about today, I don't think you'd care about what I did when I was ten.'

'Ah, start in the present day and work backwards? Genius idea. So did anything mad happen today?'

'No, not really. Nothing crazy ever happens during my days. Nothing as interesting as the type of days you have I'm sure?'

'Ah, it's not that exciting', Fionn said with a dismissive gesture.

'Oh, it's all private and confidential is it? Not allowed to discuss it on a random nice date I suppose?'

He cupped his hands under his chin and stared deep into Stephanie's eyes. 'Nah, I just don't want to bore you into ending the date early.'

Stephanie gave him a gentle smile. 'OK, fair enough.'

'I'm only joking. I honestly have had nothing happen today worth talking about.'

'What about that thing at my work, did you get any further with that?'

'Actually we do have our eyes on one person. I'm sure we'll find something on him.'

Stephanie sat up rigidly. 'Is he a member of the Lodge?'

261

'I don't know that, do I? The unhelpful staff won't exactly throw me a bone, will they?'

Stephanie smiled sheepishly. 'I suppose. Sorry. What's this guy done anyway?'

'At the moment we're tied up in another murder case and the symbol your father showed me is at the centre of that too. That's all I can say for now really, everything else is just theory until I can dig deeper.'

Stephanie folded her arms and shook her head with a solemn look on her face. 'No, I refuse to believe it. It couldn't be anybody from the Lodge. They have a strict policy for membership. Someone capable of murder would never be allowed in. People are black balled all the time if there is even the slightest question on their moral stance.'

'Black balled?' Fionn asked quietly to himself as a thought struck him.

'Not accepted.'

'Yes, I remember your father telling me. Do they formally apply to join though, yes?'

'People come in all the time hoping to join but are not accepted.'

'I see.' Fionn sat staring at the tablecloth deep in thought.

'What's wrong?'

'Nothing. These men that are not accepted, what reason have been given?'

'Oh lots of different ones. Anything from a personality clash to having opinions that are at odds with the Mason's ethos. For example, this suspect of yours couldn't have been a Mason, if someone was capable of murder there's no way they'd ever be accepted.'

'How would you know if someone is capable of murder?'

'Oh, I'm sure you would. Murderers tend to not be nice people. Only good people are accepted as Masons. They are very good judges of characters.'

'They really have a high opinion of themselves don't they? They should *all* be criminal psychologists by the sounds of it.'

Stephanie's smile disappeared and her face turned as stone cold as a forgotten statue in a damp shed. 'No, not all of them. Just the one. Mr. Cunningham is a criminal psychologist.'

'Sorry, I didn't mean to cause offence, I'm just trying to wrap my head around the whole thing.'

'It's OK. I know what you mean.'

'But tell me this,' continued Fionn, ignoring Stephanie's sudden change in mood. 'Is there a list of people that applied to be a Freemason but were rejected?'

Stephanie pouted, glanced around the table as if looking for the answer among the empty plates and dirty cutlery. She looked back up at Fionn. 'Yes, I assume so.'

'Would seeing that particular list violate any privacy, seeing as no current members would be on that list?'

'I'd have to check, but I suppose that could be OK.'

Fionn smirked and his eyes glazed over as his mind went into overdrive trying to connect the dots he had created.

'Is everything OK?' asked Stephanie after a few moments of awkward silence.

'Oh yeah, absolutely. I was just remembering back to when I was in school. There was one guy, a big fat fella, who really wanted to be on the football team. He was so passionate about it and turned up for training all the time but he was unfit and sluggish. He was never selected to play. Was never even subbed on for one minute of a match. Our coach didn't care about letting the kid have a few minutes of glory, he just wanted to win every game.'

'So what happened then', asked Stephanie leaning in closer. 'Did he burn down the gym?'

'No. He disappeared one summer and turned up on the first day of school half the size he was. He had also become a brilliant footballer. Our coach was impressed with him in training and agreed to start him in the first match of the season against the next town over.'

'And did he play well?'

'Oh he played brilliantly. Man of the match, he followed his passion and worked hard to get to where he wanted to be.'

Stephanie squinted her eyes in confusion. 'What's that got to do with your case?'

'See, he never turned up at the school for the bus to our opponent's pitch. When we arrived he was already there. In their jersey. They walked all over us and it was mainly down to him. It's amazing how being rejected can give you the motivation to achieve your goals, by any means

264

necessary. This guy had a point to prove and he sure went and proved it.'

Stephanie clasped her hands under her chin mulling over Fionn's story as he continued to stare down at the table.

Finally he looked up. 'I'm really going to need that list.'

When Billy saw Michael Behan emerge from his front door earlier than expected he gripped his steering wheel so tight that the top of his knuckles looked like snow capped mountain peaks. With a long exhale he loosened his grip and felt his anxiety begin to subside. Billy had learned to deal with his anxiety by recognising its triggers and acknowledging them as being something that either can or cannot be controlled. In this particular moment he recognised that the rise in anxiety was being caused by the unexpected movements of Behan, which was something he cannot control. Billy had been observing Behan from inside his car, which he had parked across the street from Behan's home and practice, fully expecting that he would not budge from there. He presumed at 5pm Behan would make his way upstairs, change into his regular clothes, have some dinner, watch TV and maybe go online. Then he might head to bed to try and get an early night but inevitably end up tossing and turning for several hours worrying about the visit he and Fionn had paid him. Billy assumed all of this would happen behind the walls that he sat in his car staring at and that he would not catch a glimpse of Behan the entire time. A man under the eye of the law to the extent Behan currently was wouldn't want to do anything to raise their suspicions any further.

As the evening unfolded, Billy realised he was way off with his assumptions. In fact, it was like an episode of a travel show promoting culture and tourism around Dublin's north side of the city. Behan couldn't have executed it any better if that had been what he was trying to accomplish. At 5.01pm he walked out of his office and with an awkward rhythm to his step he slowly walked north. Billy flustered to get his items together and exit the car before Behan went out of sight. He quickly caught up to Behan who was moving so sluggishly that it was a struggle to stay far enough behind not to be noticed. He observed him stroll through the gates of the National Botanic Gardens, about twenty metres ahead of him. Still making sure to keep his distance, Billy's pulse started to race as he expected to see him stop at a secret meeting point under the low hanging branches of one of the many symmetrically dispersed trees.

Instead, he sauntered stiffly up to a concession kiosk, purchased an ice-cream and then sat on a bench facing the warm glimmer of the evening sun. When he finished his ice-cream he reached into his inside pocket and pulled out a small thin book. Billy couldn't make out the title but he was confident it was a paperback novel of some kind. He sat there for over an hour with the demeanour of a vitamin D hungry nature lover soaking up the last few beams of a typical Indian summer evening.

As the first sign of dusk arrived he closed his book and slid it back inside his pocket. He stood up and looked around, enjoying the panoramic view of the thinning trees, vibrant flowers and towering glasshouses. He took a slow and deep breath of the autumn air filling his nostrils with the smell of ageing leaves and damp grass. He slowly got up and made his way towards the exit, at no point looking in Billy's direction. The saunter in his step was that of a man without a worry in the world. He took a left at the exit and Billy followed him all the way back down Botanic Road. He then turned left into the back of Glasnevin Cemetery and made a bee-line across the grass for John Kavanagh's pub. *The Gravediggers*, Billy thought to himself. He needed to remind Fionn they had to try the Guinness there.

Stephanie giggled as they entered through the same door that Fionn had first met her. 'Why do I feel like I'm breaking the law?' Within a second her giggles ceased and her body became rigid as she was met with the sound of a low pulsating alarm. 'Oh no,' she whispered. 'The alarm. I completely forgot there even was one. I've never had to unset it before.'

'Do you know the code?' asked Fionn calmly.

'No,' she replied in a panic. 'I mean, yes, I have it written down somewhere in case I was ever the last one out and had to set it.' She bolted through the office door and made a beeline for a filing cabinet. She pulled out two stacks of files and flung them on the ground. She pulled out a third and started erratically flicking through the pages contained within it. 'Come on, come on,' she muttered. 'Yes, got it,' she said just as the raucous alarm seemed to get louder as it went from an intermittent boom to a continuous blare. 'Shit, that's going to patch right through to the Guards now,' she shouted as she ran to the alarm panel and started hitting buttons forcefully with her index finger.'

'It's OK,' replied Fionn calmly. 'I'm already here. I'm *that* good.'

A sudden wave of stillness washed over the hallway as the alarm suddenly stopped. For a few seconds longer than necessary they both stood staring at the unresponsive alarm panel.

'What happens now?' asked Stephanie.

'How am I supposed to know?' replied Fionn.

'Have you never dealt with an intrusion before? How long until someone comes?'

'"Have *you* never" is a better question. You have the code, was the procedure not explained to you?'

'No it wasn't,' replied Stephanie with distress in her voice. 'I've never been the first in or last out so it's never happened to me before. What do you think is going to happen?'

'Depends on who monitors the alarm. A security company I assume. They'll probably be key holders and whoever is on duty will come over and let themselves in to check for an intrusion.'

There was still an air of panic in Stephanie's voice as she spoke. 'And when they come will you

268

be able to show them your badge and everything will be OK?'

'I could do that,' Fionn replied. 'Or, you could tell them you work here, came in after hours to get something important and was too slow resetting the alarm. Or does that sound too unbelievable.'

Stephanie smiled. 'Oh yeah, I suppose. We're not actually doing anything wrong are we?'

'No, of course not. You would be so bad at being a criminal, you know that?'

She pouted almost as if she was offended by the suggestion. 'You'd never catch me. Anyway, over here,' she said as she led him back into the office. 'I'll find that list for you,'

Several minutes went by with only three audible sounds. The clicking of a mouse, the tapping of a keyboard and the ticking of a clock. Fionn watched on as Stephanie navigated her way from file to file. 'Are you finding anything?' Fionn finally asked, unable to follow what any of the files or folders were.

'Yes I think so, I should find everything you need. I'll need a little more time though.'

'OK,' he replied, trying not to sound impatient.

'Tell me a story while I work on this?'

'A story?'

'Yeah, I'm not enjoying the silence,' said Stephanie. 'Awkward silence is not a good sign after only two dates.'

'Oh, right, I'm sorry,' he said. 'It's just, I...'

'I know,' she said. 'This is important to you. Tell me a story while I work on this. What was the scariest situation you were ever in?'

'The scariest?' asked Fionn.

'Sure,' she replied.

His eyes wandered the room as he searched his memory banks for which of the many difficult situations he had found himself in could be classified as the scariest. 'A few years ago, a call was patched through to my partner and me. A woman had called in an hour earlier, in hysterics, saying there was someone in her apartment with a knife and they were going to kill her children. It wasn't in our area so I double checked that they definitely wanted us to attend the scene but I was told that the other two Guards for that area had already gone there but had failed to check in for over twenty minutes. We thought that to be unusual and figured they could have gotten themselves into difficulty and were unable to respond. One walkie going dead was possible, but two was unlikely. We got there soon after and saw our colleague's car parked up outside the apartment block. We cautiously went up to the apartment, not sure what to expect and I remember we were both creeped out by the surprisingly silent atmosphere in the whole complex. When we got to the door we found it ajar. We called out to introduce our arrival as we slowly pushed open the door. Inside, hunched down in the middle of the hall was the woman that had called for emergency services. She was small and frail and had messy jet black hair with flecks of grey in it. I pegged her as being in her forties. She was shaking and there was blood all over her hands and her clothes. Her eyes were wide and distant. She said nothing but pointed towards her living room. We walked around the corner to see the two Guards that had arrived first lying dead on the floor in a pool of blood. I couldn't make out straight away what had happened but they had both been stabbed in an identical fashion, both in the back of the neck.

'Oh my God,' Stephanie said as she turned towards him. 'That's awful, is this the story that was all over the news? I remember reading about it. What were you thinking, what did you do?'

'Well I vomited profusely all over the floor, that was the first thing I did. The woman told us a man broke in and was holding her and her children at knife point and when the first two Guards arrived he killed them instantly and he left with her children. We told her we were going to call for additional backup, check the apartment and then check outside. She screamed hysterically and said that the man was listening and would kill one of her kids if the Guards were called. She also wouldn't let either of us leave. She said she was scared and wanted one of us to stay with her. My partner obliged and I started to take a look around the rest of the apartment. I went into the hall alone and saw that there were three rooms. The first two I entered were bedrooms, both similar in size. They were both spotless, double bed in each, large wardrobes, and had what I'd consider a classy decor. I was probably cutting corners by not checking the rooms properly but I was anxious to get out of the apartment so I could call for backup out of earshot of the woman to avoid having her go into hysterics again. As soon as I opened the third door to see the bathroom, alarm bells instantly rang.'

'What did you see?'

'No,' replied Fionn. 'I realised what it was that I hadn't seen.'

'What you hadn't seen?' Stephanie asked quizzically. 'What do you mean?'

'I didn't see any toys, any children's clothes, any little furniture, no untidiness to suggest that children lived there. Or even that a child had ever been present. I didn't have a good feeling at all so I darted back to the living area to find the woman approaching my partner from behind with a blood stained breadknife and a look in her eye I can only describe as being like she was possessed by a demon. I shouted "down" as loud as I could and with cat-like reflexes and no idea why he was doing so, my partner just hit the ground like his legs had just lost all feeling.'

'I remember now,' Stephanie interrupted. She was no longer paying any attention to the computer screen in front of her. 'It was her. The woman that stabbed two Guards to death. I can't believe you were there.'

'Well, I was. I keep saying that. I ran at her and went straight for the arm holding the knife. I only had a couple of seconds to disarm her before she regained her balance and lashed out at my partner again. He had pretty quickly figured out what was going on and he was coming at her from the other side so we were quickly able to get handcuffs on her. We were fortunate to survive that night. It was the most tragic case of Garda homicide in years. She suffered from schizophrenia and she was convinced the CIA had brainwashed her family. Her logical retaliation was to take out all the Guards. She murdered two that day but it was almost four....'

'...If it wasn't for you?' Stephanie suggested.

'Ah no, not at all, I'm not saying that. I just got lucky.'

'You think you're a hot shot hero, don't you?' boomed a voice that startled Fionn.

'But would a hero break and enter and steal private and confidential information?'

Fionn wasn't sure how long Brian Johnson had been standing there. His arms were folded and his body was rigid with fury.

Stephanie held the demeanour of a misbehaving child, fully aware that a chastisement was imminent. 'Dad, what are you doing here?'

'What am I doing here? I'm the key holder that gets called by the monitoring company when an alarm is activated. And I just so happened to be around the corner when I got the call so I came back to see what was going on. But I don't need to ask you what you're doing here because I know full well.' He looked over at the pages sitting in the printer which was still humming from its recent use.

'But Dad, I'm only trying to help the Guards, this is important, I'm doing the right thing.'

Brian raised his voice. 'If it was important Detective Fagan here would easily be able to go down the correct avenues of acquiring important information rather than manipulating a young lady into breaking the law.'

'Dad,' Stephanie exclaimed scornfully. 'Nobody is manipulating anyone, I know what I'm doing and I think we should help. There is a killer out there and we should help the Guards before anyone else dies. Going down the correct avenues, as you call them,' she said making bunny ears in the air, 'will take too long. Come on Dad.'

Brian took a long deep breath and exhaled. 'Sweetie, I know your heart is in the right place but I must put my foot down.' He looked at Fionn and his eyes seemed to darken over. 'Detective, because my daughter is naive and her intentions were good I won't press charges but I really need you to get out right now and leave this establishment alone, is that clear?' He walked over to the printer and picked up the pages that were sitting in it. He held them up with both hands and dangled them, like he was about to tear them down the middle.

'Wait, Mr. Johnson', Fionn pleaded. 'I am really sorry about this, I certainly don't mean any disrespect and we didn't think coming in this evening would set off any alarms. In fact, I am completely respectful of your wishes that the list of your members not be shared without permission. This is in fact a list of people that applied to the Freemasonry but were ultimately not accepted.'

Brian looked down at the sheets in his hand and proceeded to scan the names.

'I'm sure that isn't something you'd mind giving me, just so I can run a criminal check on those names? If there is a link between these murders and someone on the list, it means you guys made the right decision in not allowing him membership, which is a fact you'd surely be proud for the Guards to know?'

Brian grinned while still staring at the names in front of him.

Fionn gave a grin too. Had he made Brian see reason?

'There you go again, Detective. Being manipulative.' He held the sheets up to head height and ripped them up into little strips before crumpling them up and tossing them in the bin. 'Get the information through following the correct procedure and I'll be glad to hand it over. Now get out.'

Stephanie walked a deflated Fionn to the front door and held it open as he shimmied past her and exited. 'Don't mind Dad, everything is black and white with him. He's always the professional, I wouldn't take it personally.'

Fionn just made a humming sound under his breath.

'Look, I better stay here and calm him down, he'll be OK. I just need to talk to him.'

'I'm really sorry for putting you in this position. I should never have done it. I hope it won't affect your job or your relationship with him.'

'Of course it won't,' Stephanie said as she stretched out her arms to give him a hug. She squeezed him tight and as she pulled her arms away she put her hand in his jacket pocket and pulled it out again just as quick.

He reached into the same pocket and pulled out a USB key.

'Dad is useless with technology, he can barely text. He would never consider digitally copying the list.' She leaned in and gave him a peck on the cheek and sank backwards through the light beaming through the crack in the door that was closing on Fionn's astonished face.

He hadn't thought of copying it digitally either.

'Well, well, look what we have here,' Billy said as he juggled the list in one hand and his pint in the other.

'Watch your bloody pint will you,' barked Fionn, 'you'll get Guinness all over it.'

Billy put the pint down. He was highly impressed with it. The Long Hall had always had a good reputation but despite passing it no doubt thousands of times, neither he nor Fionn had been inside. Until this very moment. 'Seriously though, this is a major breakthrough,' he said, gripping the freshly printed sheet of paper like it was a priceless treasure map. 'Does any of the other names mean anything to you?'

'Nah,' said Fionn. 'Scanning through it, I don't recognise any of the other names and I had Neeve run the list for criminal records and there were no

276

hits. But I don't think I need any more than that. Our instincts were right.'

'Michael Behan,' Billy proclaimed loudly like he was introducing him to royalty. 'Right there in black in white. I'll be a nuns knickers. So what's the connection? What brings the whole thing full circle? Guy kills homeless people. Guy has a ring with a symbol on it. Symbol is related to the Freemasons. Suspect tried to join the Freemasons but was refused. Guy kills homeless people because his feelings are hurt?'

'I'm still not sure of the motive but I'm a hundred percent about Behan. He is the common denominator here.' Fionn took a long gulp as he emptied the contents of his glass. 'He seems to have an alibi, so maybe he and McGee were in it together and McGee was suffering from a guilty conscience so he threatened to confess his involvement. Maybe he felt he was taken advantage of and forced into it by Behan, maybe Adam Kelly is right and he is a hypnotist and he forced McGee to do something he normally would never have done so he wanted to confess and Behan had to do something about it.'

'So we're going to confront him and make him talk?' asked Billy.

'When you say it like that you make us sound like Bond villains, but yes, you better god damn believe we're going to confront him. We only have circumstantial evidence right now but when he realises we're one step closer to catching him by the balls he won't have such a smug look on his face, the prick. He'll break like your Granny's fine China, wait and see.'

'Are you sure we shouldn't just keep investigating and build the case first?' replied Billy.

'No, we don't have time, let's confront him with this and see how he reacts, it might be enough to get him to give up the charade.'

Billy briskly finished the last drop left in his glass. 'Right so, let's go.'

Fionn looked at Billy with a confused expression. 'We've just had two pints. And it's 12.30am.'

'Oh yeah, fair point. Tomorrow morning so?'

'First thing,' agreed Fionn.

'Another pint?'

Fionn stared into the middle distance and shook his head. 'No.'

'Are you going to call it a night?

Fionn gazed again at the same spot and then in an unpersuasive tone replied 'Sure.'

CHAPTER TWENTY FIVE

The last of the remaining crimson leaves dispersed throughout the trees that lined the street were rustling in the wind on an otherwise mild morning. The two Guards approached the dentist's door for a second visit. They both had a confident spring in their step. Despite it not yet being 9.30am, the opening time according to the plaque on the wall, the door was already open, so they walked straight into the reception area and saw the same young girl as the previous time that Behan had mentioned was an intern.

'Is he in there?' Fionn asked as he motioned his head towards the door of the office where they had previously confronted Behan.

The receptionist looked just as confused and concerned as the last time. 'Er, yes, but...'

The two Guards did not wait for an answer and continued on into the office. As they burst in Behan looked up from his desk and his face instantly turned bright red with anger.

'What the...' Behan began to talk like he was spitting venom.

'Shut the hell up, Behan and listen to me very carefully,' Fionn began. Despite the fact that the intervening sleep between last night and this morning had helped in calming him down and giving him an opportunity to collect himself, the instant sight of Behan's dislikeable face and his abrasive tones brought all of yesterday's anger and frustration right back. Finishing the night €50 in the green after an hour at a blackjack table was no longer the cause for celebration it had been and in that moment was merely a distant memory. 'We are not taking any more of your shit, you smug asshole. We will not be playing this back and forth mind game today, we are here to simply state some facts. That weird as shit ring of yours, it was worn by a person of interest, it was made by a person of interest and it's based on a design in a building run by an organisation you once tried to be a member of.' He pulled out the printed page from his inside pocket and held it in the air. Billy, who was standing in the exact same place as their previous visit, stood silently, pointed to the page and nodded. 'Now, if you think we're stupid enough to ignore these connections just because you say you were somewhere else eating and drinking like a pig then you are severely underestimating this country's police force my friend. We are so close to nailing you, I need you to understand that. I'd be surprised if you're not waking up every morning to discover you've shit the bed after having nightmares about us coming from you. You think you're a clever bastard but we'll have you real soon, mark my words. The next time you'll see us we'll be here to put handcuffs on you.'

The only sound in the room over the next several seconds was the low hum of a computer on the dentist's desk. Michael Behan appeared to be gathering his thoughts as he sat silently with his hands pressed together and held to his mouth as if he were mid prayer. The redness in his cheeks slowly turned back to a healthy pink leaving only his bright red swollen nose to stand out. The fiery tint to it was further illuminated by a cluster of interwoven tiny blue veins that along with his dark eyes gave him a sinister appearance. He finally spoke. Calmly and slowly. 'It looks like you have me, detectives.'

Billy gave a short but audible gasp from the doorway.

Fionn stood there unmoving, apart from the increase in his heart rate as the adrenaline kicked in. 'So is there something you'd like to tell us, Dr. Behan?' he asked, addressing him correctly for the first time.

'Yes, absolutely,' replied Behan. 'Please forgive my attitude the last time you were here. I mean, you had absolutely nothing on me the last time you were here so I thought I was going to get away with it. But now I can see everything has changed.'

'Ok...' said Fionn with a slow nod, beginning to become sceptical as to the reason for the sudden U-turn in Behan's attitude.

'I mean here you are again, at first I thought you were just an obsessed Bill Murray fan trying to create your very own Groundhog Day, coming into my office and repeating the exact same bullshit you already went through.' Sarcasm had taken over his tone. 'Fantasy tales of evil rings and a murder conspiracy that you think an important member of the community like myself would be involved in. But now I see that trying to outsmart you two geniuses has been absolutely futile because here you are standing in front of me with a proverbial smoking gun. My name on a piece of paper. Proof that I almost joined a boys club that meets weekly, and raises money for charity. Wow. You got me.

Fionn breathed out heavily and heard Billy scoff dismissively from behind him. 'OK Behan, that's enough.'

'No,' shouted Behan, with the anger in his voice intensifying. 'I'm the one that's had enough of your amateur theatrics. I demand you get out now and never come back, I've been more than patient with you but I swear I've been harassed by you for the last time.' He suddenly stood up from his chair and then moved gingerly towards the door Billy was standing at with a distinctive limp in his step. He pushed past Billy and held the door open gesturing for them to leave. 'I swear to God, I will take legal action against the Gardai and the State unless you get out right now.'

Billy stepped backwards into the other side of the open doorway.

Fionn moved towards the door but then stopped half way. He looked the irate dentist up and down, studying everything about him, especially his estimated height, weight and build and tried to imagine how he would look in different clothes. 'Why are you limping, Behan?'

'What?' replied Behan abrasively.

Fionn turned nonchalantly to Billy. 'Can he not understand me? Could you translate that into asshole for me please?'

'No can do,' replied Billy. 'I don't speak it, I opted for Spanish in school, mon amie.'

'Why haven't I noticed his limp before?' asked Fionn, mostly to himself.

'He was sitting down the last time we were here, wasn't he?' suggested Billy.

'Yeah, true. Have *you* noticed the limp before?'

'Get out now,' Behan shouted.

'Yeah', replied Billy. 'He was walking around like a snail yesterday. I never thought to mention it, I assumed he sprained an ankle tripping over his self-entitlement or something.'

'Ah Billy, you should have mentioned it. It's important. How did you get it, Behan?'

'I sprained my ankle playing football, get the fuck out,' barked Behan, clearly agitated.

Fionn reached out and picked up a large green golfing umbrella that had been resting against an ugly woodworm infested dresser. In a swift motion he flipped it in the air so he was now holding it by the tip, took a large step towards Behan, reached out and gently hit him on his left ankle in a way that wouldn't particularly hurt the average person.

Behan tensed and let out a short yelp of pain.

'Soft spot right there?' Fionn asked, feigning concern. 'Do you by any chance have a bollard shaped bruise too, Spider-Man?'

In a sudden jolt of anger and panic Behan stormed past Billy like an injured animal hobbling away from oncoming headlights. He limped into his surgery where his intern was standing behind the dentist chair setting up for the first patient, unaware of the altercation that was ensuing. She barely had time to look up and before he suddenly and unexpectedly reached around the young girl with his right arm and grabbed her in a headlock. She gave out a squeal. With his right hand he grabbed a cordless dental drill off the adjacent table and held it high in the air. He turned it on and it started making a high pitched hum.

'Don't fucking move or I'll ram this right into her fucking throat.'

She let out a scream. 'Michael?' she said, sounding both scared and confused. She then said something in Spanish that sounded like a plea of some kind.

'Woah, woah,' said Billy.

'Take it easy now Behan,' added Fionn.

'Stand the fuck back you pricks,' he wailed as he manoeuvred himself and his intern past them and out into the hall.

Fionn and Billy followed gently behind with their hands held out at chest height in a pacifying position. They were keeping a distance so as not to further panic Behan but close enough to keep up with him.

Behan fumbled his way backwards through the front door and down the path towards an immaculate black Mercedes sports car parked in the driveway. He kept his eyes firmly on the two guards the entire time. He moved to the driver's side of the car and after pulling keys out of his pocket he unlocked the car door while simultaneously flinging the young girl into the nearby shrubbery like he was discarding a sack of garbage. As the door slammed closed the two Guards ran for the car, Billy for the near passenger side door and Fionn sliding across the bonnet towards the driver's side. The doors were already automatically locked and as Behan put the car in reverse, the engine roared almost as loud as the horn that he was firmly holding down. The car launched backwards out of the driveway, avoiding all the stopped cars that had heard the black sports car before they saw it. Behan manoeuvred the car ninety degrees and sped off heading south, in the direction of the city centre.

'He's not getting far on that road,' shouted Billy.

'Make sure the girl is OK, I'll go after him,' Fionn said as he ran towards the car. He suddenly stopped in his tracks and turned back around towards Billy. 'Keys,' he shouted.

Billy threw the keys which landed perfectly in Fionn's outstretched hands. 'Go get the bastard', he called as Fionn darted in the direction of the car.

CHAPTER TWENTY SIX

The siren on his car was wailing as Fionn came upon the crossroads at Hart's Corner where all three one way lanes were at a standstill. The cars started to move sideways in an effort to make room for the unmarked car. As he squeezed through the space he frantically peered down the side streets, surprised that he hadn't caught up with the Mercedes already. He wondered if it had been driven the wrong way down a one way street to get away in the opposite direction. Or maybe even down one of the cul-de-sacs, into a yard and out of sight. Suddenly something out of place caught his attention in the far horizon. He saw a black car driving slowly on the footpath. As Fionn got closer he could see petrified pedestrians screaming in fear and shouting in anger as they dodged the oncoming car. He continued through the gap that had been carved for him by the awkwardly positioned vehicles but saw that the traffic up ahead had to come to a complete standstill. He glanced to his right and scanned the street ahead. The other side of the road was completely empty so he moved across as soon as he was able to and with a clear track ahead he was able to catch up to the tardy Mercedes within seconds. He came parallel to the black car, leaving just the lane of unmoving traffic between them. As Fionn looked across he noticed the car was moving slowly, not in order to avoid hitting pedestrians unaware of its trajectory as he expected but because it was pushing a large battery operated dustbin along in front of it. The street cleaner himself somehow managed to end up inside the bin and he was staring straight at the windscreen in horror, holding on to the door handle for dear life. Fionn saw Behan look sideways and for what felt like a full minute they just stared straight at each other. Eventually a gap appeared in the traffic at the crossroads of Doyle's Corner, so Behan suddenly swung the car sideways to come away from the bin and directly alongside Fionn. He then rammed the other car from the side trying to force it onto the opposite path. Fionn pushed the steering wheel back towards Behan to try and hold steady but eventually had to hit the brakes to avoid a head-on collision with a cyclist that was frantically dismounting his bike and trying to roll onto the path. This gave Behan a free road as he accelerated further south towards the inner city. Fionn struggled to keep up and was starting to slowly drop back despite the fact his right foot was pushed right to the floor. As both cars approached the tram line intersection the pace of Behan's car started to waver, allowing Fionn to get right on his tail. As they sped past the crossroads Fionn assumed they would be continuing straight so started to inch closer hoping to ram the black car from behind. Just as he was about to reach the back bumper the car was suddenly no longer in front of him. Behan had swung a sharp left and pulled the handbrake, causing the car to do an about turn. By the time Fionn turned the car around Behan was already speeding down the hill on the tram tracks and heading south. The car vibrated loudly beneath Fionn as he accelerated down the cobblestone lined tracks in fast pursuit. He celebrated inwardly when he saw a tram up ahead that seemed to be at a standstill. There was not going to be enough space on the near side of the tram to squeeze through. The prospects immediately got twice as bad for Behan a moment later when a second tram came into view, arriving towards them from the opposite direction. It was a dead end, Behan would have to come to a complete stop. Instead of slowing down, the black Mercedes began to pick up pace. Fionn prepared himself to witness a high impact head on crash between the car and the tram. Suddenly, just seconds before the collision, Behan took a sharp left, propelling the car over the side ramps of the tracks and five feet into the air. Fionn watched on, as if in slow motion, as the car launched, bonnet first, into the air like it had been blasted from a cannon. While suspended in the air its trajectory quickly changed as the front of the car came back out of orbit and headed straight for a crash landing on the pavement. The impact caused a loud bang of metal crunching and glass smashing. The front bumper came loose and was scraping along the ground, creating a light show of sparks. The car's headlights had imploded into themselves and the windscreen was no longer there. The car rolled awkwardly into a pole and then came to a complete stop. Fionn gaped in stunned silence at the badly damaged car. He could see the silhouette of Behan's head through the back window. It was hanging completely still, in an uncomfortable forward leaning position. Fionn slowly exited his car and approached the battered vehicle. Close to a dozen curious pedestrians had already gathered around to look at the chaotic scene. The two trams were still stationary and there was an assortment of faces behind phones lining the windows as the aftermath was being recorded from all angles. Just as Fionn got within touching distance of the car it started to slowly roll back. At first he assumed the car was experiencing the laws of gravity and was rolling downwards of its own accord but suddenly he saw the brake lights flash as it once again came to a stop in the middle of an open road. 'Oh shit,' Fionn whispered under his breath. The car's engine suddenly revved into a high pitched purr as the tyres began to screech. They created a cartoon like puff of smoke as the car suddenly accelerated forward. He looked back at his own car and seeing no quick way to get it off the track decided to abandon it and give chase on foot. The Mercedes ignored the red light facing it and ploughed through the next crossroads. It hit two oncoming cars, propelling them sideways like bowling pins being knocked over by a perfectly hit strike. Behan continued down the tram tracks but this time there were no oncoming trams in his way, he had a clear road ahead of him and he could see the T-junction of Parnell Street up ahead. Fionn was a fit man but when it came to running he considered his strength to be stamina, not speed. He was not much of a sprinter, so despite running as fast as he may have ever ran before, the car he was chasing was getting further away from him by the second. Already out of breath, Fionn slowed down as he got to the junction. At that exact moment the bumper that had been scraping along the ground came loose and fell in under the front wheels causing them to seize up. The car slowed suddenly and was now drifting forward at the speed of about five kilometres per hour.

Fionn went to the window of the first car that had been hit at the crossroads. It was a small red Ford and the engine was dead with smoke billowing from under the bonnet. The only occupant was an old woman in the driver's seat. He held up his badge and shouted through the window, 'Are you OK?'

The woman looked flustered but opened her door a few inches, 'Yes I'm OK, thank you, don't worry about me, get that mad man.'

Fionn had already turned away once he heard the word OK and continued towards the second car, once again holding up his badge. It was a large Toyota with a taxi plate on its roof. He opened the passenger door and looked in. 'Everyone OK?' he asked.

'What the Jesus?' the driver said in a thick Dublin accent. 'What a bleedin' arsehole, are you going after him or what?'

Fionn looked in the back seat and saw a young Asian couple embracing each other. Judging by the way they were dressed, the bags they had beside them and the direction they were coming from he guessed they had just arrived in Dublin Airport and were on the way to their hotel. They both looked shaken from the crash and were cowering at the presence of Fionn, perhaps not understanding he was a policeman in civil clothes.

He decided to jump in the passenger seat as the car was still running and facing in the right direction. 'Catch me up to that car will you, please?' asked Fionn.

The driver gave a quick chuckle and put the car in gear. 'No problemo, pal,' he said and immediately took off after the snail paced Mercedes.

Within seconds they had caught up to Behan so Fionn ordered the driver to a stop. 'That's close enough,' he said with the door already open. 'Welcome to Dublin,' he shouted loudly into the back seat as he exited the car, causing the Asian couple to jump with fright.

He ran quickly alongside Behan's car and jumped onto where the windshield should have been. He grabbed the inside of the dashboard for support, cutting his arm on broken glass in the process. He pulled his body in towards the car and found himself inches from Behan's face. 'Stop the car you psycho, you're going to kill someone.'

Behan stared at him with the same dark eyes he had seen behind the Spider-Man mask several days previously. There was no emotion in Behan's face, as if he were not even present.

Suddenly, he could feel his body take flight. Float in a way he had no control over. For a split second all he could see was white, like a plane entering the clouds. He felt a jolt of pain that went all the way from the top of his head down his neck and into his chest.

The bumper had freed itself from under the sliding wheels and glided sideways across the road like an abandoned bob-sleigh. The sudden acceleration had thrust Fionn into the car causing him to land on his head, connecting painfully with a piece of metal between the two front seats, which sent him into a momentary daze. The metal object came loose and fell down onto the floor of the passenger side seat. As Fionn regained his focus he found himself sitting in the passenger seat the wrong way up, lying awkwardly on his hands, his neck contorted and the cushion of the seat restricting his ability to breathe. He looked down at what his head had just knocked loose out of the cup holder and realised it was a gun. As he struggled to free his hands to reach the gun he suddenly saw an arm stretch slowly past his eyes. He sat helplessly as he watched Behan's fingers come within an inch of the weapon. Suddenly it stopped moving and remained suspended in front of him as if frozen in time. He glanced sideways and saw Behan's beetroot coloured face as he appeared to be straining torturously. He realised the seatbelt was restricting him and he wasn't able to stretch far enough.

Onlookers ducked and dived as the car bounced over a pedestrian island and continued the wrong direction down a one way road, passing alongside the Henry Street shopping district.

Fionn wriggled to get free from his own bodily entanglement and was able to reach out to grab the gun. He held it out and aimed it at Behan's face. 'Stop the car,' he demanded.

Behan's eyes widened into a bulbous bloodshot stare. 'Fuckin' shoot me,' he shouted with intense anger.

Fionn made no reply.

The approaching drivers were pressing hard on their horns and manoeuvring frantically onto the footpath in an attempt to avoid the oncoming wreck.

'You can't, can you?' Behan said with a maniacal laugh. 'You're not allowed to, or you'll get arrested, you idiot.'

'I'll tell you what I *won't* get arrested for,' said Fionn. Then with a brisk motion he rammed the base of the gun into the middle of Behan's forehead. He heard a crunch as he followed up with a swipe across the centre of his face. 'Breaking your nose.'

Behan let out a painful wail as blood started to pour out of his nose. Fionn flung the gun into the back seat and threw both hands on the steering wheel, trying to take control of the car. He managed to overpower Behan's grip and swerved abruptly in order to narrowly avoid a car that was stopped at a traffic light like a helpless rabbit in headlights.

Just as the car was approaching the Quays, Behan leaned forward and bit down hard on Fionn's arm, causing him to roar in pain and let go of the wheel. Now with full control of the wheel again, Behan decided to plough through a gap he saw between two cars, aiming for the Millennium

Bridge, a pedestrianised walkway joining both sides of the river that was opened in 1999 to celebrate the arrival of the twenty-first century. The car went straight into the railings that separated the beginning of the bridge from the end of the boardwalk. Fionn had tensed his body and raised his hands to his face in anticipation of a sudden impact with the wall. He said a brief silent prayer to the God he had lost touch with that his airbag would activate. Neither the airbag activated nor was there a harsh impact as the car went straight through the brittle wall and into the river.

The adrenaline that had been pumping around his body elevated to an even higher level and his priority suddenly changed from stopping Behan to staying alive. The car tipped over the edge and landed in the river, broken headlights first, as if it were slowly driving down the wall of the riverbank. A sluggish puff of mud mushroomed around the water as Fionn fell through the smashed windshield and into the murky abyss. He struggled to break free from the slimy algae that gripped him but as the water level was low he was able to quickly get his head above the water and take a deep breath. He looked upwards and saw Behan clutching his side anxiously trying to free himself from the safety belt that had him trapped in his seat and facing vertically down into the water. As Fionn moved closer to the car he heard a creaking sound and as if in slow motion he jumped sideways to avoid it as it fell forward submerging itself upside down in the river. Air bubbles began to float to the top of the water and pop softly.

Fionn watched on for about thirty seconds before deciding Behan must have been trapped underneath as he had not yet resurfaced from under the low tide. Fionn trudged slowly against the water's steady current and edged close to the car. He closed his eyes, took a sharp intake of breath and ducked under the water. Upon reopening his eyes he saw dust settle back on the hazy river bed and now had a clear sight of Behan who was still in his seat but hanging motionless with one hand around his waist and the other stretched out below him. For a brief moment he reminded Fionn of the image of God in Michelangelo's "The Creation of Man". The image was quickly interrupted when he saw Behan start to squirm. He appeared to be reaching for something. As Fionn leaned into the car he could see it was the gun. It had fallen forward from the impact and was now within Behan's reach. Fionn froze motionless as Behan's swift movements unravelled before his eyes. First his fingers tipped the gun. Then he nudged it closer to him until he could get his whole hand around it. Then he grabbed the gun in his hand and slid his finger around the trigger. He raised it and pointed it at Fionn, inches from his face. He had to make a swift fight or flight decision. Moving away would be pointless, he would move too sluggishly under water. Reaching for the gun was futile, it would take a thousand times longer to reach the gun in the time it would take Behan to pull the trigger. Fionn's only thought was to hope that the gun would jam underwater. He stared motionless into Behan's cold dark eyes. A hate radiated from them like nothing he had ever seen before. Behan was rapidly running out of breath, yet he stared at Fionn motionless as if time was just standing still. Behan's face suddenly came alive with an expression Fionn could only describe as ecstatic fury. A victorious grin came across Behan's face as he stared at him upside down like a vicious bat hanging from a ceiling. Fionn was starting to lose his breath as his rapidly beating heart was draining his lungs of the oxygen he had inhaled before impact. His entire world started to fade to blackness as his vision narrowed on to the gun pointing in his face. He blinked slowly, keeping his eyes closed for a moment, unsure if he'd ever open them again. As he finally reopened his eyes he saw the gun retreat from his line of sight. As his vision refocused he saw Behan pull the gun back towards himself, he raised it to his own face and placed the muzzle into his mouth. Behan closed his eyes and pulled the trigger. A faint muffled pop sounded and a puff of red mist expanded from behind Behan's head like a rose blooming. Before the blood fully diluted into the muddy river, Fionn had already come above water for a sharp intake of breath, it stung his lungs so painfully it felt like he had inhaled a bag of nails.

CHAPTER TWENTY SEVEN

'I feel more like a cold beer to be honest,' said Fionn, resting his head in his hand. He stared at the beer taps with both mental and physical exhaustion clearly showing in his facial expression.

'What are you talking about? Nonsense,' protested Billy. 'How will you be able to rate Frank Ryan's pints by sipping on watery American piss?'

'I was thinking maybe something German? A weißbier.'

Billy had suggested heading across to Smithfield to get out of the city centre and give Fionn a chance to get his thoughts together. But the idea wasn't entirely selfless as he had also seen an opportunity to continue the hunt for the best Guinness and visit a pub he had never been to. He had heard great things about Frank Ryan's, although reports that dogs walked around freely, feeding off crisps offered down by patrons were so far unfounded. Unless perhaps it was nap time. 'But what if this is the exact moment you discover the best pint in Dublin, and you decide to pass it up because you're too focused on putting your lederhosen on? I could be wallowing in quintessential black stuff and you're too busy singing traditional Oktoberfest songs.'

'Billy, I have drank here plenty of times. The Guinness is grand, but I doubt it's much different than the last time I was here. You fire away though.'

'Where are all the dogs?' Billy enquired.

'What?' replied Fionn curtly, confused by the question.

'Nothing,' replied Billy. 'Pint of Guinness please,' he said as he turned towards the nonchalant bar man. 'And a pint of whatever German weißbier you might have, bitte danke,'

'Will Carlsberg do?' the bar man asked as he raised a glass to the tap and started to pour.'

'Perfect,' replied Billy.

Fionn just rolled his shoulders, not having the energy to protest that it was neither German nor a weißbier.

'So,' said Billy as he turned back towards Fionn. 'We got him, eh?'

'We sure did,' replied Fionn solemnly.

'Are you happy?' asked Billy, raising his voice as three musicians in the opposite corner started into some traditional tunes using their respective fiddle, tin whistle and uilleann pipe.

'I suppose,' said Fionn as he grimaced at the sounds. He never cared much for Irish traditional music. He considered himself a big music fan and an appreciator of all genres from rock to techno and from heavy metal to ska but two styles he could never bring himself to enjoy were country music and traditional Irish music. This was possibly due to those being the only types his parents listened to when he was growing up. 'Behan and McGee were working together, the ring led us to them. They created their specific design for God knows what reason, some nut ball ethnic cleansing manifesto, McGee being a jewellery maker made them one each. Invoiced themselves I assume to claim back tax that was never paid, not realising they were leaving a massive trail of breadcrumbs leading us right to them. Behan was rejected from joining The Freemasons so he joined his like-minded friend to start their own new world order agenda by ridding their city of its poorest citizens, the homeless. They may or may not be amateur hypnotists, I'm not sure, the jury is still out on that one. They're not great at covering their tracks, so they quickly realised that we were on to them. Behan first tried to threaten me into keeping my nose out of the case, but failed. Then after an argument he murdered his accomplice and framed him as the only perpetrator. Finally, when we backed him into a corner, he panicked and tried to make a run for it. When faced with the humiliation of being caught, he decided to take the easy way out. I think that sums it up. Did I miss anything?'

'Well, his alibi, we assume that's somehow bullshit?' suggested Billy.

'Of course. Actually, hang on.' Fionn pulled his phone out of his pocket and started to dial. He sat still staring at the musicians while the phone rang on the other side.

'Fionn, are you OK? I just heard about what happened,' Neeve asked with affectionate concern in her voice. 'Where are you? It sounds like Riverdance is going on around you.'

'I'm fine, thanks Neeve. Don't worry about me, it's all good. Listen, were you looking into this guy Behan's alibi? That he was down the country in a hotel the night McGee was murdered? I'm assuming the hotel has no record of him but I need that confirmed for my report.'

'Ah Fionn, I don't think you should worry about it right now,' replied Neeve, sounding even more concerned. 'You should go home after what just happened,'

'Neeve, please, talk to me.'

'Sorry but actually the hotel has confirmed Behan and his wife were guests that night.'

Fionn rolled his eyes so Billy would know it wasn't what they wanted to hear. 'Oh great, now we'll have to get CCTV off them to confirm it wasn't actually him that was there. Nothing is straightforward about this job is it?'

'Actually, that's what I've been working on all morning. I'm looking at footage right now. I'm sorry Fionn, it's definitely him. The times don't make sense, I don't think Behan killed McGee.'

Fionn lost all colour in his face as it turned the same shade as the head on his pint.

'Besides,' continued Neeve. 'Joanna said the man that tried to kill her had an Irish name. Michael isn't very Irish.'

Fionn dropped his head sideways like a boxer receiving a knockout blow. He stood silently with nothing to say.

'Look, there is one thing that popped up in my research that I thought was interesting, but not sure if it's relevant,' continued Neeve. 'His sister is deceased. In fact, she was murdered in the city centre, walking home late at night, three years ago.'

'No way,' replied Fionn as he sat up in his seat animatedly. 'Behan was a suspect, wasn't he?'

'No,' said Neeve. 'The murderer was arrested pretty soon afterwards and is currently serving life in prison. Seemed like an open shut case, there were several witnesses, he was off his head on drugs and she was in the wrong place at the wrong time.'

'Still though, that'd mess you up, your sister being murdered. No wonder he's an asshole. Who did it anyway?'

'A guy called John Byrne, of no fixed abode,' replied Neeve.

'He was homeless?'

'Apparently so, is that important?'

'I'm not sure,' responded Fionn. 'Seems curious, I'll keep that fact in mind. Thanks Neeve, I owe you big time.'

'OK, but hang on there's one more thing,' continued Neeve. 'I just went over the Coroner's report on McGee and something it said got me thinking. It's the way he's described as having slight hands. Apparently it's helpful for anyone working with small objects. Like the way you hear about piano fingers. Skinny fingers can find their way around the keys better.'

'Shit,' Fionn said gently. 'The ring doesn't fit does it?'

'It would have been like a hula hoop on any of his fingers,' replied Neeve.

Fionn didn't reply. He slowly lifted the phone away from his ear and pressed the end call button. 'It wasn't Behan', he said to Billy

His partner let out a long blow of breath and looked to the musicians intently as if he was hanging on every note they played as his mind wandered. 'So I assume the ring is not actually McGee's?

Fionn didn't answer and bowed his head in his hands as he tried to think back over everything he thought he knew. He took all the pieces apart and tried to put them back in place in an order they made sense. He reached into his inside pocket and pulled out the water soaked list of names he had been carrying on him since he last saw Stephanie. He carefully unfolded the wet page so as not to damage it and started to study it once again, as if looking for something he had overlooked before. He knew there was nothing new that would stand out, at this point he had memorised most of the names by heart but he figured he had nowhere else to start from.

Billy on the other hand just let his eyes roam the room trying to find something to talk about in order to change the subject and take Fionn's dejected mind off the problems at hand. He noticed the passion in the musicians' faces as if the music they were playing was the most important thing they would ever do. He saw a group of locals sitting at an adjacent table. Gently swaying their heads, a look of pride and enjoyment in their faces, probably family and friends of the musicians. He looked at the barman standing behind the counter. His arms folded, staring into the middle distance. It wasn't clear whether he was being moved or bored by the music. He then looked to a group of tourists that were edging closer to the musicians with their phones held in front of their faces. One of them turned the phone on themselves and announced loudly to their camera in a North American accent that he was live from a real Irish pub, listening to a private musical performance. He seemed to be incredibly drunk as he unsteadily raised his half glass to the camera in a 'cheers' gesture. The tourist then turned the camera back to the musicians as the rest of the group followed suit with theirs, recording the proceedings and being completely oblivious of the dirty looks they were getting from the adjacent table. 'Look at those gobshites,' Billy said. 'People these days, they're too busy recording their lives as proof that it happened, that they miss out on living it in the first place.'

Fionn winced slightly and then offered a half smile as he shook his head. He turned back to redirect his attention to the group, observing their jovial interactions with their phones. The music had stopped and the musician holding the uilleann pipe started to introduce the next song. Out of a group of six, one was recording himself, two were recording the musicians, two were scrolling on theirs and only one seemed fully engaged with what the musician had to say. He announced loudly and with pride in his voice that the next tune was by the great Seamus Ennis.

'I must admit I've never heard of Seamus Ennis,' confessed Billy. 'But I know good Trad music when I hear it and you'd be facing bad chances of finding a better session in town than this one right here. These tourists don't know how lucky they are.' He turned to Fionn who was staring at the list of names and noticed he had a detached and empty expression on his face like he had just been hypnotised. 'You OK, Pal?' Billy asked, concerned that delayed shock may have taken hold of his partner.

Fionn did not reply and continued to focus blankly on the piece of soggy paper.

'Fagan? Back in the room now, please.'

Fionn finally broke his trance and without moving his body, glanced sideways at Billy with a raised eyebrow. 'You are actually spot on, you know? It's something they want to remember isn't it? That's what everyone does when they want to remember something.'

'What?' asked Billy, still concerned Fionn may be in shock.

'What these guys are doing, taking photos and videos. We all like souvenirs when we do something special, don't we? A fridge magnet when we travel. A photo at a party. A video from a gig.' He turned his body towards Billy and stared him intensely in the eyes as he continued. 'And when you accomplish something special, what do you do, Billy?'

'Accomplish something?' asked Billy, perplexed. 'I can't think of what you might mean.'

'I mean professionally. Think of a case you're proud of, do you just leave it there in your memory? Forever more?

Billy sat silently as he considered the question. 'I suppose I have newspaper clippings of a few articles that I'm mentioned in. The good ones of course, when I saved the day, and when I was referred to as a legend and all that.'

One of Fionn's eyebrows arched, crawling up his forehead as he gave Billy a sceptical look. 'I don't think you've ever been referred to as a legend by anyone,' he said as he shuffled excitedly in his seat. 'But you've just proved my point.'

'I have?' replied Billy, confused.

'Yes. It's the ring. Such a small thing connects everything and spells it all out. It was a cheap piece of crap. It was made to symbolise something specific but its value or quality wasn't important to the people that wanted it. That's what doesn't add up. The ring was put on a shelf with other valuable jewellery to make it look like McGee owned it and treasured it. But compared to how valuable everything else was in his collection, it doesn't make sense why he'd care about a cheap ring.

'Maybe he was proud of making it nonetheless?' reasoned Billy.

'But he had loads of photos of it on file. I saw them at the crime scene, along with all of his other work. McGee had two types of collections. There was his valuable collection he kept on a shelf, all expensive, rare and beautiful. Then there was the work he created. He used to photograph every job he did to remember it. He would have kept a record of everything he created. Like any artist would. It wouldn't have mattered how small the job or how cheap it was to make. But if he had his own copy of the ring he wouldn't have needed so many photos of it on file too. It didn't even fit him.

So it must have been planted there. Behan didn't kill McGee, someone else did. The owner of the second ring. There were two of them and I know who the other person is. I've always known.' Fionn hopped off his stool and pivoted on one leg as he trudged stiffly towards the door. 'I need to make a call, ' he mumbled behind him, leaving Billy with his open mouth slowly dropping like he was starting to lose feeling in his chin.

Outside Fionn surveyed the street as he put the phone to his ear and waited through the dial tone. He took the page with names out of his pocket and looked at it one more time.

'Fionn, what is it now, are you OK?' said Neeve in a professional tone mixed with maternal type concern.

'Yes, yes,' replied Fionn quickly. 'I just need a favour, urgently. Is Joanna Quinn still in hospital?'

'I believe so, yes.'

'Can you please pay her a visit, right now? I need you to show her a photo of the man that tried to kill her.'

CHAPTER TWENTY EIGHT

Garda Luke O'Loughlin stood in the shadows of the alleyway that linked Bachelors Walk to Abbey Street. He was starting to feel the chill of the night air as he shuffled from one foot to the other. He was thinking about how chuffed he was with himself for no longer being nervous in these types of situations. The first couple of times the danger was palpable, like he could taste his own fear in the air he was breathing. Trying to remember his exit plan for each and every eventuality used to make it even more stressful. By now however, it was well within his comfort zone. He considered himself a professional. He thought about how he should write a book about his experiences and wondered to what extent he'd be celebrated as a legend. Then he thought about how he actually missed the adrenaline rush he used to get in the beginning. Especially that unforgettable first time when everything went exactly to plan. Then he changed his mind and agreed that nothing can beat the feeling of having it all figured out. Having seen an opportunity to rid the streets of scumbag junkie dealers and at the same time achieving such substantial personal gain, he genuinely considered himself Dublin's version of Robin Hood. Rob from the scumbags, rid them from the streets. That would be his version of the famous slogan.

Aaron Doran gingerly entered the dark alleyway, walking unevenly footed out of sight from any other pedestrians. He heard the voice before he saw the person.

'Right on time, good man yourself,' said O'Loughlin.

'How's it going?' Aaron said with an unenthusiastic half wave. 'Are you Mr. T?'

'Yes, I bloody well am,' said O'Loughlin proudly. He had decided to come up with an alter ego for his extracurricular business venture and decided his name would be a no-brainer as his childhood hero was the character Mr T, from the A-Team, played by B.A. Baracus. Although he wasn't even born when the show first aired, he was raised on repeats of American 80's TV shows. MacGyver and Knight Rider were great. Miami Vice was brilliant. The A-Team was the greatest. He knew from a young age that he wanted to join the army where he could go on to do great things, just like his heroes. After quitting it while still in his first year he decided to join the Guards instead but quickly realised he was destined for something better, so he was always looking out for new opportunities where he could apply his particular skills. He never really thought about what his skills were but he just knew he had them and that he was far superior to everyone around him. Physically and Intellectually. They were all fools. He pitied them.

'I heard you're the guy to talk to about getting my hands on a bit of Bird Feed?' said Aaron, ignoring O'Loughlin's proverbial peacocking.

'Bird Feed?' mocked O'Loughlin. 'That's a new one. But yes I got the best and for the cheapest price. Show me your money.'

Aaron pulled a wad of €20 notes out of his pocket and dangled them in front of the Guard. 'Here you go, can I have my H now please?'

O'Loughlin took a small bag of heroin out of his inside pocket. The same one he had recently removed from a person's mouth. He threw it at Aaron with one hand and snatched the money with the other. 'You know, you don't look much like a junkie,' he said looking down at his clean runners.

'You don't look much like a Guard,' retorted Aaron with a menacing grin.

O'Loughlin went rigid. 'What the hell? What makes you think I'm a Guard?' He suddenly felt that rush of adrenaline that he missed so much, yet, at this particular moment it was not welcome. He sensed something was off. Fight or flight. Or freeze. He felt that one of those was about to happen.

'Ooops have I upset you, Guard?' Aaron unzipped the front of his hoodie revealing a wire around his neck. 'I think your comrades are on to you.'

O'Loughlin's face turned so red with anger it almost illuminated the dark alley. He reached out to snatch at Aaron's collar but missed. Arron had taken a brisk step back, dodging the oncoming swipe. O'Loughlin crouched slightly and then pounced, like a cat trying to capture a mouse, using the momentum to dig his shoulder into Aaron's chest as he passed. Aaron barely moved but O'Loughlin wouldn't have known either way as he did not look back and increased the speed of his walk as he approached the brightness of the eerily lit street. As he turned left he walked straight into the path of a mobile phone that was being pushed towards his face.

'Garda Luke O'Loughlin, you are under arrest.'

O'Loughlin couldn't see the face of the person at first as the phone was obstructing his view. After a few dazed seconds he tilted his head and focused his eyes on the man standing in front of him as recognition finally came to him. 'Lyons?' he said in a flustered tone.

Detective David Lyons seemed like a towering figure before him, despite being shorter than him. He stood tall and rigid like a statue of a historical figure. He showed no emotion as he stared at O'Loughlin, still holding the phone firmly in front of him. As his focus shifted to the screen he could see Aaron sheepishly arrive into frame behind O'Loughlin's shoulder.

'What the hell is this shit?' O'Loughlin said. 'If you want to arrest someone, arrest this junkie right here, he's got a bag of heroin on him.'

'Oh come on now Lukey boy, you're sounding desperate.' Lyons held his palm out towards Aaron, who instinctively pulled his wired mic from around his neck and a small box from under his t-shirt, handing them both to the steadily standing Detective.

'You set me up,' muttered O'Loughlin between gritted teeth.

'We've been on to you for a while, Mr T,' continued Lyons, ignoring the statement. 'What sort of a stupid name is that anyway? You think you're Dublin's answer to Pablo Escobar or something, don't you? You cocky shit, thought you could do what you like and the rest of us are just a bunch of idiots with no comprehension of the superiority of your intelligence? Well here you are, caught rotten.' Lyons let out a high pitched menacing chuckle that sounded like a small motorbike backfiring. 'You should see the look on your face right now. Actually I'm recording it aren't I, I can show you later. You look like you're shitting yourself, have you shit yourself? Is there shit in your pants right now? I think I can smell it.'

Aaron interrupted timidly. 'I'm done now, right?'

Lyons stopped recording and lowered the phone. 'I didn't say you could talk, shut the hell up, what are you saying?'

'We're even,' he said with a crack in his voice. 'I don't have to do this for you anymore.'

'What's going on?' scoffed O'Loughlin. 'You're blackmailing a junkie to take down one of your own, Lyons? You've got nothing on me, this is entrapment, and it'll never hold up, I'm out of here.'

Lyons' eyes turned black, like someone just turned a light off in his head. He leaned into O'Loughlin and briskly swung a full force punch to the side of his head, causing him to drop as if he suddenly lost all feeling in his legs. Lyons took two large steps to where Aaron was standing and proceeded to swing in slaps across his face and ears. Using his forehand from the left and his backhand from the right he made contact seven times in about three and a half seconds. Aaron offered no retaliation, just raised his hands and cowered in self-defence.

'Don't ever speak to me again you idiot, if I wanted to hear you make a sound I'd have asked all the bitches in the house to say hey-ho.' Lyons then turned back to O'Loughlin who was on the ground, lying on his side. He hunched down over him and dug his knee into his back. 'And you listen to me, asshole. I am a goddamn saint in a world of vicious wolves. I am doing the Lord's work with angels watching over me, I work magic and miracles with my bare hands and I am here to bring you down, do you understand me?'

'You're a bloody psycho, you prick,' muttered O'Loughlin, finding it hard to talk or even breathe with the pain being inflicted into his back. 'And if you think you're going to arrest me…'

He didn't get to finish the sentence, Lyons had already placed a handcuff on his wrist.

CHAPTER TWENTY NINE

Billy had been sitting silently as he waited for Fionn to return from the call he had stepped outside to make. He had felt invisible as several people hustled around him, paying no attention to his presence. He sat on the bar stool silently for several minutes, observing every single detail of his surroundings. When Fionn finally returned with a slow shuffle and his head bowed Billy felt a jolt of nervousness in the pit of his stomach. Like his instinct was telling him something was erroneous. 'You OK, chief?' he asked with a tenseness in his tone.

'I feel so stupid,' said Fionn solemnly. 'He was right here in front of my eyes this whole time.'

'Wow,' replied Billy. 'You're sure?'

'I am,' said Fionn with no particular emotion in his voice. He took out his mobile phone, held it up, adjusted some settings and took a photograph.

'What the hell are you doing?' asked Billy.

Fionn typed some words and put his phone away again, ignoring Billy's question. He just stared ahead of him deep in thought as he re-lived every moment of all the wrong turns and the many wrong decisions that had been made right up to this point.

'OK, so what are we waiting for?' asked Billy.

Fionn continued to sit silently. He was waiting for a text to come through.

CHAPTER THIRTY

Neeve was frantically racing through dark sterile corridors of the Mater Hospital, looking for Joanna's room. As she came to the end of one particularly long hall she briskly turned the corner and came face to face with David Lyons. 'Wow, Dave,' she said with surprise as she caught her balance, preventing herself from falling directly into his chest. 'What are you doing here?'

'Oh, you know, just a routine health check after a compromising incident,' he replied in a tone that feigned humility.

'I heard you caught Mr. T,' said Neeve. 'Fair play to you. I'm impressed, I must say.'

'Just tell me I'm the best, darling. That's all the reward I need. The approval of a strong beautiful woman, it's what I live for.' He took a loud deep breath and swelled out his chest.

'I think that's called having Mommy issues,' muttered Neeve through the side of her mouth. 'I'm still none the wiser of how you did it, though. How the hell did you single handedly lure him in? You had to have needed help?'

'I did it all by myself, I recorded a deal, the buyer got away,' replied Lyons defiantly.

'How did you record it, by dangling a boom mic from the roof?' replied Neeve sarcastically.

'Look darlin', don't question me.' Lyons' voice went low and sounded like a wicked rasp. 'I'm a professional and I'm about to be acknowledged as legitimate fucking rock star. I think it's in your interest not to cross me rather than second guessing my methods. You should be keeping me sweet,' he said with a suggestive wink.

Neeve stared at him straight in his shiny dilated eyes. 'I don't want you to ever call me darling again. I'd stick your balls in your mouth to shut you up except I think you'd get too much pleasure from sucking them. I have no interest in keeping you sweet. You can't sweeten something as sour or as rotten as you, not with all the sugar in Willy Wonka's factory. And if you don't come down off that pedestal of yours pretty quick I'll make a formal request to investigate your methods. Illegally involving a civilian in an investigation comes with penalties far greater than any scouts badge you can expect for bringing in Mr T. So watch yourself David, you got it?

Lyons stood rigid with his arms folded defensively. His face formed a sour scowl. 'Loud and clear Ms. Bello,' he said through gritted teeth.

Neeve bluntly brushed by him and headed for Joanna's room, taking a few short seconds to take a deep breath and refocus. As she entered the room she knocked gently on the door. Joanna was sitting up in bed with her family around her. One of her daughters was half lying on the bed holding her hand. There was a sense of peace and calmness in the room. 'Hi, Joanna,' she said softly. 'How are you? You're looking a lot better.' She looked around the room with a smile. 'Hello everyone, my name is Neeve, I'm a friend.'

Joanna smiled. She seemed pleased to see the Guard that had been so kind to her, but she suddenly looked concerned as to why she was there. 'Is something wrong?' she asked, skipping the pleasantries.

'No, not at all, don't worry,' said Neeve calmly. 'In fact, we might be closer to finding the person that tried to kill you. I'm here for your help. I want to show you a photograph of a person and I want you to tell me if you recognise them. Can you do that?

Joanna nodded yes, slowly but firmly.

Neeve placed a tablet on the bedside table, faced it towards Joanna and started recording. She then took a mobile phone out of her pocket and held up the screen directly in front of Joanna's face. 'Do you recognise this person?'

Joanna stared at a photo of Billy.

CHAPTER THIRTY ONE

There was a sharp smell of sweat and dampness where Fionn and Billy stood.

Billy wasn't used to such an ominous environment. 'I said, what are we waiting for?' he repeated. The walk from Frank Ryan's took fifteen minutes and he had to ask every question throughout the duration at least twice.

Fionn examined the photo he had just taken. It was taken from far away and it was grainy but he believed the quality was good enough to work. He pressed send. He then turned and stared Billy in the eyes intently. 'Sorry, I just need to focus and make sure I do this properly.'

'You've been a million miles away since we were in the pub,' replied Billy. 'Will you please just catch me up here so I can back you up?'

'Yes, sorry, of course,' said Fionn. 'I want to make sure the evidence can be used in court. I've just sent his photo to Neeve, so she can show Joanna. But of course it only works if it's picked out of a line so I sent Neeve five photos of random people Joanna hasn't met as well as one of our man right there. I'm betting she picks him out of the group of photos.'

'Is that why you took a photo of me in the pub?' inquired Billy. 'Did you consult my agent about that first?'

'Yeah, sorry.' Fionn remained deadpan, offering no response to Billy's quip. 'I didn't have enough pictures in my gallery that I could use so I took one of you and added it in. She's never met you so it'll do the trick. So thank you. Now let's go say hello. It's time to bring him in.'

They walked over and stood as close as they could get, which was about half a metre and between a thick pane of glass. He was sipping on a cup of coffee and focused on the screen in front of him. Suddenly he looked up and when he noticed Fionn he didn't say anything but gave a whole hearted smile. Fionn studied his face. He was smiling brightly, but Fionn noticed his eyes did not mirror his mouth. They were lifeless and wicked, almost reptile-like. Dark. Detached. Unemotional. Fionn had never noticed this before and mentally kicked himself for that. You can tell a lot about a person from their eyes, they always give away the truth. He always prided himself on being a good judge of character and realised he let his emotions blind him and had been purposely distracted and manipulated. 'Hello Seamus,' he finally said.

The fake smile immediately sank like the last second of a summer sunset leaving just a face of darkness. The blank expression on his face seemed better suited to his dead eyes. He looked down when he spoke. 'I don't usually go by that name,' said Jim in a flat tone.

'I suppose it depends who you're talking to, doesn't it?' replied Fionn. 'You certainly introduced yourself as Seamus to the Freemasons, for example. And I'm not your friend. I don't make friends with murderers, I arrest them.'

'You better step inside,' the bookmaker said as he hit a button that released the door.

Fionn and Billy stepped inside. It looked unchanged to Fionn from the last time he stood there four days earlier. The two Guards stood at the door on the inside of the compact office with their suspect sitting visibly uncomfortable and leering up at them. Everything about his body language said; guilty. He may as well be screaming it through a megaphone from the roof. His arms were folded, he was fidgeting in his seat, his lips were rolled so far inward they were not even visible. He had gone as white as a sheet on a laundry detergent commercial and sweat glistened from his brow. He may have been acting guilty but Fionn was already sure of his culpability and didn't need any signs to confirm this.

'I thought you were going to be my best customer,' Jim sneered.

'You were one of the first people I spoke to, do you know that? Said Fionn. '"Jim Rogers", I was told by someone. "Speak to him, he's such a good guy, he'll be able to help." You sent me on some wild goose chase, didn't you?

'I suppose there's no point acting surprised, is there?' replied Jim. 'If I say I have no idea what you're talking about you'll no doubt just scoff at me?'

Billy scoffed dismissively. 'You bet.'

'Actually, Guard, I don't bet,' responded Jim in a dull emotionless manner. 'That would be incredibly bad for business. Shareholders don't cash in their dividends to buy their own products. I have never placed a bet in my life. I don't think I'd be a great gambler anyway. I don't think I have

319

enough emotion to get any fun out of it. My friend Fionn here is a good gambler though. The best kind. The kind you can make a lot of money off of. And two things I am good at are spotting weaknesses and making money. The first time you came in here I saw straight away that you cared more about the fact that you were in a bookies than whatever it was that you were investigating.'

Fionn stood silently trying to keep his temper under control. As a Guard he was well used to his character being attacked by people that didn't know him but he was taking these words personally.

It was Billy that spoke first. 'Stop acting like you're so smart, we're here now aren't we? We've caught you, haven't we?'

'Dear oh dear,' said Jim. 'I've gotten ahead of myself with all of the excitement. Yes of course you're here but I suppose I better ask, just to be sure, what do you think I've actually done?'

'I'll certainly tell you how I see it from my point of view Jim,' Fionn said. 'And probably the same point of view the prosecutors will give the jury during the trial of Seamus Rogers. Or Jim as you like to be known. It hadn't occurred to me that Jim is short for James. And James in Irish is Seamus. When I was going through the list of names of men that tried but failed to join the Freemasons the name "Seamus Rogers" meant nothing to me. I never associated that name with Jim, the guy I questioned that owns the bookies. Not until I was looking at the list again and someone said the name Seamus just as I read your name. The coincidence made me pause and then it occurred to me that it's the same name. Seamus and Jim. We thought we had it solved, you know. We thought it was all caused by one guy, a guy called Michael Behan. Is he a friend of yours by any chance?' Fionn stared intently at Jim.

'At the moment I'll choose to claim I've never heard of anyone with that name,' replied Jim in a condescending tone.

'He's dead,' Billy proclaimed matter-of-factly from his usual stance at the door.

Jim attempted to show no reaction but a swift flinch and sudden flutter of his eyes showed the information had shocked him.

'Would you like to know how?' asked Fionn.

Jim just sat and moved his frantic gaze from Fionn to Billy back and forth every second.

'Of course you would, Behan has been your partner in all this. When he attacked me in the Spider-Man mask you didn't pull me inside and lock the door to protect me, you were protecting him. I was sure it was him and him alone that was responsible for all of the murders, but there was a major loose end I couldn't get my head around, his alibi. I was so intent on chasing one person I didn't consider there were two people involved. You were murdering homeless people together but it was you that killed Peter McGee. I realised it when my partner here said something earlier that reminded me of the first time we met. He said "bad chances," and it took me back to the slip of paper I handed you with that first bet I made. I remembered how I was studying the name so hard until you placed your hand on it and took it. And there, buried deep in my memories, was the image of your hand, with a ring on your wedding finger. One of those minor observations you make and store in the back of your head, not expecting it to be of any importance, I'm just disappointed I never looked at it more closely. Your old friend Buzzer is the one man on the street you actually do care about, but he knows you, so you made sure was snuggled up in a hotel room the nights you went on a rampage so he'd be none the wiser of what you were up to. But when he told you that I showed him a drawing of the symbol you have on the ring you wear on your wedding finger, you immediately removed it. The last time we spoke I couldn't understand why I thought you were married. It was because you had been wearing a ring up until then. Once you realised we were somehow onto the ring you had to cover that particular loose end so you paid McGee a visit, probably just to ask him to destroy all records of it being made. He was killed by his own gun so I assume you didn't go there with the intention of killing him, but he must not have wanted to play ball, and after a struggle he ended up dead. So you decided to go in a different direction and stage it to look like a suicide. If we did follow the trail of the ring it would stop with him. You underestimated us, you thought we'd chalk it down to guilt for committing the murders or insanity or both and close the case. But we found the receipts that lead to Behan, who you had advised to get out of town for a couple of nights as soon as his attack on me failed. After it failed and once McGee ended up dead you were worried we'd find the origin of the rings, so you planted yours and told Behan to just flaunt his and spin a tall tale about not getting the second one he ordered. Which he did with confidence because he believed he was untouchable because of his alibi and the fact that McGee was about to take the fall. But when you killed McGee and planted your ring in his collection to make it look like it was his, it stood out like a sore thumb. It was his proud collection and the ring was nothing to be proud of. He kept photographic records of everything he made, he would have never needed his own copy of the ring. Besides, you thought locking his bedroom door from the inside and hiding a ladder on a wall would be enough to make it look like suicide. And Behan thought we had nothing on him until I noticed the damage I had done to his ankle right outside that door. Neither of you are as smart as you think you are.'

The expression of deficiency on Jim's face was slowly being replaced with defeat.

'You are right about me, you know,' continued Fionn. 'I did enjoy my time here. So much so I almost forgot why I was here in the first place. I came here because you volunteer for a homeless charity. You have a connection to the victims. A wolf disguised as a saint. Pretending to care for them but instead you were drugging them, using your amateur hypnotism and then murdering them. Once I started putting the pieces together and worked backwards it led back to you Jim. We've come full circle.' Fionn's phone gave a ping sound from his pocket. He slid it out of his pocket, held it close to his leg and peered down. It was a thumb up emoji from Neeve. No other information.

'Really, Detective? A ring? That's all you have on me? Who do you think I am, Bilbo Baggins? I don't mean to make assumptions but accusing me of killing four homeless people because of a ring, that I know you have no proof I ever owned, is a little far-fetched isn't it?'

'Interesting that you think four people have been murdered. Where did you get that from?' asked Fionn.

Billy folded his arms and smirked.

Jim hummed awkwardly to himself. 'I must have read it in the papers,' he said, feigning confidence.

'Like hell you did,' said Fionn. 'There was never a report of four people because the fourth person you threw in the river was rescued. You assumed she died but she's alive and recovering excellently.'

Panic started to show in Jim's face as the colour drained from his skin.

'In fact, my colleague has just paid her a visit right now. You might find it interesting that she was presented with six photos of random people and asked if any of them was the person that drugged her and then pushed her into the river.' Fionn took his phone out of his pocket. 'She was certain one of them was. Would you like to see who she picked out?' He held up the phone showing a photo he had taken of Jim just minutes earlier. 'Did you forget you even introduced yourself to her? You told her what your Irish name was, Seamus.'

Jim stared at the photo as his bottom lip quivered.

Behind Fionn, Billy leaned forward. 'Gotcha, asshole,' he said triumphantly.

'You messed with the wrong woman,' continued Fionn. 'She'll be out of hospital tomorrow and once she is she will be making an official statement to us. That will give us enough to be able to search your house and I'm confident we'll find a lot more evidence there.'

'I guess you have it all figured out, don't you?' said Jim solemnly.

'Absolutely not,' replied Fionn. 'I still have a lot of figuring out to do. I know it started with you and Behan trying to join the Freemasons, you got rejected, took a symbol from their window, you both stuck it on a ring like a pair of lovebird teenagers and then went around killing homeless people. I know that's how it happened, but I don't for the life of me know why.'

Jim looked around the room for nothing in particular as he seemed to be considering his next move. 'Our views were too extreme for the Masons,' he finally said. 'I don't think I'm committing a crime by telling you that. We thought we could belong to an organisation that wanted to work together to better the county but they don't care at all. They have no interest in making any real difference to the world. Just a glorified boys club is all they are. Standing around drinking tea, slapping themselves on the back for holding their powerful titles, giving each other high powered jobs and once in a while raising money for some useless charity. They're not doing anything worthwhile. Certainly not what actually needs to be done. They can go to hell.'

'Ouch,' said Billy. 'You're sounding fairly bitter that they rejected you there, chief.'

'And the symbol?' continued Fionn. 'DeWolf, wasn't it? I would have considered him a suspect if he hadn't died over a hundred years ago. I learned he didn't care much for the impoverished people of Ireland. He wanted them killed, didn't he?'

'Homeless people are in poverty, aren't they?' offered Billy.

'Yes indeed,' agreed Fionn. 'Our poorest citizens I would think. Wouldn't you say so, Jim? Weren't you looking to get rid of them just like your hero, DeWolf?'

'I don't have any vendetta against poor people,' protested Jim. 'Most poor people still contribute to our society and the economy. Homeless junkies, however, are a parasite on society. They contribute nothing and all they do is take handouts, steal and kill.'

'So your answer is to kill them first?' asked Fionn.

'I didn't say that,' replied Jim. 'I'm not saying I killed anyone.'

'We know you're a killer,' declared Fionn. 'You and your fellow visionary, Behan, decided you'd do the Devil's work and go around drugging and hypnotising them and throwing them into the river to drown.'

Jim's eyebrows darted up his forehead like they had developed a mind of their own and were trying to escape his face. He let out a short one syllabled burst of laughter. 'That's a good one, is that what your lying little witness is telling you happened? She has some imagination, sitting there in her luxury St James' hospital bed. Probably the most luxurious accommodation she's had in years.'

'You're talking bullshit, Rogers,' replied Fionn. 'Right down to what hospital she's in, don't pretend you know what you're talking about.'

'You're the one talking bullshit Guard. Give me a break. Joining the Freemasons and having a grudge against homeless people are not crimes. One junkie liar is not enough to convict me. It's my word against hers. The more you talk the more I realise you have nothing on me.'

'I've got the journey figured out as to how we got here,' replied Fionn. 'The evidence and our witness will help everything else fall into place. Your vanity and egoism let you down. Believing you should have your own symbol like you think you are Batman and then putting it on a ring like you're members of the Captain Planet team. That led to our first lead, which led to you taking out McGee. You knew I was the one investigating it so Behan tried to threaten me out on the street right outside here that day. But the symbol led to him and now it leads to you and the evidence will speak for itself. If I were you I wouldn't feel too confident.'

'But what evidence? You don't have any evidence that I did anything,' protested Jim. 'Stop trying to trick me into confessing that I've actually committed a crime.'

'There were skin fibres and hair found in McGee's room that didn't belong to him or any relation of his,' stated Fionn. He pointed at a coffee cup that was sitting on the table. 'How confident are you that once we get your DNA there will be none of it found at the scene of the crime?'

The resolve in Jim's face suddenly fell away like a weathered cliffside succumbing to the relentless erosion of truth. 'Maybe I was there recently as a customer checking out his work,' he said with half-hearted conviction.

Fionn laughed. 'Maybe indeed. Perhaps if you put all the evidence together it's pretty incriminating but not enough by itself. But when a jury hears our witness tell them the story of when you tried to kill her, you're finished. It's not just your word against hers. It's yours verses hers and a bucket load of evidence.'

'We're done talking now, chief,' repeated Billy. 'Now comes the bit where we arrest you. I'm sure you've seen it on TV plenty of times so the process shouldn't come as too much of a surprise.'

'What about all my customers?' asked Jim desperately. 'What am I going to do, leave them in here to run the place themselves?'

Billy turned and walked back out into the main foyer. He took out his police badge and held it high. 'Listen up ladies and gentleman, due to a police issue we are politely asking that you vacate the premises immediately.'

There were five gentlemen in total. No ladies. They all looked up at Billy and stared at him blankly. One man pointed to the screen he had been looking at and then reverted his gaze to the horse race he had been following. It didn't take long for all five to go back to what they were doing.

Billy lowered his badge and raised his voice. 'I said, get the hell out, now.'

After a few seconds the man concentrating on the horse race looked back at Billy and quickly jumped out of his stool and bolted for the door. The velocity caused his stool to fall over and the other men to look up and then follow suit. Within five seconds the entire shop was void of customers.

'That took a few seconds to sink in,' Billy said as he turned back towards Fionn. 'But they got there eventually and.....' His sentence had been cut short. He had turned to see Fionn up against the wall with a sawn off shotgun being pressed into his face by Jim.

'Get back in here,' Jim said.

Billy quickly stepped back inside the office area.

'Think about what you're doing here, Jim,' Fionn said, trying to defuse the situation. 'This is only going to make things worse for you.'

'Shut the hell up, I know exactly what I'm doing,' snapped Jim. 'You think you're going to take me? No chance. You're like hungry bears on the side of the stream, you think you can see me swimming around in front of you like a helpless little fish? I'm not a fish, I'm in the shadows of the trees and ready to pounce on you like a wolf. That's what you called me wasn't it? I'm more than happy with being a wolf and guess what? I'm right behind you.' Jim stepped backwards out through the door. 'And before you even notice I'm there it's already too late.' He slammed the door, took a set of keys out of his back pocket and locked it shut. He then sprinted out the front door, locking that behind him too. And then he was gone. Somewhere into the hectic city night brightly lit by a swollen moon that was illuminous and fit to be howled at.

CHAPTER THIRTY TWO

Joanna had gone to sleep feeling happier than she had been in a long time. Her family had been looking for her. They had been worried about her and they missed her. As she lay in bed with them gathered around, laughing and joking, she realised she was truly loved unconditionally. Not only that, but she realised that the love was there all along. She hadn't felt it because it was her that had stopped loving herself. But as she drifted off to sleep she did so feeling safe and happy. She was looking forward to getting discharged the next day and going home. Earlier, it had been difficult to bring herself to look at the photo of the man that had drugged her and had tried to kill her. It caused her to relive the situation in her mind. The nice female Guard had reassured her that there was nothing to be afraid of anymore. She also said that her being able to identify him was going to lead to his arrest and he would not be able to hurt anyone else. Even though that gave her solace and she lay down to sleep feeling proud and at peace, she couldn't banish the image of her attacker from her mind. As she finally drifted off, his face was the last thing she saw.

She had been sleeping great. She was probably in the deepest sleep she had been in for quite a long time. She was definitely the most comfortable she had been in weeks. So what woke her? She hadn't been having a nightmare. She hadn't been dreaming at all. She had been in a sweet state of serene emptiness. She slowly opened her eyes to see the doctor had come in to check up on her. She felt a sudden wave of irritation come over her to have her sleep abruptly interrupted. Her vision was blurry and foggy as the figure in front of her started to come into focus. The first thing she noticed was that he wasn't dressed in hospital attire, he was wearing normal clothes. As her line of vision rose up the man's body she noticed he was holding something under his arm. She couldn't see it properly, it was metal and cylindrical. She opened and closed her eyes rapidly in an attempt to expel the murkiness of her vision. As her gaze rose up to see the person's face she could see a pair of intense eyes looking down at her. Did she know who this was? It wasn't any of her family or friends, she knew that for sure. As her focus finally started to sharpen, so did the realisation that the person in front of her was not a complete stranger. She knew she had seen his face before. Briefly but very recently. She didn't know his name, she wasn't sure if she was ever even told his name. But the next emotion she felt was panic. Where had the nice woman Garda gone to?

CHAPTER THIRTY THREE

Fionn lay in an uncomfortable position. He started reliving the events of the day. Move by move, like a retrospective game of chess. He had been in control some of the time. He had been at a severe disadvantage during others. He thought back to all the times when he should have made a different move. Instead of Red he should have betted on Black. Instead of a hit he should have held. Instead of folding he should have gone all in. It was the last part that he was most infuriated with himself about. The final furlong. He was in the lead but his horse collapsed from underneath him and he was flung face first into the turf. Jim Rogers had escaped arrest and he only had himself to blame for that. He wanted to show off. Reveal the wolf to the world, but instead he had been outsmarted and outran. He should have just arrested him and got it over with instead of letting his ego feast on his own self-proclaimed brilliance. Pathetic. One split second of taking his eyes off of him and Jim had reached under his desk, pulled the gun out and pointed it in his face. He couldn't even remember what he was thinking at the exact moment he stared straight into the large round barrel. He remembered experiencing an overwhelming bout of panic and defeat but he couldn't remember what his exact thoughts were. And before he even had time for his life to flash before his eyes, as he expected it to, Jim was gone. Within fifteen minutes every Guard on duty in the whole city was out looking for him. A photo of Jim was circulating around the entire county. It would be on the national news by the next morning. But Jim was nowhere to be seen. He hadn't gone back to his house, he wasn't found on the streets and his car had been untouched. As he felt his eyes get heavy his thoughts went back to Joanna. He started reliving the conversation with Jim and he started cursing himself for having such a big mouth and talking too much. He basically presented Jim with everything he needed to know on a silver platter with smoked salmon and capers on the side. Firstly, he presented Joanna as the only witness and the only thing standing between Jim and freedom. All the circumstantial evidence would be thrown out by a judge. His DNA in McGee's room could be logically explained by a good solicitor. But Joanna's compelling testimony would be the main thing that puts him away. Jim knew what he had to do. Secondly, he had told Jim she was in hospital and was getting out tomorrow. He knew what he needed to do and how long he had to do it. Thirdly, and this was the one that frustrated him most, Jim had bluffed by suggesting he knew she was in St. James' hospital. Fionn had walked straight into the trap by telling him he was wrong. Because of where the original incident happened there was logically only two possible A&E departments Joanna would have been rushed to. St. James or the Mater Hospital. Fionn had practically acknowledged she was in the Mater. Jim knew what he had to do, how long he had to do it and where he had to go. Joanna is in serious and immediate danger. Fionn too knew what he had to do. Protect her and take down Jim.

CHAPTER THIRTY FOUR

Jim Rogers kicked the door to the hospital room open and burst in loudly and brashly with his sawn off shotgun pointed out in front of him. It looked like a metal finger pointing in judgement. He didn't have patience for light footedness any longer. He had blagged his way past reception with his gun shoved down his trousers, made his way onto the correct floor and quietly approached Joanna Quinn's room. He was pleased to find her full name when flicking through a tabloid paper in a 24 hour newsagents. It was an ideal distraction while dodging the view of the Garda cars that had been looking for him. He guessed his own name and probably even his picture would be in tomorrow's edition.

The sudden thud startled Joanna. She hadn't been sleeping and had been staring at the door, only to see the man that tried to kill her burst in and point a gun at her. Her instant reflex was to raise her hands in the air and take in a deep breath in order to let out a scream, the loudest she could be physically capable of.

Jim anticipated the scream and darted to within a metre of Joanna with the gun pointed directly into her face. 'I swear to God, if you scream I will find all the family that you have and stab them in their sleep. Do you understand?'

The sudden cruelty of the statement winded Joanna and she choked on her breath as she tried not to make noise. She noticed Jim look around the room agitatedly as if he was considering his next move. 'Are you going to kill me?' she finally asked.

'Yes of course I am,' he replied calmly and coldly.

Joanna kept her cool. It almost didn't seem real. 'Are you going to shoot me here, now?'

Jim gave no reply, he just stared at her with burning hate in his misty grey eyes. They reminded Joanna of a husky dog. Except far more wicked. 'Everyone will hear the gun and you'll never get out of here,' she said with a quiver in her voice.

'Who's going to stop me with this in my hand?' He took a step closer to her bed. Three quarters a metre away.

'But, but, why?' Joanna pleaded.

'Oh come on you can't be that thick,' replied Jim. 'You're the witness that identified me, if you're gone so are the charges. The cops won't be able to prove a thing, and they practically admitted that to me.'

'No,' replied Joanna softly. 'I mean, why me in the first place. Why did you try to kill me? I've never done anything to anyone.' She fought hard to control the lump in her throat but felt water build in her eyes nonetheless.

'Are you joking?' Jim replied in a jeering voice. 'Every one of you junkie scumbags are the same. You are an embarrassment to this beautiful city, harassing hard working people going about their business, a disease that must be cured. This country would be a better place with all of you gone. You're not overdosing on heroin quick enough for my liking.'

Joanna took a deep breath and spoke slowly. 'I have never taken an illegal drug in my life, I have never stolen as much as a cup of tea. I have worked hard my whole career and never did anything bad to anyone. I don't deserve this.'

'Oh spare me the sob story you stupid bitch,' snarled Jim. 'If you're thick enough to end up on the street it was only a matter of time before you did all of those things. I know exactly how you people think and act, I've seen it time and time again. Leeching off decent upstanding people like me. Robbing and killing good people to feed your disgusting habits. One of you killed my friend's sister and I tell you what he has been a hero to this entire society after what he's done to help me cull you people. And now he's gone too, because of you. Since someone like you took away his sister his main purpose in life was to avenge her and to make this city a better place. Do you want to know when I got my moment of clarity? I was at a cash machine one day and two strung out junkies completely off their faces came up to me with a syringe full of their AIDs blood and threatened me with it. They took my wallet and the €500 I had just taken out to pay a bill. I ran and I ran until I realised what a useless coward I was being. I realised I should have stood up to them. I realised I had failed to stand up to lesser people my entire life and in that moment I decided it was all going to chance. Not anymore. I wanted to kill those two and their diseased bodies with my bare hands. I spent the entire night walking around the city centre looking for them but I never found them. Hopefully they died of an overdose in a filthy alley drenched in rat piss.'

'So instead of them you wanted to kill me?'

'Shut the hell up, you're making me sound like a serial killer.' Jim's voice had turned frantic and erratic. 'I wasn't alone either, my good friend Michael was a great man. A pillar of his community. He felt exactly like me. Together we were going to cleanse the country. Between us we were already making a difference. But he's gone now. Yes, you. And everyone like you. The lowest, most useless scum of our society.'

'You killed those other three homeless people didn't you?'

'Yes of course we did, you idiot, have you not been paying attention?' Jim took another step towards Joanna.

Half a metre. Close enough.

Jim pressed the stock of his gun into his shoulder as he stared down the sawn off barrel directly at Joanna's face. 'I wish I could say it's not personal or that I don't take any pleasure in this but neither of those things are true. It's time to end this.'

Suddenly a cloud of white filled his vision and swallowed him up, as if a volcano had erupted and engulfed his entire body.

The loud whack of the door had woken Fionn up instantly. He heard brisk shuffles and sudden movements but no voices. He quickly but gently slid under the bed and saw two feet approaching.

'I swear to God, if you scream I will find any family you have and stab them in their sleep. Do you understand?'

It was Jim for sure. He had been right about what Jim was going to do next.

After they had been locked into the Bookmakers they were trapped for twenty minutes until a crew of firemen were eventually able to break down the door to get them out. Most modern buildings have emergency push bars to be able to escape a building safely but not an old listed building on Dame Street such as this one. As they waited to be let out Billy became anxious and claustrophobic. Fionn on the other hand sat calmly with his head in his hands for the first five minutes and then, looking up at the TV screens that were still showing the American horse races, turned to the same thing he always does when he needs to take his mind off something. He had asked Billy to bet €50 on a horse in a race that was about to start, he was going to do the same and whichever one finished ahead of the other won all of the money. Billy was reluctant to play along but eventually agreed once the pot was reduced to one pint of Guinness. It was when Fionn started studying the names and odds of the horses that one in particular caught his eye. "Hospital Blues." The odds weren't favourable at 13/1 but there was something about the name that seemed to jump out of the screen and smack him across the face. It suddenly struck

Fionn that he knew exactly where Jim would be going next and that it was really important that he got there first.

Fionn had indeed made it there first. He nervously crept into Joanna's room to see her peacefully asleep in her hospital bed. He reached out and grabbed the fire extinguisher that was mounted beside the door. Jim could arrive at any second and he felt more defensively prepared with something to protect himself. He gently woke Joanna up. She didn't seem to recognise him at first. They had only met once so he wasn't surprised by her initial confusion. The extinguisher he was holding under his arm seemed to frighten her so he placed it down and explained why he was there. He caught her up on what had just happened less than an hour earlier. That Jim was on the loose and that Fionn had reason to believe he may be on his way there right now so he was going to spend the night in the room in case he did arrive. Fionn was struck by how brave Joanna was as she agreed to his plan without protest and portrayed little fear as she asked questions. Fionn would lie on the ground beside Joanna's bed, but on the far side. If Jim came in, he wouldn't know Fionn was there so Joanna had to just get Jim to within a half a metre of her bed and Fionn would be able to take him down. He had left out the part about the gun so as not to scare her too much but he knew Jim would have to get close to the bed if he intended to take a shot. A sawn off shotgun fired from the door would certainly injure but would not be guaranteed to kill as the pellets would spread across the room like fresh paint flicked from a saturated brush. Fionn made himself a makeshift mattress out of thick blankets and lay in silence thinking about the mistakes he had made that led to this situation. After about thirty minutes his exhaustion got the better of him and he drifted off to sleep.

'Are you going to kill me?' he heard Joanna say. The courage was still thick in her voice, the gun hadn't caused her to panic, so now he had to do his bit. He slowly and quietly slid under the bed clutching the extinguisher in a bear hug as if protecting it like a priceless vase. He could see Jim's feet. He readjusted his position, raised the nozzle and pointed it outwards, as if he was opening a giant pen knife. Jim was about a metre away. He had to choose his moment carefully. He felt like he was standing at a slot machine waiting for the exact right time to pull the lever. A second too soon would mean the outcome will be ineffective, a second too late would mean he'll miss his chance and everything will be lost. Joanna had a gun pointed at her. There was a lot more at stake than money. Jim took another step forward. "But, but, why?" he heard Joanna say desperately. Brilliantly done, he thought. She was doing great. He took out his phone and hit the record voice memo button. He then lay still while he listened to Jim make a robust confession as to his motive, then he implicated Behan, then he admitted to committing three murders between them. Fionn felt like the slot machine was endlessly spitting out coins. He had hit the jackpot. Then, Jim took another step forward. Half a metre. He could hear him say 'it's time to end this. He knew it was time to go all in. He shoved the nozzle of the extinguisher out from under the bed, pointed it upwards towards Jim's face, and squeezed on the handle so tightly that his knuckles seized up into a cramp. A whoosh sound echoed as an explosion of white powder blew up around Jim, engulfing his body. The whoosh was followed by a loud bang that shook the walls like an earthquake had hit the entire city. Jim had pulled the trigger but the impact of the blast from the fire extinguisher had sent the shotgun in an upwards motion away from the trajectory of Joanna. The contents of the shell had been blasted into the ceiling causing fragments of white plasterboard to rain down on the bed. Fionn speedily slid out from under the bed and pounced on Jim who had dropped his weapon and was attempting to wipe the foam from his eyes. He elbowed Jim in the throat, winding him even further, he pushed him to the ground, causing him to fall face first with a dull smack. He sat on him, digging his knee into the small of his back which caused Jim to let out an agonising bark. He pulled both his hands behind his back, contorting the restrained man's shoulders in the process and placed handcuffs on him. 'Seamus Rogers,' declared Fionn. 'I am placing you under arrest for the suspicion of four counts of murder and for the attempted murder of Joanna Quinn. Twice.' He turned and looked up at Joanna, who was looking on with a triumphant grin. 'It's over,' he said.

EPILOGUE

ONE DAY LATER

'So we did it. We actually did it,' declared Billy.

'I wouldn't exactly say that,' replied Fionn, taking a sip of his pint.

'You literally just said this is the best pint you've ever had,' chuckled Stephanie.

'Thank you,' replied Billy loudly as he turned to Stephanie.

'No, I mean, yes,' replied Fionn, holding his hands up in surrender. 'OK this might be number one on the list so far, but I just feel like I still haven't found the best pint, you know what I mean?'

Neeve looked at Stephanie. 'This is quite the eventful day for you. You get to meet Fionn's friends and find out that The Gravediggers pub does the best pint in Dublin. She held up her pint of lager in anticipation of cheers.

Stephanie clinked her wine glass against Neeve's pint and grinned. 'Not that the quality of Guinness matters to us.' She turned into Fionn and put her hand on his knee. 'And not that today could ever come close to how exciting yesterday was. For all of you. You're all heroes.

Neeve smiled gently and nodded her gratitude. Billy grinned cheerily and pushed his chest out like a proud peacock.

Fionn sank his face in his hands. 'I don't feel much of a hero, to be honest,' he said sombrely.

'What are you talking about,' Stephanie said with surprise. 'Of course you are.'

'I just think back to when I arrived at Joanna's room yesterday. When she saw me she was afraid of me. It made me think back to when I met her, I wasn't pleasant to her. She didn't deserve that. I don't feel like I saved the day, I feel more like all I did was make amends.'

'Oh don't be silly,' said Neeve. 'You act like a bollox but deep down you're a good person and you have a big heart. People don't see that, they think that someone is either a people's person or not a people's person. They either care about other people or they only care about themselves. I think there are two other kinds of people. There are those that don't care about people but pretend that they do. Think middle management in a large company, for example. They only care about profit but they read somewhere that happier staff means more productivity which means more profit, so they trick the staff into thinking they are valued so they'll work harder.'

'Or psychopaths,' Billy added. 'They would fall into that category too maybe?'

'I thought that's what I just described,' said Neeve to a low murmur of polite chuckles. 'Anyway,' she continued, turning back to Fionn. 'You are the fourth kind. You are a people's person. You care deeply about others. From the people you love, right down to people you don't even know.'

Fionn blushed a little and then turned to Stephanie and smiled awkwardly.

'But you don't show it,' said Neeve. 'You portray on the outside that you're full of bravado. That you are cynical and egotistical and anyone would think you're the kind of person that doesn't care about anyone else. Except maybe Billy, you blatantly care about him. Maybe too much.'

'You're pretty much describing everyone there, Neeve,' said Billy.

'Neeve, if you're trying to wingman me here you are doing completely the opposite,' protested Fionn. 'You are being my torpedo man.'

Billy turned to Stephanie and winked. 'Better leave now, before he gets all bravado with you.'

'No it's OK,' said Stephanie. 'I agree with you, Neeve,' she clasped his knee tighter, 'and you did amazingly. Two murderers can't hurt anyone ever again, thanks to you. Thanks to all of you.'

'Thanks Steph.' said Fionn with a dejected smile, 'But it didn't go as well as it could have.'

'Ah so what,' said Billy. 'We got there in the end, that's all that matters, you can't always be right.'

'Oh, Billy,' said Fionn in a jeering tone. 'I'll tell you something that was definitely not right. Your stupid theory that a fire extinguisher will stop a gun from shooting. I can tell you first hand you were talking bollox.'

Billy arched his eyebrows. 'Did you use foam or $co2$?'

'$Co2$,' replied Fionn.

'Ah it's the foam that does that, you used the wrong one,' he replied confidently.

'Yeah, it was actually the foam I used, you jackass,' replied Fionn as he laughed.

Billy returned a guilty laugh and Stephanie smiled but Neeve was staring into the distance like something else was on her mind.

'What's the matter Detective Bello,' said Fionn. 'Are we boring you?'

'Sorry,' she said. 'I'm just thinking about Bagman.'

'Another hero of the day, according to Corcoran,' said Billy. 'I think he was more impressed with Lyons catching the elusive Mr. T than us catching two murderers. He's a cocky arsehole.'

'I'm not buying it,' said Neeve. 'Something stinks about his statement. It doesn't add up. He's leaving details out. I think he broke the law to catch O'Loughlin. He thinks he's bloody Denzel Washington in "Training Day".'

'Really?' said Fionn. 'I might have to take a gander. Let's have a look at that next week, see what we find.'

They all sat silently as they thought, except Stephanie who sat with a confused look on her face. She had no idea who Lyons was nor had she ever seen Training Day.

'Right,' Fionn said, finally breaking the silence. 'That's enough talking shop. Who's coming for a night at the dog races?'

Acknowledgements:

My gratitude to Writer's Garage for their exceptional editing and invaluable feedback. Big thanks to Ali for giving me confidence to share my work. To the prolific Jo Nesbo, whose work has always inspired me. Simone, even though she doesn't recall, her dare motivated me to embark on this journey. Thank you to my friends and family for putting up with me being in their lives. Above all, this, and everything beyond, is dedicated to Tom.
And thank YOU for reading.